THE WRONG HAT

Frank saw one of his club members across the street staring at Lin in amazement. Frank's face darkened and he put his hand on his brother's shoulder.

"Lin," he said, "while your running with our crowd here in Boston, you don't want to wear that style of hat, you know."

The cowpuncher stopped dead short. "You've made it plain," he said, slanting his steady eyes down into Frank's. "Run along with your crowd and I'll not bother you more. And one more thing: If you see me on the street, don't try any talk—for I'm liable to close your jaw up for you."

LIN McLEAN

Owen Wister

A TOM DOHERTY ASSOCIATES BOOK
NEW YORK

This is a work of fiction. All the characters and events portrayed in this book are either products of the author's imagination or are used fictitiously.

LIN MCLEAN

All new material in this edition is copyright © 1998 by Tom Doherty Associates

A Forge Book
Published by Tom Doherty Associates, Inc.
175 Fifth Avenue
New York, NY 10010

Forge® is a registered trademark of Tom Doherty Associates, Inc.

ISBN: 0-812-58044-3

First Tor edition: June 1998

Printed in the United States of America

0 9 8 7 6 5 4 3 2 1

DEDICATION

MY DEAR HARRY MERCER: When Lin McLean was only a hero in manuscript, he received his first welcome and chastening beneath your patient roof. By none so much as by you has he in private been helped and affectionately disciplined, and now you must stand godfather to him upon this public page.

Always yours,

OWEN WISTER.

Philadelphia, 1897.

CONTENTS

CHAPTER I

How Lin McLean Went East

IN THE old days, the happy days, when Wyoming was a Territory with a future instead of a State with a past, and the unfenced cattle grazed upon her ranges by prosperous thousands, young Lin McLean awaked early one morning in cow camp, and lay staring out of his blankets upon the world. He would be twenty-two this week. He was the youngest cow-puncher in camp. But because he could break wild horses, he was earning more dollars a month than any man there, except one. The cook was a more indispensable person. None save the cook was up, so far, this morning. Lin's brother punchers slept about him on the ground, some motionless, some shifting their prone heads to burrow deeper from the increasing day. The busy work of spring was over, that of the fall, or beef round-up, not yet come. It was mid-July, a lull for these hard-riding bachelors of the saddle, and many unspent dollars stood to Mr. McLean's credit on the ranch books.

"What's the matter with some variety?" muttered the boy in his blankets.

The long range of the mountains lifted clear in the air. They slanted from the purple folds and furrows of the pines that richly cloaked them, upward into rock and grassy bareness until they broke remotely into bright peaks, and filmed into the distant lavender of the north and the south. On their western side the streams ran into Snake or into Green River, and so at length met the Pacific. On this side, Wind River flowed forth from them, descending out of the Lake of the Painted Meadows. A mere trout-brook it was up there at the top of the divide, with easy riffles and stepping-stones in many places; but down here, outside the mountains, it was become a streaming avenue, a broadening course, impetuous between its two tall green walls of cottonwood-trees. And so it wound away like a vast green ribbon across the lilac-gray sage-brush and the yellow, vanishing plains.

"Variety, you bet!" young Lin repeated, aloud.

He unrolled himself from his bed, and brought from the garments that made his pillow a few toilet articles. He got on his long boy legs and limped blithely to the margin. In the mornings his slight lameness was always more visible. The camp was at Bull Lake Crossing, where the fork from Bull Lake joins Wind River. Here Lin found some convenient shingle-stones, with dark, deepish water against them, where he plunged his face and energetically washed, and came up with the short curly hair shining upon his round head. After enough looks at himself in the dark water, and having knotted a clean, jaunty handkerchief at his throat, he returned with his slight limp to camp, where they were just sitting at breakfast to the rear of the cook-shelf of the wagon.

"Bugged up to kill!" exclaimed one, perceiving Lin's careful dress.

"He sure has not shaved again?" another inquired, with concern.

"I 'ain't got my opera-glasses on," answered a third.

"He has spared that pansy-blossom mustache," said a fourth.

"My spring crop," remarked young Lin, rounding on this last one, "has juicier prospects than that rat-eaten catastrophe of last year's hay which wanders out of your face."

"Why, you'll soon be talking yourself into a regular man," said the other.

But the camp laugh remained on the side of young Lin till breakfast was ended, when the ranch foreman rode into camp.

Him Lin McLean at once addressed. "I was wantin' to speak to you," said he.

The experienced foreman noticed the boy's holiday appearance. "I understand you're tired of work," he remarked.

"Who told you?" asked the bewildered Lin.

The foreman touched the boy's pretty handkerchief. "Well, I have a way of taking things in at a glance," said he. "That's why I'm foreman, I expect. So you've had enough work?"

"My system's full of it," replied Lin, grinning. As the foreman stood thinking, he added, "And I'd like my time."

Time, in the cattle idiom, meant back-pay up to date.

"It's good we're not busy," said the foreman.

"Meanin' I'd quit all the same?" inquired Lin, rapidly, flushing.

"No—not meaning any offence. Catch up your horse. I want to make the post before it gets hot."

The foreman had come down the river from the ranch at Meadow Creek, and the post, his goal, was Fort Washakie. All this part of the country formed the Shoshone Indian Reservation, where, by permission, pastured the herds whose owner would pay Lin his time at Washakie. So the young cow-puncher flung on his saddle and mounted.

"So-long!" he remarked to the camp, by way of farewell. He might never be going to see any of them again; but the cow-punchers were not demonstrative by habit.

"Going to stop long at Washakie?" asked one.

"Alma is not waiter-girl at the hotel now," another mentioned.

"If there's a new girl," said a third, "kiss her one for me, and tell her I'm handsomer than you."

"I ain't a deceiver of women," said Lin.

"That's why you'll tell her," replied his friend.

"Say, Lin, why are you quittin' us so sudden, anyway?" asked the cook, grieved to lose him.

"I'm after some variety," said the boy.

"If you pick up more than you can use, just can a little of it for me!" shouted the cook at the departing McLean.

This was the last of camp by Bull Lake Crossing, and in the foreman's company young Lin now took the road for his accumulated dollars.

"So you're leaving your bedding and stuff with the outfit?" said the foreman.

"Brought my tooth-brush," said Lin, showing it in the breast-pocket of his flannel shirt.

"Going to Denver?"

"Why, maybe."

"Take in San Francisco?"

"Sounds slick."

"Made any plans?"

"Gosh, no!"

"Don't want anything on your brain?"

"Nothin' except my hat, I guess," said Lin, and broke into cheerful song:

" ' 'Twas a nasty baby anyhow,
    And it only died to spite us;
'Twas afflicted with the cerebrow
    Spinal meningitis!' "

They wound up out of the magic valley of Wind River, through the bastioned gullies and the gnome-like mystery of dry water-courses, upward and up to the level of the huge sage-brush plain above. Behind lay the deep valley they had climbed from, mighty, expanding, its trees like bushes, its cattle like pebbles, its opposite side towering also to the edge of this upper plain. There it lay, another world. One step farther away from its rim, and the two edges of the plain had flowed together over it like a closing sea, covering without a sign or ripple the great country which lay sunk beneath.

"A man might think he'd dreamed he'd saw that place," said Lin to the foreman, and wheeled his horse to the edge again. "She's sure there, though," he added, gazing down. For a moment his boy face grew thoughtful. "Shucks!" said he then, abruptly, "where's any joy in money that's comin' till it arrives? I have most forgot the feel o' spot-cash."

He turned his horse away from the far-winding vision of the river, and took a sharp jog after the foreman, who had not been waiting for him. Thus they crossed the eighteen miles of high plain, and came down to Fort Washakie, in the valley of Little Wind, before the day was hot.

His roll of wages once jammed in his pocket like an old handkerchief, young Lin precipitated himself out of the post-trader's store and away on his horse up the stream among the Shoshone tepees to an unexpected entertainment—a wolf-dance. He had meant to go and see what the new waiter-girl at the hotel looked like, but put this off promptly to attend the dance. This hospitality the Shoshone Indians were extending to some visiting Ute friends, and the neighborhood was assembled to watch the ring of painted naked dancers.

The post-trader looked after the galloping Lin. "What's he quitting his job for?" he asked the foreman.

"Same as most of 'em quit."

"Nothing?"

"Nothing."

"Been satisfactory?"

"Never had a boy more so. Good-hearted, willing, a plumb dare-devil with a horse."

"And worthless," suggested the post-trader.

"Well—not yet. He's headed that way."

"Been punching cattle long?"

"Came in the country about seventy-eight, I believe, and rode for the Bordeaux Outfit most a year, and quit. Blew in at Cheyenne till he went broke, and worked over on to the Platte. Rode for the C. Y. Outfit most a year, and quit. Blew in at Buffalo. Rode for Balaam awhile on Butte Creek. Broke his leg. Went to the Drybone Hospital, and when the fracture was commencing to knit pretty good he broke it again at the hog-ranch across the bridge. Next time you're in Cheyenne get Dr. Barker to tell you about that. McLean drifted to Green River last year and went up over on to Snake, and up Snake, and was around with a prospecting outfit on Galena Creek by Pitchstone Cañon. Seems he got interested in some Dutchwoman up there, but she had trouble—died, I think they said—and he came down by Meteetsee to Wind River. He's liable to go to Mexico or Africa next."

"If you need him," said the post-trader, closing his ledger, "you can offer him five more a month."

"That'll not hold him."

"Well, let him go. Have a cigar. The bishop is expected for Sunday, and I've got to see his room is fixed up for him."

"The bishop!" said the foreman. "I've heard him highly spoken of."

"You can hear him preach to-morrow. The bishop is a good man."

"He's better than that; he's a man," stated the foreman—"at least, so they tell me."

Now, saving an Indian dance, scarce any possible event at the Shoshone agency could assemble in one spot so many sorts of inhabitants as a visit from this bishop. Inhabitants of four colors gathered to view the wolf-dance this afternoon—red men, white men, black men, yellow men. Next day, three sorts came to church at the agency. The Chinese laundry was absent. But because, indeed (as the foreman said), the bishop was not only a good man but a man, Wyoming held him in respect and went to look at him. He stood in the agency church and held the Episcopal service this Sunday morning for some brightly glittering army officers and their families, some white cavalry, and some black infantry; the agency doctor, the post-trader, his foreman, the government scout, three gamblers, the waiter-girl from the hotel, the stage-driver, who was there because she was; old Chief Washakie, white-haired and royal in blankets, with two royal Utes splendid beside him; one benchful of squatting Indian children, silent and marvelling; and, on the back bench, the commanding officer's new hired-girl, and, beside her, Lin McLean.

Mr. McLean's hours were already various and successful. Even at the wolf-dance, before he had wearied of its monotonous drumming and pageant, his roving eye had rested upon a girl whose eyes he caught resting upon him. A look, an approach, a word, and each was soon content with the other. Then, when her duties called her to the post from him and the stream's border, with a promise for next day he sought the hotel and found the three gamblers anxious to make his acquaintance; for when a cow-puncher has his pay many people will take an interest in him. The three gamblers did not know that Mr. McLean could play cards. He left them late in the evening fat with their money, and sought the tepees of the Arapahoes. They lived across the road from the Shoshones, and among their tents the boy remained until morning. He was here in church now, keeping his promise to see the bishop with the girl of yesterday; and while he gravely looked at the bishop, Miss Sabina Stone allowed his arm to encircle her waist. No soldier had achieved this yet, but Lin was the first cow-puncher she had seen, and he had given her the handkerchief from round his neck.

The quiet air blew in through the windows and door, the pure, light breath from the mountains; only, passing over their foot-hills it had caught and carried the clear aroma of the sage-brush. This it brought into church, and with this seemed also to float the peace and great silence of the plains. The little melodeon in the corner, played by one of the ladies at the post, had finished accompanying the hymn, and now it prolonged a few closing chords while the bishop paused before his address, resting his keen eyes on the people. He was dressed in a plain suit of black with a narrow black tie. This was because the Union Pacific Railroad, while it had delivered him correctly at Green River, had despatched his robes towards Cheyenne.

Without citing chapter and verse the bishop began:

"And he arose, and came to his father. But when he was yet a great way off, his father saw him, and had compassion, and ran, and fell on his neck and kissed him."

The bishop told the story of that surpassing parable, and then proceeded to draw from it a discourse fitted to the drifting destinies in whose presence he found himself for one solitary morning. He spoke unlike many clergymen. His words were chiefly those which the people round him used, and his voice was more like earnest talking than preaching.

Miss Sabina Stone felt the arm of her cow-puncher loosen slightly, and she looked at him. But he was looking at the bishop, no longer gravely but with wide-open eyes, alert. When the narrative reached the elder brother in the field, and how he came to the house and heard sounds of music and dancing, Miss Stone drew away from her companion and let him watch the bishop, since he seemed to prefer that. She took to reading hymns vindictively. The bishop himself noted the sun-browned boy face and the wide-open eyes. He was too far away to see anything but the alert, listening position of the young cow-puncher. He could not discern how that, after he had left the music and dancing and begun to draw morals, attention faded from those eyes that seemed to watch him, and they filled with dreaminess. It was very hot in church. Chief Washakie went to sleep, and so did a corporal; but Lin McLean sat in the same alert position till Miss Stone pulled him and asked if he intended to sit down through the hymn. Then church was out. Officers, Indians, and all the people dispersed through the great sunshine to their dwellings, and the cow-puncher rode beside Sabina in silence.

"What are you studying over, Mr. McLean?" inquired the lady, after a hundred yards.

"Did you ever taste steamed Duxbury clams?" asked Lin, absently.

"No, indeed. What's them?"

"Oh, just clams. Yu' have drawn butter, too." Mr. McLean fell silent again.

"I guess I'll be late for settin' the colonel's table. Good-bye," said Sabina, quickly, and swished her whip across the pony, who scampered away with her along the straight road across the plain to the post.

Lin caught up with her at once and made his peace.

"Only," protested Sabina, "I ain't used to gentlemen taking me out and—well, same as if I was a collie-dog. Maybe it's Wind River politeness."

But she went riding with him up Trout Creek in the cool of the afternoon. Out of the Indian tepees, scattered wide among the flat levels of sage-brush, smoke rose thin and gentle, and vanished. They splashed across the many little running channels which lead water through that thirsty soil, and though the range of mountains came no nearer, behind them the post, with its white, flat buildings and green trees, dwindled to a toy village.

"My! but it's far to everywheres here," exclaimed Sabina, "and it's little you're sayin' for yourself to-day, Mr. McLean. I'll have to do the talking. What's that thing now, where the rocks are?"

"That's Little Wind River Cañon," said the young man. "Feel like going' there, Miss Stone?"

"Why, yes. It looks real nice and shady like, don't it? Let's."

So Miss Stone turned her pony in that direction.

"When do your folks eat supper?" inquired Lin.

"Half-past six. Oh, we've lots of time! Come on."

"How many miles per hour do you figure that cayuse of yourn can travel?" Lin asked.

"What are you a-talking about, anyway? You're that strange to-day," said the lady.

"Only if we try to make that cañon, I guess you'll be late settin' the colonel's table," Lin remarked, his hazel eyes smiling upon her. "That is, if your horse ain't good for twenty miles an hour. Mine ain't, I know. But I'll do my best to stay with yu'."

"Your're the teasingest man—" said Miss Stone,

pouting. "I might have knowed it was ever so much further nor it looked."

"Well, I ain't sayin' I don't want to go, if yu' was desirous of campin' out to-night."

"Mr. McLean! Indeed, and I'd do no such thing!" and Sabina giggled.

A sage-hen rose under their horses' feet, and hurtled away heavily over the next rise of ground, taking a final wide sail out of sight.

"Something like them partridges used to," said Lin, musingly.

"Partridges?" inquired Sabina.

"Used to be in the woods between Lynn and Salem. Maybe the woods are gone by this time. Yes, they must be gone, I guess."

Presently they dismounted and sought the stream bank.

"We had music and dancing at Thanksgiving and such times," said Lin, his wiry length stretched on the grass beside the seated Sabina. He was not looking at her, but she took a pleasure in watching him, his curly head and bronze face, against which the young mustache showed to its full advantage.

"I expect you used to dance a lot," remarked Sabina, for a subject.

"Yes. Do yu' know the Portland Fancy?"

Sabina did not, and her subject died away.

"Did anybody ever tell you you had good eyes?" she inquired next.

"Why, sure," said Lin, waking for a moment; "but I like your color best. A girl's eyes will mostly beat a man's."

"Indeed, I don't think so!" exclaimed poor Sabina, too much expectant to perceive the fatal note of routine with which her transient admirer pronounced this gallantry. He informed her that hers were like the sea, and she told him she had not yet looked upon the sea.

"Never?" said he. "It's a turrible pity you've never saw salt water. It's different from fresh. All around home it's blue—awful blue in July—around Swampscott and Marblehead and Nahant, and around the islands. I've swam there lots. Then our home bruck up and we went to board in Boston." He snapped off a flower in reach of his long arm. Suddenly all dreaminess left him.

"I wonder if you'll be settin' the colonel's table when I come back?" he said.

Miss Stone was at a loss.

"I'm goin' East to-morrow—East, to Boston."

Yesterday he had told her that sixteen miles to Lander was the farthest journey from the post that he intended to make—the farthest from the post and her.

"I hope nothing 'ain't happened to your folks?" said she.

"I 'ain't got no folks," replied Lin, "barring a brother. I expect he is taking good care of himself."

"Don't you correspond?"

"Well, I guess he would if there was anything to say. There 'ain't been nothin'."

Sabina thought they must have quarrelled, but learned that they had not. It was time for her now to return and set the colonel's table, so Lin rose and went to bring her horse. When he had put her in her saddle he noticed him step to his own.

"Why, I didn't know you were lame!" cried she.

"Shucks!" said Lin. "It don't cramp my style any." He had sprung on his horse, ridden beside her, leaned and kissed her before she got any measure of his activity.

"That's how," said he; and they took their homeward way galloping. "No," Lin continued, "Frank and me never quarrelled. I just thought I'd have a look at this Western country. Frank, he thought dry-goods was good enough for him, and so we're both satisfied, I expect. And that's a lot of years now. Whoop ya!" he suddenly sang out, and fired his six-shooter at a jack-rabbit, who strung himself out flat and flew over the earth.

Both dismounted at the parade-ground gate, and he kissed her again when she was not looking, upon which she very properly slapped him; and he took the horses to the stable. He sat down to tea at the hotel, and found the meal consisted of black potatoes, gray tea, and a guttering dish of fat pork. But his appetite was good, and he remarked to himself that inside the first hour he was in Boston he would have steamed Duxbury clams. Of Sabina he never thought again, and it is likely that she found others to take his place. Fort Washakie was one hundred and fifty miles from the railway, and men there were many and girls were few.

The next morning the other passengers entered the stage with resignation, knowing the thirty-six hours of evil that lay before them. Lin climbed up beside the driver. He had a new trunk now.

"Don't get full, Lin," said the clerk, putting the mail-sacks in at the store.

"My plans ain't settled that far yet," replied Mr. McLean.

"Leave it out of them," said the voice of the bishop, laughing, inside the stage.

It was a cool, fine air. Gazing over the huge plain down in which lies Fort Washakie, Lin heard the faint notes of the trumpet on the parade-ground, and took a good-bye look at all things. He watched the American flag grow small, saw the circle of steam rising away down by the hot springs, looked at the bad lands beyond, chemically pink and rose amid the vast, natural, quiet-colored plain. Across the spreading distance Indians trotted at wide spaces, generally two large bucks on one small pony, or a squaw and papoose—a bundle of parti-colored rags. Presiding over the whole rose the mountains to the west, serene, lifting into the clearest light. Then once again came the now tiny music of the trumpet.

"When do yu' figure on comin' back?" inquired the driver.

"Oh, I'll just look around back there for a spell," said Lin. "About a month, I guess."

He had seven hundred dollars. At Lander the horses are changed; and during this operation Lin's friends gathered and said, where was any sense in going to Boston when you could have a good time where you were? But Lin remained sitting safe on the stage. Toward evening, at the bottom of a little dry gulch some eight feet deep, the horses decided it was a suitable place to stay. It was the bishop who persuaded them to change their minds. He told the driver to give up beating, and unharness. Then they were led up the bank, quivering, and a broken trace was spliced with rope. Then the stage was forced on to the level ground, the bishop proving a strong man, familiar with the gear of vehicles. They crossed through the pass among the quaking asps and the pines, and, reaching Pacific Springs, came down again into open country. That afternoon the stage put its passengers down on the railroad platform at Green River; this was the route in those days before the mid-winter catastrophes of frozen passengers led to its abandonment. The bishop was going west. His robes had passed him on the up stage during the night. When the reverend gentleman heard this he was silent for a very short moment, and then laughed vigorously in the baggage-room.

"I can understand how you swear sometimes," he said to Lin McLean; "but I can't, you see. Not even at this."

The cow-puncher was checking his own trunk to Omaha.

"Good-bye and good luck to you," continued the

bishop, giving his hand to Lin. "And look here—don't you think you might leave that 'getting full' out of your plans?"

Lin gave a slightly shamefaced grin. "I don't guess I can, sir," he said. "I'm givin' yu' straight goods, yu' see," he added.

"That's right. But you look like a man who could stop when he'd had enough. Try that. You're man enough—and come and see me whenever we're in the same place."

He went to the hotel. There were several hours for Lin to wait. He walked up and down the platform till the stars came out and the bright lights of the town shone in the saloon windows. Over across the way piano-music sounded through one of the many open doors.

"Wonder if the professor's there yet?" said Lin, and he went across the railroad tracks. The bartender nodded to him as he passed through into the back room. In that place were many tables, and the flat clicking and rattle of ivory counters sounded pleasantly through the music. Lin did not join the stud-poker game. He stood over a table at which sat a dealer and a player, very silent, opposite each other, and whereon were painted sundry cards, numerals, and the colors red and black in squares. The legend "Jacks pay" was also clearly painted. The player placed chips on whichever insignia of fortune he chose, and the dealer slid cards (quite fairly) from the top of a pack that lay held within a skeleton case made with some clamped bands of tin. Sometimes the player's pile of chips rose high, and sometimes his sumptuous pillar of gold pieces was lessened by one. It was very interesting and pretty to see; Lin had much better have joined the game of stud-poker. Presently the eye of the dealer met the eye of the player. After that slight incident the player's chip pile began to rise, and rose steadily, till the dealer made admiring comments on such a run of luck. Then the player stopped, cashed in, and said good-night, having nearly doubled the number of his gold pieces.

"Five dollars' worth," said Lin, sitting down in the vacant seat. The chips were counted out to him. He played with unimportant shiftings of fortune until a short while before his train was due, and then, singularly enough, he discovered he was one hundred and fifty dollars behind the game.

"I guess I'll leave the train go without me," said Lin, buying five dollars' worth more of ivory counters. So that train came and went, removing eastward Mr. McLean's trunk.

During the hour that followed his voice grew dogged and his remarks briefer, as he continually purchased more chips from the now surprised and sympathetic dealer. It was really wonderful how steadily Lin lost—just as steadily as his predecessor had won after that meeting of eyes early in the evening.

When Lin was three hundred dollars out, his voice began to clear of its huskiness and a slight humor revolved and sparkled in his eye. When his seven hundred dollars had gone to safer hands and he had nothing left at all but some silver fractions of a dollar, his robust cheerfulness was all back again. He walked out and stood among the railroad tracks with his hands in his pockets, and laughed at himself in the dark. Then his fingers came on the check for Omaha, and he laughed loudly. The trunk by this hour must be nearing Rawlins; it was going east anyhow.

"I'm following it, you bet," he declared, kicking the rail. "Not yet though. Nor I'll not go to Washakie to have 'em josh me. And yonder lays Boston." He stretched his arm and pointed eastward. Had he seen another man going on in this fashion alone in the dark, among side-tracked freight cars, he would have pitied the poor fool. "And I guess Boston'll have to get along without me for a spell, too," continued Lin. "A man don't want to show up plumb broke like that younger son did after eatin' with the hogs the bishop told about. His father was a jim-dandy, that hog chap's. Hustled around and set 'em up when he come back home. Frank, he'd say to me 'How do you do, brother?' and he'd be wearin' a good suit o' clothes and—no, sir, you bet!"

Lin now watched the great headlight of a freight train bearing slowly down into Green River from the wilderness. Green River is the end of a division, an epoch in every train's journey. Lanterns swung signals, the great dim thing slowed to its standstill by the coal chute, its locomotive moved away for a turn of repose, the successor backed steaming to its place to tackle a night's work. Cars were shifted, heavily bumping and parting.

"Hello, Lin!" A face was looking from the window of the caboose.

"Hello!" responded Mr. McLean, perceiving above his head Honey Wiggin, a good friend of his. They had not met for three years.

"They claimed you got killed somewheres. I was sorry to hear it." Honey offered his condolence quite sincerely.

"Bruck my leg," corrected Lin, "if that's what they meant."

"I expect that's it," said Honey. "You've had no other trouble?"

"Been boomin'," said Lin.

From the mere undertone in their voices it was plain they were good friends, carefully hiding their pleasure at meeting.

"Wher're yu' bound?" inquired Honey.

"East," said Lin.

"Better jump in here, then. We're goin' west."

"That just suits me," said Lin.

The busy lanterns wagged among the switches, the steady lights of the saloons shone along the town's wooden façade. From the bluffs that wall Green River the sweet, clean sage-brush wind blew down in currents freshly through the coal-smoke. A wrench passed through the train from locomotive to caboose, each fettered car in turn strained into motion and slowly rolled over the bridge and into silence from the steam and the bells of the railroad yard. Through the open windows of the caboose great dull-red cinders rattled in, and the whistles of distant Union Pacific locomotives sounded over the open plains ominous and long, like ships at sea.

Honey and Lin sat for a while, making few observations and far between, as their way is between whom flows a stream of old-time understanding. Mutual whiskey and silence can express much friendship, and eloquently.

"What are yu' doing at present?" Lin inquired.

"Prospectin'."

Now prospecting means hunting gold, except to such spirits as the boy Lin. To these it means finding gold. So Lin McLean listened to the talk of his friend Honey Wiggin as the caboose trundled through the night. He saw himself in a vision of the near future enter a bank and thump down a bag of gold-dust. Then he saw the new, clean money the man would hand him in exchange, bills with round zeroes half covered by being folded over, and heavy, satisfactory gold pieces. And then he saw the blue water that twinkles beneath Boston. His fingers came again on his trunk check. He had his ticket, too. And as dawn now revealed the gray country to him, his eye fell casually upon a mile-post: "Omaha, 876." He began to watch for them:—877, 878. But the trunk would really get to Omaha.

"What are yu' laughin' about?" asked Honey.

"Oh, the wheels."

"Wheels?"

"Don't yu' hear 'em?" said Lin. " 'Variety,' they keep a-sayin'. 'Variety, variety.' "

"Huh!" said Honey, with scorn. " 'Ker-chunk-a-chunk' 's all I make it."

"You're no poet," observed Mr. McLean.

As the train moved into Evanston in the sunlight, a gleam of dismay shot over Lin's face, and he ducked his head out of sight of the window, but immediately raised it again. Then he leaned out, waving his arm with a certain defiant vigor. But the bishop on the platform failed to notice this performance, though it was done for his sole benefit, nor would Lin explain to the inquisitive Wiggin what the matter was. Therefore, very naturally, Honey drew a conclusion for himself, looked quickly out of the window, and, being disappointed in what he expected to see, remarked, sulkily, "Do yu' figure I care what sort of a lookin' girl is stuck on yu' in Evanston?" And upon this young Lin laughed so loudly that his friend told him he had never seen a man get so foolish in three years.

By-and-by they were in Utah, and, in the company of Ogden friends, forgot prospecting. Later they resumed freight trains and journeyed north. In Idaho they said good-bye to the train hands in the caboose, and came to Little Camas, and so among the mountains near Feather Creek. Here the berries were of several sorts, and growing riper each day; and the bears in the timber above knew this, and came down punctually with the season, making variety in the otherwise even life of the prospectors. It was now August, and Lin sat on a wet hill making mud-pies for sixty days. But the philosopher's stone was not in the wash at that placer, nor did Lin gather gold-dust sufficient to cover the nail of his thumb. Then they heard of an excitement at Obo, Nevada, and, hurrying to Obo, they made some more mud-pies.

Now and then, eating their fat bacon at noon, Honey would say, "Lin, wher're yu' goin'?"

And Lin always replied, "East." This became a signal for drinks.

For beauty and promise, Nevada is a name among names. Nevada! Pronounce the word aloud. Does it not evoke mountains and clear air, heights of untrodden snow and valleys aromatic with the pine and musical with falling waters? Nevada! But the name is all. Abomination of desolation presides over nine-tenths of the place. The sun beats down as on a roof of zinc, fierce and dull. Not a drop of water to a mile of sand. The mean ash-dump landscape stretches on from nowhere to nowhere, a spot of mange. No portion of the earth is more lacquered with paltry, unimportant ugliness.

There is gold in Nevada, but Lin and Honey did not find it. Prospecting of the sort they did, besides proving unfruitful, is not comfortable. Now and again, losing patience, Lin would leave his work and stalk about and gaze down at the scattered men who stooped or knelt in the water. Passing each busy prospector, Lin would read on every broad, upturned pair of overalls the same label, "Levi Strauss, No. 2," with a picture of two lusty horses hitched to one of these garments and vainly struggling to split them asunder. Lin remembered he was wearing a label just like that too, and when he considered all things he laughed to himself. Then, having stretched the ache out of his long legs, he would return to his ditch. As autumn wore on, his feet grew cold in the mushy gravel they were sunk in. He beat off the sand that had stiffened on his boots, and hated Obo, Nevada. But he held himself ready to say "East" whenever he saw Honey coming along with the bottle. The cold weather put an end to this adventure. The ditches froze and filled with snow, through which the sordid gravel heaps showed in a dreary fashion; so the two friends drifted southward.

Near the small new town of Mesa, Arizona, they sat down again in the dirt. It was milder here, and, when the sun shone, never quite froze. But this part of Arizona is scarcely more grateful to the eye than Nevada. Moreover, Lin and Honey found no gold at all. Some men near them found a little. Then in January, even though the sun shone, it quite froze one day.

"We're seein' the country, anyway," said Honey.

"Seein' hell," said Lin, "and there's more of it above ground than I thought."

"What'll we do?" Honey inquired.

"Have to walk for a job—a good-payin' job," responded the hopeful cow-puncher. And he and Honey went to town.

Lin found a job in twenty-five minutes, becoming assistant to the apothecary in Mesa. Established at the drug-store, he made up the simpler prescriptions. He had studied practical pharmacy in Boston between the ages of thirteen and fifteen, and, besides this qualification, the apothecary had seen him when he first came into Mesa, and liked him. Lin made no mistakes that he or any one ever knew of; and, as the mild weather began, he materially increased the apothecary's business by persuading him to send East for a soda-water fountain. The ladies of the town clustered around this entertaining novelty, and while sipping vanilla and lemon bought knickknacks. And the gentlemen of the town discovered that whiskey with soda and strawberry syrup was delicious, and produced just as competent effects. A group of them were generally standing in the shop and shaking dice to decide who should pay for the next, while Lin administered to each glass the necessary ingredients. Thus money began to come to him a little more steadily than had been its wont, and he divided with the penniless Honey.

But Honey found fortune quickly, too. Through excellent card-playing he won a pinto from a small Mexican horse-thief who came into town from the South, and who cried bitterly when he delivered up his pet pony to the new owner. The new owner, being a man of the world and agile on his feet, was only slightly stabbed that evening as he walked to the dance-hall at the edge of the town. The Mexican was buried on the next day but one.

The pony stood thirteen two, and was as long as a steamboat. He had white eyelashes, pink nostrils, and one eye was bright blue. If you spoke pleasantly to him, he rose instantly on his hind-legs and tried to beat your face. He did not look as if he could run, and that was what made him so valuable. Honey travelled through the country with him, and every gentleman who saw the pinto and heard Honey became anxious to get up a race. Lin always sent money for Wiggin to place, and he soon opened a bank account, while Honey, besides his racing-bridle, bought a silver-inlaid one, a pair of forty-dollar spurs, and a beautiful saddle richly stamped. Every day (when in Mesa) Honey would step into the drug-store and inquire, "Lin, wher're yu' goin'?"

But Lin never answered any more. He merely came to the soda-water fountain with the whiskey. The passing of days brought a choked season of fine sand and hard blazing sky. Heat rose up from the ground and hung heavily over man and beast. Many insects sat out in the sun rattling with joy; the little tearing river grew clear from the swollen mud, and shrank to a succession of standing pools; and the fat, squatting cactus bloomed everywhere into butter-colored flowers big as tulips in the sand. There were artesian wells in Mesa, and the water did not taste very good; but if you drank from the standing pools where the river had been, you repaired to the drug-store almost immediately. A troop of wandering players came dot-ting along the railroad, and, reaching Mesa, played a brass-band up and down the street, and announced the powerful drama of "East Lynne." Then Mr. McLean thought of the Lynn marshes that lie between there and Chelsea, and of the sea that must look so cool. He forgot them while following the painful fortunes of the Lady Isabel; but, going to bed in the back part of the drug-store, he remembered how he used to beat everybody swimming in the salt water.

"I'm goin'," he said. Then he got up, and, striking the light, he inspected his bank account. "I'm sure goin'," he repeated, blowing the light out, "and I can buy the fatted calf myself, you bet!" for he had often thought of the bishop's story. "You bet!" he remarked once more in a muffled voice, and was asleep in a minute. The apothecary was sorry to have him go, and Honey was deeply grieved.

"I'd pull out with yer," he said, "only I can do business round Yuma and westward with the pinto."

For three farewell days Lin and Honey roved together in all sorts of places, where they were welcome, and once more Lin rode a horse and was in his native element. Then he travelled to Deming, and so through Denver to Omaha, where he was told that his trunk had been sold for some months. Besides a suit of clothes for town wear, it had contained a buffalo coat for his brother—something scarce to see in these days.

"Frank'll have to get along without it," he observed, philosophically, and took the next eastbound train.

If you journey in a Pullman from Mesa to Omaha without a waistcoat, and with a silk handkerchief knotted over the collar of your flannel shirt instead of a tie, wearing, besides, tall, highheeled boots, a soft, gray hat with a splendid brim, a few people will notice you, but not the majority. New Mexico and

Colorado are used to these things. As Iowa, with its
immense rolling grain, encompasses you, people will
stare a little more, for you're getting near the East,
where cow-punchers are not understood. But in
those days the line of cleavage came sharp-drawn at
Chicago. West of there was still tolerably west, but
east of there was east indeed, and the Atlantic Ocean
was the next important stopping-place. In Lin's new
train, good gloves, patent-leathers, and silence prevailed throughout the sleeping-car, which was for
Boston without change. Had not home memories begun impetuously to flood his mind, he would have
felt himself conspicuous. Town clothes and conven-
tions had their due value with him. But just now the
boy's single-hearted thoughts were far from any sur-
roundings, and he was murmuring to himself, "To-
morrow! to-morrow night!"

There were ladies in that blue plush car for Boston
who looked at Lin for thirty miles at a stretch; and by
the time Albany was reached the next day one or two
of them commented that he was the most attractive-
looking man they had ever seen! Whereas, beyond
his tallness, and wide-open, jocular eyes, eyes that
seemed those of a not highly conscientious wild animal, there was nothing remarkable about young Lin
except stage effect. The conductor had been annoyed to have such a passenger; but the cow-
puncher troubled no one, and was extremely silent.
So evidently was he a piece of the true frontier that
curious and hopeful fellow-passengers, after watching him with diversion, more than once took a seat
next to him. He met their chatty inquiries with mono-
syllables so few and so unprofitable in their quiet politeness that the passengers soon gave him up. At
Springfield he sent a telegram to his brother at the
great dry-goods establishment that employed him.

The train began its homestretch after Worcester,
and whirled and swung by hills and ponds he began

to watch for, and through stations with old wayside names. These flashed on Lin's eye as he sat with his hat off and his forehead against the window, looking: Wellesley. Then, not long after, Riverside. That was the Charles River, and did the picnic woods used to be above the bridge or below? West Newton; Newtonville; Newton. "Faneuil's next," he said aloud in the car, as the long-forgotten home-knowledge shone forth in his recollection. The traveller seated near said, "Beg pardon?" but, turning, wondered at the all-unconscious Lin, with his forehead pressed against the glass. The blue water flashed into sight, and soon after they were running in the darkness between high walls; but the cow-puncher never moved, though nothing could be seen. When the porter announced "Boston," he started up and followed like a sheep in the general exodus. Down on the platform he moved along with the slow crowd till some one touched him, and, wheeling round, he seized both his brother's hands and swore a good oath of joy.

There they stood—the long, brown fellow with the silk handkerchief knotted over his flannel shirt, greeting tremendously the spruce civilian, who had a rope-colored mustache and bore a faint-hearted resemblance to him. The story was plain on its face to the passers-by; and one of the ladies who had come in the car with Lin turned twice, and smiled gently to herself.

But Frank McLean's heart did not warm. He felt that what he had been afraid of was true; and he saw he was being made conspicuous. He saw men and women stare in the station, and he saw them staring as he and his Western brother went through the streets. Lin strode along, sniffing the air of Boston, looking at all things, and making it a stretch for his sleek companion to keep step with him. Frank thought of the refined friends he should have to introduce his brother to; for he had risen with his sal-

ary, and now belonged to a small club where the
paying-tellers of banks played cards every night,
and the head clerk at the Parker House was presi-
dent. Perhaps he should not have to reveal the
cow-puncher to these shining ones. Perhaps the
cow-puncher would not stay very long. Of course he
was glad to see him again, and he would take him to
dine at some obscure place this first evening. But
this was not Lin's plan. Frank must dine with him, at
the Parker House. Frank demurred, saying it was he
that should be host.

"And," he added, "they charge up high for wines at
Parker's." Then for the twentieth time he shifted a
sidelong eye over his brother's clothes.

"You're goin' to take your grub with me," said Lin.
"That's all right, I guess. And there ain't any 'no'
about it. Things is not the same like as if father was
livin'—(his voice softened)—and here to see me
come home. Now I'm good for several dinners with
wines charged up high, I expect, nor it ain't nobody
in this world, barrin' just Lin McLean, that I've any
need to ask for anything. 'Mr. McLean,' says I to Lin,
'can yu' spare me some cash?' 'Why, to be sure, you
bet!' And we'll start off with steamed Duxbury
clams." The cow-puncher slapped his pocket, where
the coin made a muffled chinking. Then he said,
gruffly, "I suppose Swampscott's there yet?"

"Yes," said Frank. "It's a dead little town, is Swampscott."

"I guess I'll take a look at the old house to-
morrow," Lin pursued.

"Oh, that's been pulled down since— I forget the
year they improved that block."

Lin regarded in silence his brother, who was speaking so jauntily of the first and last home they had
ever had.

"Seventy-nine is when it was," continued Frank.

"So you can save the trouble of travelling away down to Swampscott."

"I guess I'll go to the graveyard, anyway," said the cow-puncher in his offish voice, and looking fixedly in front of him.

They came into Washington Street, and again the elder McLean uneasily surveyed the younger's appearance.

But the momentary chill had melted from the heart of the genial Lin. "After to-morrow," said he, laying a hand on his brother's shoulder, "yu' can start any lead yu' please, and I guess I can stay with yu' pretty close, Frank."

Frank said nothing. He saw one of the members of his club on the other side of the way, and the member saw him, and Frank caught diverted amazement on the member's face. Lin's hand weighed on his shoulder, and the stress became too great. "Lin," said he, "while you're running with our crowd, you don't want to wear that style of hat, you know."

It may be that such words can in some way be spoken at such a time, but not in the way that these were said. The frozen fact was irrevocably revealed in the tone of Frank's voice.

The cow-puncher stopped dead short, and his hand slid off his brother's shoulder. "You've made it plain," he said, evenly, slanting his steady eyes down into Frank's. "You've explained yourself fairly well. Run along with your crowd, and I'll not bother yu' more with comin' round and causin' yu' to feel ashamed. It's a heap better to understand these things at once, and save making a fool of yourself any longer 'n yu' need to. I guess there ain't no more to be said, only one thing. If yu' see me around on the street, don't yu' try any talk, for I'd be liable to close your jaw up, and maybe yu'd have more of a job explainin' that to your crowd than you've had makin' me see what kind of a man I've got for a brother."

Frank found himself standing alone before any reply to these sentences had occurred to him. He walked slowly to his club, where a friend joked him on his glumness.

Lin made a sore failure of amusing himself that night; and in the bright, hot morning he got into the train for Swampscott. At the graveyard he saw a woman lay a bunch of flowers on a mound and kneel, weeping.

"There ain't nobody to do that for this one," thought the cow-puncher, and looked down at the grave he had come to see, then absently gazed at the woman.

She had stolen away from her daily life to come here where her grief was shrined, and now her heart found it hard to bid the lonely place good-bye. So she lingered long, her thoughts sunk deep in the motionless past. When she at last looked up, she saw the tall, strange man re-enter from the street among the tombs, and deposit on one of them an ungainly lump of flowers. They were what Lin had been able hastily to buy in Swampscott. He spread them gently as he had noticed the woman do, but her act of kneeling he did not imitate. He went away quickly. For some hours he hung about the little town, aimlessly loitering, watching the salt water where he used to swim.

"Yu' don't belong any more, Lin," he miserably said at length, and took his way to Boston.

The next morning, determined to see the sights, he was in New York, and drifted about to all places night and day, till his money was mostly gone, and nothing to show for it but a somewhat pleasure-beaten face and a deep hatred of the crowded, scrambling East. So he suddenly bought a ticket for Green River, Wyoming, and escaped from the city that seemed to numb his good humor.

When, after three days, the Missouri lay behind

him and his holiday, he stretched his legs and took heart to see out of the window the signs of approaching desolation. And when on the fourth day civilization was utterly emptied out of the world, he saw a bunch of cattle, and, galloping among them, his spurred and booted kindred. And his manner took on that alertness a horse shows on turning into the home road. As the stage took him toward Washakie, old friends turned up every fifty miles or so, shambling out of a cabin or a stable, and saying, in casual tones, "Hello, Lin, where've you been at?"

At Lander, there got into the stage another old acquaintance, the Bishop of Wyoming. He knew Lin at once, and held out his hand, and his greeting was hearty.

"It took a week for my robes to catch up with me," he said, laughing. Then, in a little while, "How was the East?"

"First-rate," said Lin, not looking at him. He was shy of the conversation's taking a moral turn. But the bishop had no intention of reverting—at any rate, just now—to their last talk at Green River, and the advice he had then given.

"I trust your friends were all well?" he said.

"I guess they was healthy enough," said Lin.

"I suppose you found Boston much changed? It's a beautiful city."

"Good enough town for them that likes it, I expect," Lin replied.

The bishop was forming a notion of what the matter must be, but he had no notion whatever of what now revealed itself.

"Mr. Bishop," the cow-puncher said, "how was that about that fellow you told about that's in the Bible somewheres?—he come home to his folks, and they—well there was his father saw him comin'—" He stopped, embarrassed.

Then the bishop remembered the wide-open eyes,

and how he had noticed them in the church at the agency intently watching him. And, just now, what were best to say he did not know. He looked at the young man gravely.

"Have yu' got a Bible?" pursued Lin. "For, excuse me, but I'd like yu' to read that onced."

So the bishop read, and Lin listened. And all the while this good clergyman was perplexed how to speak—or if indeed to speak at this time at all—to the heart of the man beside him for whom the parable had gone so sorely wrong. When the reading was done, Lin had not taken his eyes from the bishop's face.

"How long has that there been wrote?" he asked.

He was told about how long.

"Mr. Bishop," said Lin, "I 'ain't got good knowledge of the Bible, and I never figured it to be a book much on to facts. And I tell you I'm more plumb beat about it's having that elder brother, and him being angry, down in black and white two thousand years ago, than—than if I'd seen a man turn water into wine, for I'd have knowed that ain't so. But the elder brother is facts—dead-sure facts. And they knowed about that, and put it down just the same as life two thousand years ago!"

"Well," said the bishop, wisely ignoring the challenge as to miracles, "I am a good twenty years older than you, and all that time I've been finding more facts in the Bible every day I have lived."

Lin meditated. "I guess that could be," he said. "Yes; after that yu've been a-readin', and what I know for myself that I didn't know till lately, I guess that could be."

Then the bishop talked with exceeding care, nor did he ask uncomfortable things, or moralize visibly. Thus he came to hear how it had fared with Lin his friend, and Lin forgot altogether about its being a parson he was delivering the fullness of his heart to.

"And come to think," he concluded, "it weren't home I had went to back East, layin' round them big cities, where a man can't help but feel strange all the week. No, sir! yu' can blow in a thousand dollars like I did in New York, and it'll not give yu' any more home feelin' than what cattle has put in a stock-yard. Nor it wouldn't have in Boston neither. Now this country here" (he waved his hand towards the endless sagebrush), "seein' it onced more, I know where my home is, and I wouldn't live nowheres else. Only I 'ain't got no father watching for me to come up Wind River."

The cow-puncher stated this merely as a fact, and without any note of self-pity. But the bishop's face grew very tender, and he looked away from Lin. Knowing his man—for had he not seen many of this kind in his desert diocese?—he forbore to make any text from that last sentence the cow-puncher had spoken. Lin talked cheerfully on about what he should now do. The round-up must be somewhere near Du Noir Creek. He would join it this season, but next he should work over to the Powder River country. More business was over there, and better chances for a man to take up some land and have a ranch of his own. As they got out at Fort Washakie, the bishop handed him a small book, in which he had turned several leaves down, carefully avoiding any page that related of miracles.

"You need not read it through, you know," he said, smiling; "just read where I have marked, and see if you don't find some more facts. Good-bye—and always come and see me."

The next morning he watched Lin riding slowly out of the post towards Wind River, leading a single packhorse. By-and-by the little moving dot went over the ridge. And as the bishop walked back into the parade-ground, thinking over the possibilities in that untrained manly soul, he shook his head sorrowfully.

CHAPTER II

The Winning of the Biscuit-shooter

It was quite clear to me that Mr. McLean could not know the news. Meeting him to-day had been unforeseen—unforeseen and so pleasant that the thing had never come into my head until just now, after both of us had talked and dined our fill, and were torpid with satisfaction.

I had found Lin here at Riverside in the morning. At my horse's approach to the cabin, it was he and not the postmaster who had come precipitately out of the door.

"I'm turrible pleased to see yu'," he had said, immediately.

"What's happened?" said I, in some concern at his appearance.

And he piteously explained: "Why, I've been here all alone since yesterday!"

This was indeed all; and my hasty impressions of shooting and a corpse gave way to mirth over the child and his innocent grievance that he had blurted out before I could get off my horse.

Since when, I inquired of him, had his own company become such a shock to him?

"As to that," replied Mr. McLean, a thought ruffled, "when a man expects lonesomeness he stands it like he stands anything else, of course. But when he has figured on finding company—say—" he broke off (and vindictiveness sparkled in his eye)—"when you're lucky enough to catch yourself alone, why, I suppose yu' just take a chair and chat to yourself for hours.—You've not seen anything of Tommy?" he pursued with interest.

I had not; and forthwith Lin poured out to me the pent-up complaints and sociability with which he was bursting. The foreman had sent him over here with a sackful of letters for the post, and to bring back the week's mail for the ranch. A day was gone now, and nothing for a man to do but sit and sit. Tommy was overdue fifteen hours. Well, you could have endured that, but the neighbors had all locked their cabins and gone to Buffalo. It was circus week in Buffalo. Had I ever considered the money there must be in the circus business? Tommy had taken the outgoing letters early yesterday. Nobody had kept him waiting. By all rules he should have been back again last night. Maybe the stage was late reaching Powder River, and Tommy had had to lay over for it. Well, that would justify him. Far more likely he had gone to the circus himself and taken the mail with him. Tommy was no type of man for postmaster. Except drawing the allowance his mother in the East gave him first of every month, he had never shown punctuality, that Lin could remember. Never had any second thoughts, and awful few first ones. Told bigger lies than a small man ought, also.

"Has successes, though," said I, wickedly.

"Huh!" went on Mr. McLean. "Successes! One ice-cream-soda success. And she"—Lin's still wounded male pride made him plaintive—"why, even that girl quit him, once she got the chance to appreciate how insignificant he was compared with the size of his words. No, sir. Not one of 'em retains interest in Tommy."

Lin was unsaddling and looking after my horse, just because he was glad to see me. Since our first acquaintance, that memorable summer of Pitchstone Cañon when he had taken such good care of me and such bad care of himself, I had learned pretty well about horses and camp craft in general. He was an entire boy then. But he had been East since, East by a route of his own discovering—and from his account of that journey it had proved, I think, a sort of spiritual experience. And then the years of our friendship were beginning to roll up. Manhood of the body he had always richly possessed; and now, whenever we met after a season's absence and spoke those invariable words which all old friends upon this earth use to each other at meeting—"You haven't changed, you haven't changed at all!"—I would wonder if manhood had arrived in Lin's boy soul. And so to-day, while he attended to my horse and explained the nature of Tommy (a subject he dearly loved just now), I looked at him and took an intimate, superior pride in feeling how much more mature I was than he, after all.

There's nothing like a sense of merit for making one feel aggrieved, and on our return to the cabin Mr. McLean pointed with disgust to some firewood.

"Look at those sorrowful toothpicks," said he: "Tommy's work."

So Lin, the excellent hearted, had angrily busied himself, and chopped a pile of real logs that would last a week. He had also cleaned the stove, and nailed up the bed, the pillow-end of which was on the floor. It appeared the master of the house had been sleeping in it the reverse way on account of the slant. Thus had Lin cooked and dined alone, supped alone, and sat over some old newspapers until bed-time alone with his sense of virtue. And now here it was long after breakfast, and no Tommy yet.

"It's good yu' come this forenoon," Lin said to me. "I'd not have had the heart to get up another dinner just for myself. Let's eat rich!"

Accordingly, we had richly eaten, Lin and I. He had gone out among the sheds and caught some eggs (that is how he spoke of it), we had opened a number of things in cans, and I had made my famous dish of evaporated apricots, in which I managed to fling a suspicion of caramel throughout the stew.

"Tommy'll be hot about these," said Lin joyfully, as we ate the eggs. "He don't mind what yu' use of his canned goods—pickled salmon and truck. He is hospitable all right enough till it comes to an egg. Then he'll tell any lie. But shucks! Yu' can read Tommy right through his clothing. 'Make yourself at home, Lin,' says he, yesterday. And he showed me his fresh milk and his stuff. 'Here's a new ham,' says he; 'too bad my damned hens 'ain't been layin'. The sons-o'-guns have quit on me ever since Christmas.' And away he goes to Powder River for the mail. 'You swore too heavy about them hens,' thinks I. Well, I expect he may have travelled half a mile by the time I'd found four nests."

I am fond of eggs, and eat them constantly—and in Wyoming they were always a luxury. But I never forget those that day, and how Lin and I enjoyed them thinking of Tommy. Perhaps manhood was not quite established in my own soul at that time—and perhaps that is the reason why it is the only time I have ever known which I would live over again, those years when people said, "You are old enough to know better"—and one didn't care!

Salmon, apricots, eggs, we dealt with them all

properly, and I had some cigars. It was now that the news came back into my head.

"What do you think of—" I began, and stopped.

I spoke out of a long silence, the slack, luxurious silence of digestion. I got no answer, naturally, from the torpid Lin, and then it occurred to me that he would have asked me what I thought, long before this, had he known. So, observing how comfortable he was, I began differently.

"What is the most important event that can happen in this country?" said I.

Mr. McLean heard me where he lay along the floor of the cabin on his back, dozing by the fire; but his eyes remained closed. He waggled one limp, open hand slightly at me, and torpor resumed her dominion over him.

"I want to know what you consider the most important event that can happen in this country," said I, again, enunciating each word with slow clearness.

The throat and lips of Mr. McLean moved, and a sulky sound came forth that I recognized to be meant for the word "War." Then he rolled over so that his face was away from me, and put an arm over his eyes.

"I don't mean country in the sense of United States," said I. "I mean this country here, and Bear Creek, and—well, the ranches southward for fifty miles, say. Important to this section."

"Mosquitoes'll be due in about three weeks," said Lin. "Yu' might leave a man rest till then."

"I want your opinion," said I.

"Oh, misery! Well, a raise in the price of steers."

"No."

"Yu' said yu' wanted my opinion," said Lin. "Seems like yu' merely figure on givin' me yours."

"Very well," said I. "Very well, then."

I took up a copy of the Cheyenne *Sun*. It was five weeks old, and I soon perceived that I had read it three weeks ago; but I read it again for some minutes now.

"I expect a railroad would be more important," said Mr. McLean, persuasively, from the floor.

"Than a rise in steers?" said I, occupied with the Cheyenne *Sun*. "Oh yes. Yes, a railroad certainly would."

"It's got to be money, anyhow," stated Lin, thoroughly wakened. "Money in some shape."

"How little you understand the real wants of the country!" said I, coming to the point. "It's a girl."

Mr. McLean lay quite still on the floor.

"A girl," I repeated. "A new girl coming to this starved country."

The cow-puncher took a long, gradual stretch and began to smile. "Well," said he, "yu' caught me—if that's much to do when a man is half-witted with dinner and sleep." He closed his eyes again and lay with a specious expression of indifference. But that sort of thing is a solitary entertainment, and palls. "Starved," he presently muttered. "We are kind o' starved that way, I'll admit. More dollars than girls to the square mile. And to think of all of us nice, healthy, young—bet yu' I know who she is!" he triumphantly cried. He had sat up and levelled a finger at me with the throw-down jerk of a marksman. "Sidney, Nebraska."

I nodded. This was not the lady's name—he could not recall her name—but his geography of her was accurate.

One day in February my friend, Mrs. Taylor, over on Bear Creek, had received a letter—no common event for her. Therefore, during several days she had all callers read it just as naturally as she had them all see the new baby; and baby and letter had both been brought out for me. The letter was signed,

"Ever your afectionite frend
    "KATIE PECK,"

and was not easy to read, here and there. But you
could piece out the drift of it, and there was Mrs.
Taylor by your side, eager to help you when you
stumbled. Miss Peck wrote that she was overworked
in Sidney, Nebraska, and needed a holiday. When the
weather grew warm she should like to come to Bear
Creek and be like old times. "Like to come and be
like old times" filled Mrs. Taylor with sentiment and
the cow-punchers with expectation. But it is a long
way from February to warm weather on Bear Creek,
and even cow-punchers will forget about a new girl if
she does not come. For several weeks I had not
heard Miss Peck mentioned, and old girls had to do.
Yesterday, however, when I paid a visit to Miss Molly
Wood (the Bear Creek schoolmistress), I found her
keeping in order the cabin and the children of the
Taylors, while they were gone forty-five miles to the
stage station to meet their guest.

"Well," said Lin, judicially, "Miss Wood is a lady."

"Yes," said I, with deep gravity. For I was thinking
of an occasion when Mr. McLean had discovered that
truth somewhat abruptly.

Lin thoughtfully continued. "She is—she's—she's—
what are you laughin' at?"

"Oh, nothing. You don't see quite so much of Miss
Wood as you used to, do you?"

"Huh! So that's got around. Well, o' course I'd
ought t've knowed better, I suppose. All the same,
there's lots and lots of girls do like gettin' kissed
against their wishes—and you know it."

"But the point would rather seem to be that she—"

"Would rather seem! Don't yu' start that professor
style o' yours, or I'll—I'll talk more wickedness in
worse language than ever yu've heard me do yet."

"Impossible!" I murmured, sweetly, and Master Lin
went on.

"As to point—that don't need to be explained to
me. She's a lady all right." He ruminated for a mo-

ment. "She has about scared all the boys off, though," he continued. "And that's what you get by being refined," he concluded, as if Providence had at length spoken in this matter.

"She has not scared off a boy from Virginia, I notice," said I. "He was there yesterday afternoon again. Ridden all the way over from Sunk Creek. Didn't seem particularly frightened."

"Oh, well, nothin' alarms him—not even refinement," said Mr. McLean, with his grin. "And she'll fool your Virginian like she done the balance of us. You wait. Shucks! If all the girls were that chilly, why, what would us poor punchers do?"

"You have me cornered," said I, and we sat in a philosophical silence, Lin on the floor still, and I at the window. There I looked out upon a scene my eyes never tired of then, nor can my memory now. Spring had passed over it with its first, lightest steps. The pastured levels undulated in emerald. Through the many-changing sage, that just this moment of to-day was lilac, shone greens scarce a week old in the dimples of the foot-hills; and greens new-born beneath to-day's sun melted among them. Around the doublings of the creek in the willow thickets glimmered skeined veils of yellow and delicate crimson. The stream poured turbulently away from the snows of the mountains behind us. It went winding in many folds across the meadows into distance and smallness, and so vanished round the great red battlement of wall beyond: Upon this were falling the deep hues of afternoon—violet, rose, and saffron, swimming and meeting as if some prism had dissolved and flowed over the turrets and crevices of the sandstone. Far over there I saw a dot move.

"At last!" said I.

Lin looked out of the window. "It's more than Tommy," said he, at once; and his eyes made it out before mine could. "It's a wagon. That's Tommy's bald-faced horse alongside. He's fooling to the fin-ish," Lin severely commented, as if, after all this de-lay, there should at least be a homestretch.

Presently, however, a homestretch seemed likely to occur. The bald-faced horse executed some lively ma-noeuvres, and Tommy's voice reached us faintly through the light spring air. He was evidently howling the remarkable strain of yells that the cow-punchers invented as the speech best understood by cows—"Oi-ee, yah, whoop-yah-ye-ee, oooo-oop, oop, oop-oop-oop-oop-yah-hee!" But that gives you no idea of it. Alphabets are worse than photographs. It is not the lungs of every man that can produce these ef-fects, nor even from armies, eagles, or mules were such sounds ever heard on earth. The cow-puncher invented them. And when the last cow-puncher is laid to rest (if that, alas! have not already befallen) the yells will be forever gone. Singularly enough, the cattle appeared to appreciate them. Tommy always did them very badly, and that was plain even at this distance. Nor did he give us a homestretch, after all. The bald-faced horse made a number of evolutions and returned beside the wagon.

"Showin' off," remarked Lin. "Tommy's showin' off." Suspicion crossed his face, and then certainty. "Why, we might have knowed that!" he exclaimed, in dudgeon. "It's her." He hastened outside for a better look, and I came to the door myself. "That's what it is," said he. "It's the girl. Oh yes. That's Taylor's buckskin pair he traded Balaam for. She come by the stage all right yesterday, yu' see, but she has been too tired to travel, yu' see, or else, maybe, Taylor wanted to rest his buckskins—they're four-year-olds. Or else—anyway, they laid over last night at Powder River, and Tommy he has just laid over too, yu' see, holdin' the mail back on us twenty-four hours—and that's your postmaster!"

It was our postmaster, and this he had done, quite

as the virtuously indignant McLean surmised. Had I taken the same interest in the new girl, I suppose that I too should have felt virtuously indignant.

Lin and I stood outside to receive the travellers. As their cavalcade drew near, Mr. McLean grew silent and watchful, his whole attention focused upon the Taylors' vehicle. Its approach was joyous. Its gear made a cheerful clanking, Taylor cracked his whip and encouragingly chirruped to his buckskins, and Tommy's apparatus jingled musically. For Tommy wore upon himself and his saddle all the things you can wear in the Wild West. Except that his hair was not long, our postmaster might have conducted a show and minted gold by exhibiting his romantic person before the eyes of princes. He began with a black-and-yellow rattlesnake skin for a hat-band, he continued with a fringed and beaded shirt of buckskin, and concluded with large, tinkling spurs. Of course, there were things between his shirt and his heels, but all leather and deadly weapons. He had also a riata, a cuerta, and tapaderos, and frequently employed these Spanish names for the objects. I wish that I had not lost Tommy's photograph in Rocky Mountain costume. You must understand that he was really pretty, with blue eyes, ruddy cheeks, and a graceful figure; and, besides, he had twenty-four hours' start of poor dusty Lin, whose best clothes were elsewhere.

You might have supposed that it would be Mrs. Taylor who should present us to her friend from Sidney, Nebraska; but Tommy on his horse undertook the office before the wagon had well come to a standstill. "Good friends of mine, and gentlemen, both," said he to Miss Peck; and to us, "A lady whose acquaintance will prove a treat to our section."

We all bowed at each other beneath the florid expanse of these recommendations, and I was proceeding to murmur something about its being a long journey and a fine day when Miss Peck cut me short, gayly:

"Well," she exclaimed to Tommy, "I guess I'm pretty near ready for them eggs you've spoke so much about."

I have not often seen Mr. McLean lose his presence of mind. He needed merely to exclaim, "Why, Tommy, you told me your hens had not been laying since Christmas!" and we could have sat quiet and let Tommy try to find all the eggs that he could. But the new girl was a sore embarrassment to the cow-puncher's wits. Poor Lin stood by the wheels of the wagon. He looked up at Miss Peck, he looked over at Tommy, his features assumed a rueful expression, and he wretchedly blurted,

"Why, Tommy, I've been and eat 'em."

"Well, if that ain't!" cried Miss Peck. She stared with interest at Lin as he now assisted her to descend.

"All?" faltered Tommy. "Not the four nests?"

"I've had three meals, yu' know," Lin reminded him, deprecatingly.

"I helped him," said I. "Ten innocent, fresh eggs. But we have left some ham. Forgive us, please."

"I declare!" said Miss Peck, abruptly, and rolled her sluggish, inviting eyes upon me. "You're a case, too, I expect."

But she took only brief note of me, although it was from head to foot. In her stare the dull shine of familiarity grew vacant, and she turned back to Lin McLean. "You carry that," said she, and gave the pleased cow-puncher a hand valise.

"I'll look after your things, Miss Peck," called Tommy, now springing down from his horse. The egg tragedy had momentarily stunned him.

"You'll attend to the mail first, Mr. Postmaster!" said the lady, but favoring him with a look from her large eyes. "There's plenty of gentlemen here." With that her glance favored Lin. She went into the cabin, he following her close, with the Taylors and myself in the rear. "Well, I guess I'm about collapsed!" said she, vigorously, and sank upon one of Tommy's chairs.

The fragile article fell into sticks beneath her, and Lin leaped to her assistance. He placed her upon a firmer foundation. Mrs. Taylor brought a basin and towel to bathe the dust from her face, Mr. Taylor produced whiskey, and I found sugar and hot water. Tommy would doubtless have done something in the way of assistance or restoratives, but he was gone to the stable with the horses.

"Shall I get your medicine from the valise, deary?" inquired Mrs. Taylor.

"Not now," her visitor answered; and I wondered why she should take such a quick look at me.

"We'll soon have yu' independent of medicine," and Lin, gallantly. "Our climate and scenery here has frequently raised the dead."

"You're a case, anyway!" exclaimed the sick lady with rich conviction.

The cow-puncher now sat himself on the edge of Tommy's bed, and, throwing one leg across the other, began to raise her spirits with cheerful talk. She steadily watched him—his face sometimes, sometimes his lounging, masculine figure. While he thus devoted his attentions to her, Taylor departed to help Tommy at the stable, and good Mrs. Taylor, busy with supper for all of us in the kitchen, expressed her joy at having her old friend of childhood for a visit after so many years.

"Sickness has changed poor Katie some," said she. "But I'm hoping she'll get back her looks on Bear Creek."

"She seems less feeble than I had understood," I remarked.

"Yes, indeed! I do believe she's feeling stronger. She was that tired and down yesterday with the long stage-ride, and it is so lonesome! But Taylor and I heartened her up, and Tommy came with the mail, and to-day she's real spruced-up like, feeling she's among friends."

"How long will she stay?" I inquired.

"Just as long as ever she wants! Me and Katie hasn't met since we was young girls in Dubuque, for I left home when I married Taylor, and he brought me to this country right soon; and it 'ain't been like Dubuque much, though if I had it to do over again I'd do just the same, as Taylor knows. Katie and me hasn't wrote even, not till this February, for you always mean to and you don't. Well, it'll be like old times. Katie'll be most thirty-four, I expect. Yes. I was seventeen and she was sixteen the very month I was married. Poor thing! She ought to have got some good man for a husband, but I expect she didn't have any chance, for there was a big fam'ly o' them girls, and old Peck used to act real scandalous, getting drunk so folks didn't visit there evenings scarcely at all. And so she quit home, it seems, and got a position in the railroad eating-house at Sidney, and now she has poor health with feeding them big trains day and night."

"A biscuit-shooter!" said I.

Loyal Mrs. Taylor stirred some batter in silence. "Well," said she then, "I'm told that's what the yard-hands of the railroad call them poor waiter-girls. You might hear it around the switches at them division stations."

I had heard it in higher places also, but meekly accepted the reproof.

If you have made your trans-Missouri journeys only since the new era of dining-cars, there is a quantity of things you have come too late for, and will never know. Three times a day in the brave days of old you sprang from your scarce-halted car at the summons of a gong. You discerned by instinct the right direction, and, passing steadily through doorways, had taken, before you knew it, one of some sixty chairs in a room of tables and catsup bottles. Behind the chairs, standing attention, a platoon of Amazons, thick-wristed, pink-and-blue, began immediately a swift chant. It hymned the total bill-of-fare at a blow. In this inexpressible ceremony the name of every dish went hurtling into the next, telescoped to shapelessness. Moreover, if you stopped your Amazon in the middle, it dislocated her, and she merely went back and took a fresh start. The chant was always the same, but you never learned it. As soon as it began, your mind snapped shut like the upper berth in a Pullman. You must have uttered appropriate words—even a parrot will—for next you were eating things—pie, ham, hot cakes—as fast as you could. Twenty minutes of swallowing, and all aboard for Ogden, with your pile-driven stomach dumb with amazement. The Strasburg goose is not dieted with greater velocity, and "biscuit-shooter" is a grand word. Very likely some Homer of the railroad yards first said it—for what men upon the present earth so speak with imagination's tongue as we Americans?

If Miss Peck had been a biscuit-shooter, I could account readily for her conversation, her equipped deportment, the maturity in her round, blue, marble eye. Her abrupt laugh, something beyond gay, was now sounding in response to Mr. McLean's lively sallies, and I found him fanning her into convalescence with his hat. She herself made but few remarks, but allowed the cow-puncher to entertain her, merely exclaiming briefly now and then, "I declare!" and "If you ain't!" Lin was most certainly engaging, if that was the lady's meaning. His wide-open eyes sparkled upon her, and he half closed them now and then to look at her more effectively. I suppose she was worth it to him. I have forgotten to say that she was handsome in a large California-fruit style. They made a good-looking pair of animals. But it was in the presence of Tommy that Master Lin shone more energetically than ever, and under such shining Tommy was transparently restless. He tried, and failed, to bring the conversation his way, and took to rearranging the mail and the furniture.

"Supper's ready," he said, at length. "Come right in, Miss Peck; right in here. This is your seat—this one, please. Now you can see my fields out of the window."

"You sit here," said the biscuit-shooter to Lin; and thus she was between them. "Them's elegant!" she presently exclaimed to Tommy. "Did you cook 'em?"

I explained that the apricots were of my preparation.

"Indeed!" said she, and returned to Tommy, who had been telling her of his ranch, his potatoes, his horses. "And do you punch cattle, too?" she inquired of him.

"Me?" said Tommy, slightingly; "gave it up years ago; too empty a life for me. I leave that to such as like it. When a man owns his own property"—Tommy swept his hand at the whole landscape—"he takes to more intellectual work."

"Lickin' postage-stamps," Mr. McLean suggested, sourly.

"You lick them and I cancel them," answered the postmaster; and it does not seem a powerful rejoinder. But Miss Peck uttered her laugh.

"That's one on you," she told Lin. And throughout this meal it was Tommy who had her favor. She partook of his generous supplies; she listened to his romantic inventions, the trails he had discovered, the bears he had slain; and after supper it was with Tommy, and not with Lin, that she went for a little walk.

"Katie was ever a tease," said Mrs. Taylor of her childhood friend, and Mr. Taylor observed that there was always safety in numbers. "She'll get used to the ways of this country quicker than our little school-marm," said he.

Mr. McLean said very little, but read the new-arrived papers. It was only when bedtime dispersed us, the ladies in the cabin and the men choosing various spots outside, that he became talkative again for a while. We lay in the blankets we had spread on some soft, dry sand in preference to the stable, where Taylor and Tommy had gone. Under the contemplative influence of the stars, Lin fell into generalization.

"Ever notice," said he, "how whiskey and lyin' act the same on a man?"

I did not feel sure that I had.

"Just the same way. You keep either of 'em up long enough, and yu' get to require it. If Tommy didn't lie some every day, he'd get sick."

I was sleepy, but I murmured assent to this, and trusted he would not go on.

"Ever notice," said he, "how the victims of the whiskey and lyin' habit get to increasing the dose?"

"Yes," said I.

"Him roping six bears!" pursued Mr. McLean, after further contemplation. "Or any bear. Ever notice how the worser a man's lyin' the silenter other men'll get? Why's that, now?"

I believe that I made a faint sound to imply that I was following him.

"Men don't get took in. But ladies now, they—"

Here he paused again, and during the next interval of contemplation I sank beyond his reach.

In the morning I left Riverside for Buffalo, and there or thereabouts I remained for a number of weeks. Miss Peck did not enter my thoughts, nor did I meet any one to remind me of her, until one day I stopped at the drug-store. It was not for drugs, but gossip, that I went. In the daytime there was no place

like the apothecary's for meeting men and hearing
the news. There I heard how things were going everywhere, including Bear Creek.

All the cow-punchers liked the new girl up there,
said gossip. She was a great addition to society. Re-
ported to be more companionable than the school-
marm, Miss Molly Wood, who had been raised too far
east, and showed it. Vermont, or some such dude
place. Several had been in town buying presents for
Miss Katie Peck. Tommy Postmaster had paid high
for a necklace of elk-tushes the government scout at
McKinney sold him. Too bad Miss Peck did not enjoy
good health. Shorty had been in only yesterday to
get her medicine again. Third bottle. Had I heard the
big joke on Lin McLean? He had promised her the
skin of a big bear he knew the location of, and
Tommy got the bear.

Two days after this I joined one of the round-up
camps at sunset. They had been working from Salt
Creek to Bear Creek, and the Taylor ranch was in visiting distance from them again, after an interval of
gathering and branding far across the country. The
Virginian, the gentle-voiced Southerner, whom I had
last seen lingering with Miss Wood, was in camp. Silent three-quarters of the time, as was his way, he sat
gravely watching Lin McLean. That person seemed silent also, as was not his way quite so much.

"Lin," said the Southerner, "I reckon you're failin'."

Mr. McLean raised a sombre eye, but did not trouble to answer further.

"A healthy man's laigs ought to fill his pants," pursued the Virginian.

The challenged puncher stretched out a limb and
showed his muscles with young pride.

"And yu' cert'nly take no comfort in your food,"
his ingenious friend continued, slowly and gently.

"I'll eat you a match any day and place yu' name,"
said Lin.

"It ain't sca'cely hon'able," went on the Virginian, "to waste away durin' the round-up. A man owes his strength to them that hires it. If he is paid to rope stock he ought to rope stock, and not leave it dodge or pull away."

"It's not many dodge my rope," boasted Lin, imprudently.

"Why, they tell me as how that heifer of the Sidney-Nebraska brand got plumb away from yu', and little Tommy had to chase after her."

Lin sat up angrily amid the laughter, but reclined again. "I'll improve," said he, "if yu' learn me how yu' rope that Vermont stock so handy. Has she promised to be your sister yet?" he added.

"Is that what they do?" inquired the Virginian, serenely. "I have never got related that way. Why, that'll make Tommy your brother-in-law, Lin!"

And now, indeed, the camp laughed a loud, merciless laugh.

But Lin was silent. Where everybody lives in a glass-house the victory is to him who throws the adroitest stone. Mr. McLean was readier witted than most, but the gentle, slow Virginian could be a master when he chose.

"Tommy has been recountin' his wars up at the Taylors'," he now told the camp. "He has frequently campaigned with General Crook, General Miles, and General Ruger, all at onced. He's an exciting fighter, in conversation, and kep' us all scared for mighty nigh an hour. Miss Peck appeared interested in his statements."

"What was you doing at the Taylors' yourself?" demanded Lin.

"Visitin' Miss Wood," answered the Virginian, with entire ease. For he also knew when to employ the plain truth as a bluff. "You'd ought to write to Tommy's mother, Lin, and tell her what a dare-devil her son is gettin' to be. She would cut off his allowance and bring him home, and you would have the runnin' all to yourself."

"I'll fix him yet," muttered Mr. McLean. "Him and his wars."

With that he rose and left us.

The next afternoon he informed me that if I was riding up the creek to spend the night he would go for company. In that direction we started, therefore, without any mention of the Taylors or Miss Peck. I was puzzled. Never had I seen him thus disconcerted by woman. With him woman had been a transient disturbance. I had witnessed a series of flighty romances, where the cow-puncher had come, seen, often conquered, and moved on. Nor had his affairs been of the sort to teach a young man respect. I am putting it rather mildly.

For the first part of our way this afternoon he was moody, and after that began to speak with appalling wisdom about life. Life, he said, was a serious matter. Did I realize that? A man was liable to forget it. A man was liable to go sporting and helling around till he waked up some day and found all his best pleasures had become just a business. No interest, no surprise, no novelty left, and no cash in the bank. Shorty owed him fifty dollars. Shorty would be able to pay that after the round-up, and he, Lin, would get his time and rustle altogether some five hundred dollars. Then there was his homestead claim on Box Elder, and the surveyors were coming in this fall. No better location for a home in this country than Box Elder. Wood, water, fine land. All it needed was a house and ditches and buildings and fences, and to be planted with crops. Such chances and considerations should sober a man and make him careful what he did. "I'd take in Cheyenne on our wedding-trip and after that I'd settle right down to improving Box Elder," concluded Mr. McLean, suddenly.

His real intentions flashed upon me for the first time. I had not remotely imagined such a step.

"*Marry* her!" I screeched in dismay. "Marry *her*!"

I don't know which word was the worse to emphasize at such a moment, but I emphasized both thoroughly.

"I didn't expect yu'd act that way," said the lover. He dropped behind me fifty yards and spoke no more.

Not at once did I beg his pardon for the brutality I had been surprised into. It is one of those speeches that, once said, is said forever. But it was not that which withheld me. As I thought of the tone in which my friend had replied, it seemed to me sullen, rather than deeply angry or wounded—resentment at my opinion not of her character so much as of his choice! Then I began to be sorry for the fool, and schemed for a while how to intervene. But have you ever tried intervention? I soon abandoned the idea, and took a way to be forgiven, and to learn more.

"Lin," I began, slowing my horse, "you must not think about what I said."

"I'm thinkin' of pleasanter subjects," said he, and slowed his own horse.

"Oh, look here!" I exclaimed.

"Well?" said he. He allowed his horse to come within about ten yards.

"Astonishment makes a man say anything," I proceeded. "And I'll say again you're too good for her—and I'll say I don't generally believe in the wife being older than the husband."

"What's two years?" said Lin.

I was near screeching out again, but saved myself. He was not quite twenty-five, and I remembered Mrs. Taylor's unprejudiced computation of the biscuit-shooter's years. It is a lady's prerogative, however, to estimate her own age.

"She had her twenty-seventh birthday last month,"

said Lin, with sentiment, bringing his horse entirely abreast of mine. "I promised her a bear-skin."

"Yes," said I, "I heard about that in Buffalo."

Lin's face grew dusky with anger. "No doubt yu' heard about it!" said he. "I don't guess yu' heard much about anything else. I ain't told the truth to any of 'em—but her." He looked at me with a certain hesitation. "I think I will," he continued. "I don't mind tellin' you."

He began to speak in a strictly business tone, while he evened the coils of rope that hung on his saddle.

"She had spoke to me about her birthday, and I had spoke to her about something to give her. I had offered to buy her in town whatever she named, and I was figuring to borrow from Taylor. But she fancied the notion of a bear-skin. I had mentioned about some cubs. I had found the cubs where the she-bear had them cached by the foot of a big boulder in the range over Ten Sleep, and I put back the leaves and stuff on top o' them little things as near as I could the way I found them, so that the bear would not suspicion me. For I was aiming to get her. And Miss Peck, she sure wanted the hide for her birthday. So I went back. The she-bear was off, and I clumb up inside the rock, and I waited a turrible long spell till the sun travelled clean around the cañon. Mrs. Bear come home though, a big cinnamon; and I raised my gun, but laid it down to see what she'd do. She scrapes around and snuffs, and the cubs start whining, and she talks back to 'em. Next she sits up awful big, and lifts up a cub and holds it to her close with both her paws, same as a person. And she rubbed her ear agin the cub, and the cub sort o' nipped her, and she cuffed the cub, and the other cub came toddlin', and away they starts rolling all three of 'em! I watched that for a long while. That big thing just nursed and played with them little cubs, beatin' em for a change onced in a while, and talkin', and onced in a while she'd sit up solemn and look all around so life-like that I near busted. Why, how was I goin' to spoil that? So I come away, very quiet, you bet! for I'd have hated to have Mrs. Bear notice me. Miss Peck, she laughed. She claimed I was scared to shoot."

"After you had told her why it was?" said I.

"Before and after. I didn't tell her first, because I felt kind of foolish. Then Tommy went and he killed the bear all right, and she has the skin now. Of course the boys joshed me a heap about gettin' beat by Tommy."

"But since she has taken you?" said I.

"She ain't said it. But she will when she understands Tommy."

I fancied that the lady understood. The once I had seen her she appeared to me as what might be termed an expert in men, and one to understand also the reality of Tommy's ranch and allowance, and how greatly these differed from Box Elder. Probably the one thing she could not understand was why Lin spared the mother and her cubs. A deserted home in Dubuque, a career in a railroad eating-house, a somewhat vague past, and a present lacking context—indeed, I hoped with all my heart that Tommy would win!

"Lin," said I, "I'm backing him."

"Back away!" said he. "Tommy can please a woman—him and his blue eyes—but he don't savvy how to make a woman want him, not any better than he knows about killin' Injuns."

"Did you hear about the Crows?" said I.

"About young bucks going on the war-path? Shucks! That's put up by the papers of this section. They're aimin' to get Uncle Sam to order his troops out, and then folks can sell hay and stuff to 'em. If Tommy believed any Crows—" he stopped, and suddenly slapped his leg.

"What's the matter now?" I asked.

"Oh, nothing." He took to singing, and his face grew roguish to its full extent. "What made yu' say that to me?" he asked, presently.

"Say what?"

"About marrying. Yu' don't think I'd better."

"I don't."

"Onced in a while yu' tell me I'm flighty. Well, I am. Whoop-ya!"

"Colts ought not to marry," said I.

"Sure!" said he. And it was not until we came in sight of the Virginian's black horse tied in front of Miss Wood's cabin next the Taylors' that Lin changed the lively course of thought that was evidently filling his mind.

"Tell yu'," said he, touching my arm confidentially and pointing to the black horse, "for all her Vermont refinement she's a woman just the same. She likes him dangling round her so earnest—him that nobody every saw dangle before. And he has quit spreein' with the boys. And what does he get by it? I am glad I was not raised good enough to appreciate the Miss Woods of this world," he added, defiantly—"except at long range."

At the Taylors' cabin we found Miss Wood sitting with her admirer, and Tommy from Riverside come to admire Miss Peck. The biscuit-shooter might pass for twenty-seven, certainly. Something had agreed with her—whether the medicine, or the mountain air, or so much masculine company; whatever had done it, she had bloomed into brutal comeliness. Her hair looked curlier, her figure was shapelier, her teeth shone whiter, and her cheeks were a lusty, overbearing red. And there sat Molly Wood talking sweetly to her big, grave Virginian; to look at them, there was no doubt that he had been "raised good enough" to appreciate her, no matter what had been his raising!

Lin greeted every one jauntily. "How are yu', Miss

Peck? How are yu', Tommy?" said he. "Hear the news, Tommy? Crow Injuns on the war-path."

"I declare!" said the biscuit-shooter.

The Virginian was about to say something, but his eye met Lin's, and then he looked at Tommy. Then what he did say was, "I hadn't been goin' to mention it to the ladies until it was right sure."

"You needn't to be afraid, Miss Peck," said Tommy. "There's lots of men here."

"Who's afraid?" said the biscuit-shooter.

"Oh," said Lin, "maybe it's like most news we get in this country. Two weeks stale and a lie when it was fresh."

"Of course," said Tommy.

"Hello, Tommy!" called Taylor from the lane. "Your horse has broke his rein and run down the field."

Tommy rose in disgust and sped after the animal.

"I must be cooking supper now," said Katie, shortly.

"I'll stir for yu'," said Lin, grinning at her.

"Come along then," said she; and they departed to the adjacent kitchen.

Miss Wood's gray eyes brightened with mischief. She looked at her Virginian, and she looked at me.

"Do you know," she said, "I used to be so afraid that when Bear Creek wasn't new any more it might become dull!"

"Miss Peck doesn't find it dull either," said I.

Molly Wood immediately assumed a look of doubt. "But mightn't it become just—just a little trying to have two gentlemen so very—determined, you know?"

"Only one is determined," said the Virginian.

Molly looked inquiring.

"Lin is determined Tommy shall not beat him. That's all it amounts to."

"Dear me, what a notion!"

"No, ma'am, no notion. Tommy—well, Tommy is

considered harmless, ma'am. A cow-puncher of reputation in this country would cert'nly never let
Tommy get ahaid of him that way."

"It's pleasant to know sometimes how much we
count!" exclaimed Molly.

"Why, ma'am," said the Virginian, surprised at her
flash of indignation, "where is any countin' without
some love?"

"Do you mean to say that Mr. McLean does not
care for Miss Peck?"

"I reckon he thinks he does. But there is a mighty
wide difference between thinkin' and feelin', ma'am."

I saw Molly's eyes drop from his, and I saw the
rose deepen in her cheeks. But just then a loud voice
came from the kitchen.

"You, Lin, if you try any of your foolin' with me, I'll
histe yu's over the jiste!"

"All cow-punchers—" I attempted to resume.

"Quit now, Lin McLean," shouted the voice, "or I'll
put yus through that window, and it shut."

"Well, Miss Peck, I'm gettin' most a full dose o' this
treatment. Ever since yu' come I've been doing my
best. And yu' just cough in my face. And now I'm going to quit and cough back."

"Would you enjoy walkin' out till supper, ma'am?"
inquired the Virginian as Molly rose. "You was speaking of gathering some flowers yondeh."

"Why, yes," said Molly, blithely. "And you'll come?"
she added to me.

But I was on the Virginian's side. "I must look after
my horse," said I, and went down to the corral.

Day was slowly going as I took my pony to the water. Corncliff Mesa, Crowheart Butte, these shone in
the rays that came through the cañon. The cañon's
sides lifted like tawny castles in the same light.
Where I walked the odor of thousands of wild roses
hung over the margin where the thickets grew. High
in the upper air, magpies were sailing across the si-

lent blue. Somewhere I could hear Tommy explaining loudly how he and General Crook had pumped lead into hundreds of Indians; and when supper-time brought us all back to the door he was finishing the account to Mrs. Taylor. Molly and the Virginian arrived bearing flowers, and he was saying that few cow-punchers had any reason for saving their money.

"But when you get old?" said she.

"We mostly don't live long enough to get old, ma'am," said he, simply. "But I have a reason, and I am saving."

"Give me the flowers," said Molly. And she left him to arrange them on the table as Lin came hurrying out.

"I've told her," said he to the Southerner and me, "that I've asked her twiced, and I'm going to let her have one more chance. And I've told her that if it's a log cabin she's marryin', why Tommy is a sure good wooden piece of furniture to put inside it. And I guess she knows there's not much wooden furniture about me. I want to speak to you." He took the Virginian round the corner. But though he would not confide in me, I began to discern something quite definite at supper.

"Cattle men will lose stock if the Crows get down as far as this," he said, casually, and Mrs. Taylor suppressed a titter.

"Ain't it hawses the're repawted as running off?" said the Virginian.

"Chap come into the round-up this afternoon," said Lin. "But he was rattled, and told a heap o' facts that wouldn't square."

"Of course they wouldn't," said Tommy, haughtily.

"Oh, there's nothing in it," said Lin, dismissing the subject.

"Have yu' been to the opera since we went to Cheyenne, Mrs. Taylor?"

Mrs. Taylor had not.

"Lin," said the Virginian, "did yu' ever see that opera 'Cyarmen'?"

"You bet. Fellow's girl quits him for a bull-fighter. Gets him up in the mountains, and quits him. He wasn't much good—not in her class o' sports, smugglin' and such."

"I reckon she was doubtful of him from the start. Took him to the mount'ins to experiment, where they'd not have interruption," said the Virginian.

"Talking of mountains," said Tommy, "this range here used to be a great place for Indians till we ran 'em out with Terry. Pumped lead into the red sons-of-guns."

"You bet," said Lin. "Do yu' figure that girl tired of her bull-fighter and quit him, too?"

"I reckon," replied the Virginian, "that the bull-fighter wore better."

"Fans and taverns and gypsies and sportin'," said Lin. "My! but I'd like to see them countries with oranges and bull-fights! Only I expect Spain, maybe, ain't keepin' it up so gay as when 'Carmen' happened."

The table-talk soon left romance and turned upon steers and alfalfa, a grass but lately introduced in the country. No further mention was made of the hostile Crows, and from this I drew the false conclusion that Tommy had not come up to their hopes in the matter of reciting his campaigns. But when the hour came for those visitors who were not spending the night to take their leave, Taylor drew Tommy aside with me, and I noticed the Virginian speaking with Molly Wood, whose face showed diversion.

"Don't seem to make anything of it," whispered Taylor to Tommy, "but the ladies have got their minds on this Indian truck."

"Why, I'll just explain—" began Tommy.

"Don't," whispered Lin, joining us. "Yu' know how women are. Once they take a notion, why, the more yu' deny the surer they get. Now, yu' see, him and me" (he jerked his elbow towards the Virginian) "must go back to camp, for we're on second relief."

"And the ladies would sleep better knowing there was another man in the house," said Taylor.

"In that case," said Tommy, "I—"

"Yu' see," said Lin, "they've been told about Ten Sleep being burned two nights ago."

"It 'ain't!" cried Tommy.

"Why, of course it 'ain't," drawled the ingenious Lin. "But that's what I say. You and I know Ten Sleep's all right, but we can't report from our own knowledge seeing it all right, and there it is. They get these nervous notions."

"Just don't appear to make anything special of not going back to Riverside," repeated Taylor, "but—"

"But just kind of stay here," said Lin.

"I will!" exclaimed Tommy. "Of course, I'm glad to oblige."

I suppose I was slow-sighted. All this pains seemed to me larger than its results. They had imposed upon Tommy, yes. But what of that? He was to be kept from going back to Riverside until morning. Unless they proposed to visit his empty cabin and play tricks—but that would be too childish, even for Lin McLean, to say nothing of the Virginian, his occasional partner in mischief.

"In spite of the Crows," I satirically told the ladies, "I shall sleep outside, as I intended. I've no use for houses at this season."

The cinches of the horses were tightened, Lin and the Virginian laid a hand on their saddle-horns, swung up, and soon all sound of the galloping horses had ceased. Molly Wood declined to be nervous, and crossed to her little neighbor cabin; we all parted, and (as always in that blessed country) deep sleep quickly came to me.

I don't know how long after it was that I sprang

from my blankets in half-doubting fright. But I had dreamed nothing. A second long, wild yell now gave me (I must own to it) a horrible chill. I had no pistol—nothing. In the hateful brightness of the moon my single thought was "House! House!" and I fled across the lane in my underclothes to the cabin, when round the corner whirled the two cow-punchers, and I understood. I saw the Virginian catch sight of me in my shirt, and saw his teeth as he smiled. I hastened to my blankets, and returned more decent to stand and watch the two go shooting and yelling round the cabin, crazy with their youth. The door was opened, and Taylor courageously emerged, bearing a Winchester. He fired at the sky immediately.

"B' gosh!" he roared. "That's one." He fired again. "Out and at 'em. They're running."

At this, duly came Mrs. Taylor in white with a pistol, and Miss Peck in white, staring and stolid. But no Tommy. Noise prevailed without, shots by the stable and shots by the creek. The two cow-punchers dismounted and joined Taylor. Maniac delight seized me, and I, too, rushed about with them, helping the din.

"Oh, Mr. Taylor!" said a voice. "I didn't think it of you." It was Molly Wood, come from her cabin, very pretty in a hood-and-cloak arrangement. She stood by the fence, laughing, but more at us than with us.

"Stop, friends!" said Taylor, gasping. "She teaches my Bobbie his A B C. I'd hate to have Bobbie—"

"Speak to your papa," said Molly, and held her scholar up on the fence.

"Well, I'll be gol-darned," said Taylor, surveying his costume, "if Lin McLean hasn't made a fool of me to-night!"

"Where has Tommy got?" said Mrs. Taylor.

"Didn't yus see him?" said the biscuit-shooter, speaking her first word in all this.

We followed her into the kitchen. The table was covered with tin plates. Beneath it, wedged, knelt Tommy with a pistol firm in his hand; but the plates were rattling up and down like castanets.

There was a silence among us, and I wondered what we were going to do.

"Well," murmured the Virginian to himself, "if I could have foresaw, I'd not—it makes yu' feel humiliated yu'self."

He marched out, got on his horse, and rode away. Lin followed him, but perhaps less penitently. We all dispersed without saying anything, and presently from my blankets I saw poor Tommy come out of the silent cabin, mount, and slowly, very slowly, ride away. He would spend the night at Riverside, after all.

Of course we recovered from our unexpected shame, and the tale of the table and the dancing plates was not told as a sad one. But it is a sad one when you think of it.

I was not there to see Lin get his bride. I learned from the Virginian how the victorious puncher had ridden away across the sunny sage-brush, bearing the biscuit-shooter with him to the nearest justice of the peace. She was astride the horse he had brought for her.

"Yes, he beat Tommy," said the Virginian. "Some folks, anyway, get what they want in this hyeh world."

From which I inferred that Miss Molly Wood was harder to beat than Tommy.

CHAPTER III

Lin McLean's Honey-moon

Rain had not fallen for some sixty days, and for some sixty more there was no necessity that it should fall. It is spells of weather like this that set the Western editor writing praise and prophecy of the boundless fertility of the soil—when irrigated, and of what an Eden it can be made—with irrigation; but the spells annoy the people who are trying to raise the Eden. We always told the transient Eastern visitor, when he arrived at Cheyenne and criticised the desert, that anything would grow here—with irrigation; and sometimes he replied, unsympathetically, that anything could fly—with wings. Then we would lead such a man out and show him six, eight, ten square miles of green crops; and he, if he was thoroughly nasty, would mention that Wyoming contained ninety-five thousand square miles, all waiting for irrigation and Eden. One of these Eastern supercivilized hostiles from New York was breakfasting with the Governor and me at the Cheyenne Club, and we were explaining to him the glorious future, the coming empire, of the Western country. Now the Governor was about thirty-two, and until twenty-five had never gone West far enough to see over the top of the Alleghany Mountains. I was not a pioneer myself; and why both of us should have pitied the New-Yorker's narrowness so hard I cannot see. But we did. We spoke to him of the size of the country. We told him that his State could rattle round inside Wyoming's stomach without any inconvenience to Wyoming, and he told us that this was because Wyoming's stomach was empty. Altogether I began to feel almost sorry that I had asked him to come out for a hunt, and had travelled in haste all the way from Bear Creek to Cheyenne expressly to meet him.

"For purposes of amusement," he said, "I'll admit anything you claim for this place. Ranches, cowboys, elk; it's all splendid. Only, as an investment I prefer the East. Am I to see any cowboys?"

"You shall," I said; and I distinctly hoped some of them might do something to him "for purposes of amusement."

"You fellows come up with me to my office," said the Governor. "I'll look at my mail, and show you round." So we went with him through the heat and sun.

"What's that?" inquired the New-Yorker, whom I shall call James Ogden.

"That is our park," said I. "Of course it's merely in embryo. It's wonderful how quickly any shade tree will grow here wi—" I checked myself.

But Ogden said, "with irrigation" for me, and I was entirely sorry he had come.

We reached the Governor's office, and sat down while he looked his letters over.

"Here you are, Ogden," said he. "Here's the way we hump ahead out here." And he read us the following:

"MAGAW, KANSAS, *July* 5, 188—.
"Hon. Amory W. Barker:

"SIR,—Understanding that your district is suffering from a prolonged drought, I write to say that for necessary expenses paid I will be glad to furnish you with a reasonable shower. I have operated successfully in Australia, Mexico, and several States of the Union, and am anxious to exhibit my system. If your Legislature will appropriate a sum to cover, as I said, merely my necessary expenses—say $350 (three hundred and fifty dollars)—for half an inch, I will guarantee you that quantity of rain or forfeit the money. If I fail to give you the smallest fraction of the amount contracted for, there is to be no pay. Kindly advise me of what date will be most convenient for you to have the shower. I require twenty-four hours' preparation. Hoping a favorable reply,

"I am, respectfully yours,

"ROBERT HILBRUN."

"Will the Legislature do it?" inquired Ogden, in good faith.

The Governor laughed boisterously. "I guess it wouldn't be constitutional," said he.

"Oh bother!" said Ogden.

"My dear man," the Governor protested, "I know we're new, and our women vote, and we're a good deal of a joke, but we're not so progressively funny as all that. The people wouldn't stand it. Senator Warren would fly right into my back hair." Barker was also new as Governor.

"Do you have Senators here too?" said Ogden, raising his eyebrows. "What do they look like? Are they females?" And the Governor grew more boisterous than ever, slapping his knee and declaring that these Eastern men were certainly "out of sight." Ogden, however, was thoughtful.

"I'd have been willing to chip in for that rain myself," he said.

"That's an idea!" cried the Governor. "Nothing unconstitutional about that. Let's see. Three hundred and fifty dollars—"

"I'll put up a hundred," said Ogden, promptly. "I'm out for a Western vacation, and I'll pay for a good specimen."

The Governor and I subscribed more modestly, and by noon, with the help of some lively minded gentlemen of Cheyenne, we had the purse raised. "He won't care," said the Governor, "whether it's a private enterprise or a municipal step, so long as he gets his money."

"He won't get it, I'm afraid," said Ogden. "But if he succeeds in tempting Providence to that extent, I consider it cheap. Now what do you call those people there on the horses?"

We were walking along the track of the Cheyenne and Northern, and looking out over the plain toward Fort Russell. "That is a cow-puncher and his bride," I answered, recognizing the couple.

"Real cow-puncher?"

"Quite. The puncher's name is Lin McLean."

"Real bride?"

"I'm afraid so."

"She's riding straddle!" exclaimed the delighted Ogden, adjusting his glasses. "Why do you object to their union being holy?"

I explained that my friend Lin had lately married an eating-house lady precipitately and against my advice.

"I suppose he knew his business," observed Ogden.

"That's what he said to me at the time. But you ought to see her—and know him."

Ogden was going to. Husband and wife were coming our way. Husband nodded to me his familiar offish nod, which concealed his satisfaction at meeting with an old friend. Wife did not look at me at all. But I looked at her, and I instantly knew that Lin—the fool!— had confided to her my disapproval of their marriage. The most delicate specialty upon earth is your standing with your old friend's new wife.

"Good-day, Mr. McLean," said the Governor to the cow-puncher on his horse.

"How are yu', doctor," said Lin. During his early days in Wyoming the Governor, when as yet a private citizen, had set Mr. McLean's broken leg at Drybone. "Let me make yu' known to Mrs. McLean," pursued the husband.

The lady, at a loss how convention prescribes the greeting of a bride to a Governor, gave a waddle on the pony's back, then sat up stiff, gazed haughtily at the air, and did not speak or show any more sign than a cow would under like circumstances. So the Governor marched cheerfully at her, extending his hand, and when she slightly moved out toward him her big, dumb, red fist, he took it and shook it, and made her a series of compliments, she maintaining always the scrupulous reserve of the cow.

"I say," Ogden whispered to me while Barker was pumping the hand of the flesh image, "I'm glad I came." The appearance of the puncher-bridegroom also interested Ogden, and he looked hard at Lin's leather chaps and cartridge-belt and so forth. Lin stared at the New-Yorker, and his high white collar and good scarf. He had seen such things quite often, of course, but they always filled him with the same distrust of the man that wore them.

"Well," said he, "I guess we'll be pulling for a hotel. Any show in town? Circus come yet?"

"No," said I. "Are you going to make a long stay?"

The cow-puncher glanced at the image, his bride of three weeks. "Till we're tired of it, I guess," said he, with hesitation. It was the first time that I had ever

seen my gay friend look timidly at any one, and I felt
a rising hate for the ruby-cheeked, large-eyed eating-
house lady, the biscuit-shooter whose influence was
dimming this jaunty, irrepressible spirit. I looked at
her. Her bulky bloom had ensnared him, and now she
was going to tame and spoil him. The Governor was
looking at her too, thoughtfully.

"Say, Lin," I said, "if you stay here long enough
you'll see a big show." And his eye livened into
something of its native jocularity as I told him of the
rain-maker.

"Shucks!" said he, springing from his horse impetuously, and hugely entertained at our venture.
"Three hundred and fifty dollars? Let me come in";
and before I could tell him that we had all the money
raised, he was hauling out a wadded lump of bills.

"Well, I ain't going to starve here in the road, I
guess," spoke the image, with the suddenness of a
miracle. I think we all jumped, and I know that Lin
did. The image continued: "Some folks and their
money are soon parted"—she meant me; her searching tones came straight at me; I was sure from the
first that she knew all about me and my unfavorable
opinion of her—"but it ain't going to be you *this* time,
Lin McLean. *Ged ap!*" This last was to the horse, I
maintain, though the Governor says the husband immediately started off on a run.

At any rate, they were gone to their hotel, and
Ogden was seated on some railroad ties, exclaiming:
"Oh, I like Wyoming! I am certainly glad I came."

"That's who she is!" said the Governor, remembering Mrs. McLean all at once. "I know her. She used to
be at Sidney. She's got another husband somewhere.
She's one of the boys. Oh, that's nothing in this country!" he continued to the amazed Ogden, who had
ejaculated "Bigamy!" "Lots of them marry, live together awhile, get tired and quit, travel, catch on to

a new man, marry him, get tired and quit, travel, catch on—"

"One moment, I beg," said Ogden, adjusting his glasses. "What does the law—"

"Law?" said the Governor. "Look at that place!" He swept his hand towards the vast plains and the mountains. "Ninety-five thousand square miles of that, and sixty thousand people in it. We haven't got policemen yet on top of the Rocky Mountains."

"I see," said the New-Yorker. "But—but—well, let A and B represent first and second husbands, and X represent the woman. Now, does A know about B? or does B know about A? and what do they do about it?"

"Can't say," the Governor answered, jovially. "Can't generalize. Depends on heaps of things—love—money— Did you go to college? Well, let A minus X equal B plus X, then if A and B get squared—"

"Oh, come to lunch," I said. "Barker, do you really know the first husband is alive?"

"Wasn't dead last winter." And Barker gave us the particulars. Miss Katie Peck had not served long in the restaurant before she was wooed and won by a man who had been a ranch cook, a sheep-herder, a bar-tender, a freight hand, and was then hauling poles for the government. During his necessary absences from home she, too, went out-of-doors. This he often discovered, and would beat her, and she would then also beat him. After the beatings one of them would always leave the other forever. Thus was Sidney kept in small-talk until Mrs. Lusk one day really did not come back. "Lusk," said the Governor, finishing his story, "cried around the saloons for a couple of days, and then went on hauling poles for the government, till at last he said he'd heard of a better job south, and next we knew of him he was round Leavenworth. Lusk was a pretty poor bird. Owes me ten dollars."

"Well," I said, "none of us ever knew about him when she came to stay with Mrs. Taylor on Bear Creek. She was Miss Peck when Lin made her Mrs. McLean."

"You'll notice," said the Governor, "how she has got him under in three weeks. Old hand, you see."

"Poor Lin!" I said.

"Lucky, I call him," said the Governor. "He can quit her."

"Supposing McLean does not want to quit her?"

"She's educating him to want to right now, and I think he'll learn pretty quick. I guess Mr. Lin's romance wasn't very ideal this trip. Hello! here comes Jode. Jode, won't you lunch with us? Mr. Ogden, of New York, Mr. Jode. Mr. Jode is our signal-service officer, Mr. Ogden." The Governor's eyes were sparkling hilariously, and he winked at me.

"Gentlemen, good-morning. Mr. Ogden, I am honored to make your acquaintance," said the signal-service officer.

"Jode, when is it going to rain?" said the Governor, anxiously.

Now Jode is the most extraordinarily solemn man I have ever known. He has the solemnity of all science, added to the unspeakable weight of representing five of the oldest families in South Carolina. The Jodes themselves were not old in South Carolina, but immensely so in—I think he told me it was Long Island. His name is Poinsett Middleton Manigault Jode. He used to weigh a hundred and twenty-eight pounds then, but his health has strengthened in that climate. His clothes were black; his face was white, with black eyes sharp as a pin; he had the shape of a spout—the same narrow size all the way down—and his voice was as dry and light as an egg-shell. In his first days at Cheyenne he had constantly challenged large cowboys for taking familiarities with his dignity, and they, after one moment's bewilderment, had concocted apologies that entirely met his exactions, and gave them much satisfaction also. Nobody would have hurt Jode for the world. In time he came to see that Wyoming was a game invented after his book of rules was published, and he looked on, but could not play the game. He had fallen, along with other incongruities, into the roaring Western hotch-pot, and he passed his careful, precise days with barometers and weather-charts.

He answered the Governor with official South Carolina impressiveness. "There is no indication of diminution of the prevailing pressure," he said.

"Well, that's what I thought," said the joyous Governor, "so I'm going to whoop her up."

"What do you expect to whoop up, sir?"

"Atmosphere, and all that," said the Governor. "Whole business has got to get a move on. I've sent for a rain-maker."

"Governor, you are certainly a wag, sir," said Jode, who enjoyed Barker as some people enjoy a symphony, without understanding it. But after we had reached the club and were lunching, and Jode realized that a letter had actually been written telling Hilbrun to come and bring his showers with him, the punctilious signal-service officer stated his position. "Have your joke, sir," he said, waving a thin, clean hand, "but I decline to meet him."

"Hilbrun?" said the Governor, staring.

"If that's his name—yes, sir. As a member of the Weather Bureau and the Meteorological Society I can have nothing to do with the fellow."

"Glory!" said the Governor. "Well, I suppose not. I see your point, Jode. I'll be careful to keep you apart. As a member of the College of Physicians I've felt that way about homœopathy and the faith-cure. All very well if patients will call 'em in, but can't meet 'em in consultation. But three months' drought annually, Jode! It's slow—too slow. The Western people feel that this conservative method the Zodiac does its business by is out of date."

"I am quite serious, sir," said Jode. "And let me express my gratification that you do see my point." So we changed the subject.

Our weather scheme did not at first greatly move the public. Beyond those who made up the purse, few of our acquaintances expressed curiosity about Hilbrun, and next afternoon Lin McLean told me in the street that he was disgusted with Cheyenne's coldness toward the enterprise. "But the boys would fly right at it and stay with it if the round-up was near town, you bet," said he.

He was walking alone. "How's Mrs. McLean to-day?" I inquired.

"She's well," said Lin, turning his eye from mine. "Who's your friend all bugged up in English clothes?"

"About as good a man as you," said I, "and more cautious."

"Him and his eye-glasses!" said the sceptical puncher, still looking away from me and surveying Ogden, who was approaching with the Governor. That excellent man, still at long range, broke out smiling till his teeth shone, and he waved a yellow paper at us.

"Telegram from Hilbrun," he shouted; "be here to-morrow"; and he hastened up.

"Says he wants a cart at the depot, and a small building where he can be private," added Ogden. "Great, isn't it?"

"You bet!" said Lin, brightening. The New-Yorker's urbane but obvious excitement mollified Mr. McLean. "Ever seen rain made, Mr. Ogden?" said he.

"Never. Have you?"

Lin had not. Ogden offered him a cigar, which the puncher pronounced excellent, and we all agreed to see Hilbrun arrive.

"We're going to show the telegram to Jode," said

the Governor; and he and Ogden departed on this mission to the signal service.

"Well, I must be getting along myself," said Lin; but he continued walking slowly with me. "Where're yu' bound?" he said.

"Nowhere in particular," said I. And we paced the board sidewalks a little more.

"You're going to meet the train to-morrow?" said he.

"The train? Oh yes. Hilbrun's. To-morrow. You'll be there?"

"Yes, I'll be there. It's sure been a dry spell, 'ain't it?"

"Yes. Just like last year. In fact, like all the years."

"Yes. I've never saw it rain any to speak of in summer. I expect it's the rule. Don't you?"

"I shouldn't wonder."

"I don't guess any man knows enough to break such a rule. Do you?"

"No. But it'll be fun to see him try."

"Sure fun! Well, I must be getting along. See yu' to-morrow."

"See you to-morrow, Lin."

He left me at a corner, and I stood watching his tall, depressed figure. A hundred yards down the street he turned, and seeing me looking after him, pretended he had not turned; and then I took my steps toward the club, telling myself that I had been something of a skunk; for I had inquired for Mrs. McLean in a certain tone, and I had hinted to Lin that he had lacked caution; and this was nothing but a way of saying "I told you so" to the man that is down. Down Lin certainly was, although it had not come so home to me until our little walk together just now along the boards.

At the club I found the Governor teaching Ogden a Cheyenne specialty—a particular drink, the Allston cocktail. "It's the bitters that does the trick," he was saying, but saw me and called out: "You ought to have been with us and seen Jode. I showed him the telegram, you know. He read it through, and just handed it back to me, and went on monkeying with his anemometer. Ever seen his instruments? Every fresh jigger they get out he sends for. Well, he monkeyed away, and wouldn't say a word, so I said, 'You understand, Jode, this telegram comes from Hilbrun.' And Jode, he quit his anemometer and said, 'I make no doubt, sir, that your despatch is *genuwine*.' Oh, South Carolina's indignant at me!" And the Governor slapped his knee. "Why, he's so set against Hilbrun," he continued, "I guess if he knew of something he could explode to stop rain he'd let her fly!"

"No, he wouldn't," said I. "He'd not consider that honorable."

"That's so," the Governor assented. "Jode'll play fair."

It was thus we had come to look at our enterprise— a game between a well-established, respectable weather bureau and an upstart charlatan. And it was the charlatan had our sympathy—as all charlatans, whether religious, military, medical, political, or what not, have with the average American. We met him at the station. That is, Ogden, McLean, and I; and the Governor, being engaged, sent (unofficially) his secretary and the requested cart. Lin was anxious to see what would be put in the cart, and I was curious about how a rain-maker would look. But he turned out an unassuming, quiet man in blue serge, with a face you could not remember afterwards, and a few civil, ordinary remarks. He even said it was a hot day, as if he had no relations with the weather; and what he put into the cart were only two packing-boxes of no special significance to the eye. He desired no lodging at the hotel, but to sleep with his apparatus in the building provided for him; and we set out for

it at once. It was an untenanted barn, and he asked
that he and his assistant might cut a hole in the roof,
upon which we noticed the assistant for the first
time—a tallish, good-looking young man, but with a
weak mouth. "This is Mr. Lusk," said the rain-maker;
and we shook hands, Ogden and I exchanging a
glance. Ourselves and the cart marched up Hill
Street—or Capitol Avenue, as it has become named
since Cheyenne has grown fuller of pomp and emp-
tier of prosperity—and I thought we made an unusual procession: the Governor's secretary,
unofficially leading the way to the barn; the cart, and
the rain-maker beside it, guarding his packed-up mys-
teries; McLean and Lusk, walking together in unconscious bigamy; and in the rear, Ogden nudging me in
the ribs. That it was the correct Lusk we had with us
I felt sure from his incompetent, healthy, vacant appearance, strong-bodied and shiftless—the sort of
man to weary of one trade and another, and make a
failure of wife-beating betweenwhiles. In Twenty-
fourth Street—the town's uttermost rim—the Governor met us, and stared at Lusk. "Christopher!" was
his single observation; but he never forgets a face—
cannot afford to, now that he is in politics; and, besides, Lusk remembered him. You seldom really
forget a man to whom you owe ten dollars.

"So you've quit hauling poles?" said the Governor.

"Nothing in it, sir," said Lusk.

"Is there any objection to my having a hole in the
roof?" asked the rain-maker; for this the secretary
had been unable to tell him.

"What! Going to throw your bombs through it?"
said the Governor, smiling heartily.

But the rain-maker explained at once that his was
not the bomb system, but a method attended by
more rain and less disturbance. "Not that the bomb
don't produce first-class results at times and under

circumstances," he said, "but it's uncertain and costly."

The Governor hesitated about the hole in the roof, which Hilbrun told us was for a metal pipe to conduct his generated gases into the air. The owner of the barn had gone to Laramie. However, we found a stove-pipe hole, which saved delay. "And what day would you prefer the shower?" said Hilbrun, after we had gone over our contract with him.

"Any day would do," the Governor said.

This was Thursday; and Sunday was chosen, as a day when no one had business to detain him from witnessing the shower—though it seemed to me that on week-days, too, business in Cheyenne was not so inexorable as this. We gave the strangers some information about the town, and left them. The sun went away in a cloudless sky, and came so again when the stars had finished their untarnished shining. Friday was clear and dry and hot, like the dynasty of blazing days that had gone before.

I saw a sorry spectacle in the street—the bridegroom and the bride shopping together; or, rather, he with his wad of bills was obediently paying for what she bought; and when I met them he was carrying a scarlet parasol and a bonnet-box. His biscuit-shooter, with the lust of purchase on her, was brilliantly dressed, and pervaded the street with splendor, like an escaped parrot. Lin walked beside her, but it might as well have been behind, and his bearing was so different from his wonted happy-go-luckiness that I had a mind to take off my hat and say, "Good-morning, Mrs. Lusk." But it was "Mrs. McLean" I said, of course. She gave me a remote, imperious nod, and said, "Come on, Lin," something like a cross nurse, while he, out of sheer decency, made her a good-humored, jocular answer, and said to me, "It takes a woman to know what to buy for house-keepin' "; which poor piece of hypocrisy endeared him to me more than ever. The puncher was not of the fibre to succeed in keeping appearances, but he deserved success, which the angels consider to be enough. I wondered if disenchantment had set in, or if this were only the preliminary stage of surprise and wounding, and I felt that but one test could show, namely, a coming face to face of Mr. and Mrs. Lusk, perhaps not to be desired. Neither was it likely. The assistant rain-maker kept himself steadfastly inside or near the barn, at the north corner of Cheyenne, while the bride, when she was in the street at all, haunted the shops clear across town diagonally.

On this Friday noon the appearance of the metal tube above the blind building spread some excitement. It moved several of the citizens to pay the place a visit and ask to see the machine. These callers, of course, sustained a polite refusal, and returned among their friends with a contempt for such quackery, and a greatly heightened curiosity; so that pretty soon you could hear discussions at the street corners, and by Saturday morning Cheyenne was talking of little else. The town prowled about the barn and its oracular metal tube, and heard and saw nothing. The Governor and I (let it be confessed) went there ourselves, since the twenty-four hours of required preparation were now begun. We smelled for chemicals, and he thought there was a something, but having been bred a doctor, distrusted his imagination. I could not be sure myself whether there was anything or not, although I walked three times round the barn, snuffing as dispassionately as I knew how. It might possibly be chlorine, the Governor said, or some gas for which ammonia was in part responsible; and this was all he could say, and we left the place. The world was as still and the hard, sharp hills as clear and near as ever; and the sky over Sahara is not more dry and enduring than was ours. This tenacity in the elements plainly gave Jode a malicious official pleasure. We could tell it by his talk at lunch; and when the Governor reminded him that no rain was contracted for until the next day, he mentioned that the approach of a storm is something that modern science is able to ascertain long in advance; and he bade us come to his office whenever we pleased, and see for ourselves what science said. This was, at any rate, something to fill the afternoon with, and we went to him about five. Lin McLean joined us on the way. I came upon him lingering alone in the street, and he told me that Mrs. McLean was calling on friends. I saw that he did not know how to spend the short recess or holiday he was having. He seemed to cling to the society of others, and with them for the time regain his gayer mind. He had become converted to Ogden, and the New-Yorker, on his side, found pleasant and refreshing this democracy of Governors and cow-punchers. Jode received us at the signal-service office, and began to show us his instruments with the careful pride of an orchid-collector.

"A hair hygrometer," he said to me, waving his waxlike hand over it. "The indications are obtained from the expansion and contraction of a prepared human hair, transferred to an index needle traversing the divided arc of—"

"What oil do you put on the human hair, Jode?" called out the Governor, who had left our group, and was gamboling about by himself among the tubes and dials. "What will this one do?" he asked, and poked at a wet paper disc. But before the courteous Jode could explain that it had to do with evaporation and the dew-point, the Governor's attention wandered, and he was blowing at a little fan-wheel. This instantly revolved and set a number of dial hands going different ways. "Hi!" said the Governor, delighted. "Seen 'em like that down mines. Register air velocity in feet. Put it away, Jode. You don't want that to-morrow. What you'll need, Hilbrun says, is a big old rain-gauge and rubber shoes."

"I shall require nothing of the sort, Governor," Jode retorted at once. "And you can go to church without your umbrella in safety, sir. See there." He pointed to a storm-glass, which was certainly as clear as crystal. "An old-fashioned test, you will doubtless say, gentlemen," Jode continued—though none of us would have said anything like that—"but unjustly discredited; and, furthermore, its testimony is well corroborated, as you will find you must admit." Jode's voice was almost threatening, and he fetched one corroborator after another. I looked passively at wet and dry bulbs, at self-recording, dotted registers; I caught the fleeting sound of words like "meniscus" and "terrestrial minimum thermometer," and I nodded punctually when Jode went through some calculation. At last I heard something that I could understand—a series of telegraphic replies to Jode from brother signal-service officers all over the United States. He read each one through from date of signature, and they all made any rain to-morrow entirely impossible. "And I tell you," Jode concluded, in his high, eggshell voice, "there's no chance of precipitation now, sir. I tell you, sir"—he was shrieking jubilantly—"there's not a damn' think to precipitate!"

We left him in his triumph among his glass and mercury. "Gee whiz!" said the Governor. "I guess we'd better go and tell Hilbrun it's no use."

We went, and Hilbrun smiled with a certain compassion for the antiquated scientist. "That's what they all say," he said. "I'll do my talking to-morrow."

"If any of you gentlemen, or your friends," said Assistant Lusk, stepping up, "feel like doing a little business on this, I am ready to accommodate you."

"What do yu' want this evenin'?" said Lin McLean, promptly.

"Five to one," said Lusk.

"Go yu' in twenties," said the impetuous puncher; and I now perceived this was to be a sporting event. Lin had his wad of bills out—or what of it still survived his bride's shopping. "Will you hold stakes, doctor?" he said to the Governor.

But that official looked at the clear sky, and thought he would do five to one in twenties himself. Lusk accommodated him, and then Ogden, and then me. None of us could very well be stake-holder, but we registered our bets, and promised to procure an uninterested man by eight next morning. I have seldom had so much trouble, and I never saw such a universal search for ready money. Every man we asked to hold stakes instantly whipped out his own pocketbook, went in search of Lusk, and disqualified himself. It was Jode helped us out. He would not bet, but was anxious to serve, and thus punish the bragging Lusk.

Sunday was, as usual, chronically fine, with no cloud or breeze anywhere, and by the time the church-bells were ringing, ten to one was freely offered. The biscuit-shooter went to church with her friends, so she might wear her fine clothes in a worthy place, while her furloughed husband rushed about Cheyenne, entirely his own old self again, his wad of money staked and in Jode's keeping. Many citizens bitterly lamented their lack of ready money. But it was a good thing for these people that it was Sunday, and the banks closed.

The church-bells ceased; the congregations sat inside, but outside the hot town showed no Sunday emptiness or quiet. The metal tube, the possible smell, Jode's sustained and haughty indignation, the extraordinary assurance of Lusk, all this had ended by turning every one restless and eccentric. A citizen came down the street with an umbrella. In a moment the by-standers had reduced it to a sordid tangle of ribs. Old Judge Burrage attempted to address us at the corner about the vast progress of science. The postmaster pinned a card on his back with the well-known legend, "I am somewhat of a liar myself." And all the while the sun shone high and hot, while Jode grew quieter and colder under the certainty of victory. It was after twelve o'clock when the people came from church, and no change or sign was to be seen. Jode told us, with a chill smile, that he had visited his instruments and found no new indications. Fifteen minutes after that the sky was brown. Sudden, padded, dropsical clouds were born in the blue above our heads. They blackened, and a smart shower, the first in two months, wet us all, and ceased. The sun blazed out, and the sky came blue again, like those rapid, unconvincing weather changes of the drama.

Amazement at what I saw happening in the heavens took me from things on earth, and I was unaware of the universal fit that now seized upon Cheyenne until I heard the high cry of Jode at my ear. His usual punctilious bearing had forsaken him, and he shouted alike to stranger and acquaintance: "It is no half-inch, sir! Don't you tell me!" And the crowd would swallow him, but you could mark his vociferous course as he went proclaiming to the world: "A failure, sir! The fellow's an impostor, as I well knew. It's no half-inch!" Which was true.

"What have you got to say to that?" we asked Hilbrun, swarming around him.

"If you'll just keep cool," said he—"it's only the first instalment. In about two hours and a half I'll give you the rest."

Soon after four the dropsical clouds materialized once again above open-mouthed Cheyenne. No school let out for an unexpected holiday, no herd of stampeded range cattle, conducts itself more miscellaneously. Gray, respectable men, with daughters married, leaped over fences and sprang back, prominent legislators hopped howling up and down door-steps, women waved handkerchiefs from windows and porches, the chattering Jode flew from anemometer to rain-gauge, and old Judge Burrage apostrophized Providence in his front yard, with the postmaster's label still pinned to his back. Nobody minded the sluicing downpour—this second instalment was much more of a thing than the first—and Hilbrun alone kept a calm exterior—the face of the man who lifts a heavy dumb-bell and throws an impressive glance at the audience. Assistant Lusk was by no means thus proof against success. I saw him put a bottle back in his pocket, his face already disintegrated with a tipsy leer. Judge Burrage, perceiving the rain-maker, came out of his gate and proceeded toward him, extending the hand of congratulation. "Mr. Hilbrun," said he, "I am Judge Burrage—the Honorable T. Coleman Burrage—and I will say that I am most favorably impressed with your shower."

"*His* shower!" yelped Jode, flourishing measurements.

"Why, yu' don't claim it's yourn, do yu'?" said Lin McLean, grinning.

"I tell you it's no half-inch yet, gentlemen," said Jode, ignoring the facetious puncher.

"You're mistaken," said Hilbrun, sharply.

"It's a plumb big show, half-inch or no half-inch," said Lin.

"If he's short he don't get his money," said some ignoble subscriber.

"Yes, he will," said the Governor, "or I'm a shote. He's earned it."

"You bet!" said Lin. "Fair and square. If they're goin' back on yu', doctor, I'll chip—Shucks!" Lin's hand fell from the empty pocket; he remembered his wad in the stake-holder's hands, and that he now possessed possibly two dollars in silver, all told. "I

can't chip in, doctor," he said. "That hobo over there
has won my cash, an' he's filling up on the prospect
right now. I don't care! It's the biggest show I've ever
saw. You're a dandy, Mr. Hilbrun! Whoop!" And Lin
clapped the rain-maker on the shoulder, exulting. He
had been too well entertained to care what he had in
his pocket, an his wife had not yet occurred to him.

They were disputing about the rainfall, which had
been slightly under half an inch in a few spots, but
over it in many others; and while we stood talking in
the renewed sunlight, more telegrams were brought
to Jode, saying that there was no moisture anywhere,
and simultaneously with these, riders dashed into
town with the news that twelve miles out the rain
had flattened the grain crop. We had more of such re-
ports from as far as thirty miles, and beyond that
there had not been a drop or a cloud. It staggered
one's reason; the brain was numb with surprise.

"Well, gentlemen," said the rain-maker, "I'm packed
up, and my train'll be along soon—would have been
along by this, only it's late. What's the word as to my
three hundred and fifty dollars?"

Even still there were objections expressed. He had
not entirely performed his side of the contract.

"I think different, gentlemen," said he. "But I'll un-
pack and let that train go. I can't have the law on
you, I suppose. But if you *don't* pay me" (the rain-
maker put his hands in his pockets and leaned
against the fence) "I'll flood your town."

In earthquakes and eruptions people end by expecting anything; and in the total eclipse that was
now over all Cheyenne's ordinary standards and
precedents the bewildered community saw in this
threat nothing more unusual than if he had said
twice two made four. The purse was handed over.

"I'm obliged," said Hilbrun, simply.

"If I had foreseen, gentlemen," said Jode, too
deeply grieved now to feel anger, "that I would even

be indirectly associated with your losing your money through this—this absurd occurrence, I would have declined to help you. It becomes my duty," he continued, turning coldly to the inebriated Lusk, "to hand this to you, sir." And the assistant lurchingly stuffed his stakes away.

"It's worth it," said Lin. "He's welcome to my cash."

"What's that you say, Lin McLean?" It was the biscuit-shooter, and she surged to the front.

"I'm broke. He's got it. That's all," said Lin, briefly.

"Broke! You!" She glared at her athletic young lord, and she uttered a preliminary howl.

At that long-lost cry Lusk turned his silly face. "It's my darling Kate," he said. "Why, Kate!"

The next thing that I knew Ogden and I were grappling with Lin McLean; for everything had happened at once. The bride had swooped upon her first wedded love and burst into tears on the man's neck, which Lin was trying to break in consequence. We do not always recognize our benefactors at sight. They all came to the ground, and we hauled the second husband off. The lady and Lusk remained in a heap, he foolish, tearful, and affectionate; she turned furiously at bay, his guardian angel, indifferent to the onlooking crowd, and hurling righteous defiance at Lin. "Don't yus dare lay yer finger on my husband, you sage-brush bigamist!" is what the marvellous female said.

"Bigamist?" repeated Lin, dazed at this charge. "I ain't," he said to Ogden and me. "I never did. I've never married any of 'em before her."

"Little good that'll do yus, Lin McLean! Me and him was man and wife before ever I come acrosst yus."

"You and him?" murmured the puncher.

"Her and me," whimpered Lusk. "Sidney." He sat up with a limp, confiding stare at everybody.

"Sidney who?" said Lin.

"No, no," corrected Lusk, crossly—"Sidney, Nebraska."

The stakes at this point fell from his pocket, which he did not notice. But the bride had them in safekeeping at once.

"Who are yu', anyway—when yu' ain't drunk?" demanded Lin.

"He's as good a man as you, and better," snorted the guardian angel. "Give him a pistol, and he'll make you hard to find."

"Well, you listen to me, Sidney Nebraska—" Lin began.

"No, no," corrected Lusk once more, as a distant whistle blew—"Jim."

"Good-bye, gentlemen," said the rain-maker. "That's the westbound. I'm perfectly satisfied with my experiment here, and I'm off to repeat it at Salt Lake City."

"You are?" shouted Lin McLean. "Him and Jim's going to work it again! For goodness' sake, somebody lend me twenty-five dollars!"

At this there was an instantaneous rush. Ten minutes later, in front of the ticket-windows, there was a line of citizens buying tickets for Salt Lake as if it had been Madame Bernhardt. Some rock had been smitten, and ready money had flowed forth. The Governor saw us off, sad that his duties should detain him. But Jode went!

"Betting is the fool's argument, gentlemen," said he to Ogden, McLean, and me, "and it's a weary time since I have had the pleasure."

"Which way are yu' bettin'?" Lin asked.

"With my principles, sir," answered the little signal-service officer.

"I expect I 'ain't got any," said the puncher. "It's Jim I'm backin' this time."

"See here," said I; "I want to talk to you." We went into another car, and I did.

"And so yu' knowed about Lusk when we was on them board walks?" the puncher said.

"Do you mean I ought to have—"

"Shucks! no. Yu' couldn't. Nobody couldn't. It's a queer world, all the same. Yu' have good friends, and all that." He looked out of the window. "Laramie already!" he commented, and got out and walked by himself on the platform until we had started again. "Yu' have good friends," he pursued, settling himself so his long legs were stretched and comfortable, "and they tell yu' things, and you tell them things. And when it don't make no particular matter one way or the other, yu' give 'em your honest opinion and talk straight to 'em, and they'll come to you the same way. So that when yu're ridin' the range alone sometimes, and thinkin' a lot o' things over on top maybe of some dog-goned hill, you'll say to yourself about some fellow yu' know mighty well, 'There's a man is a good friend of mine.' And yu' mean it. And it's so. Yet when matters is serious, as onced in a while they're bound to get, and yu're in a plumb hole, where is the man then—your good friend? Why, he's where yu' want him to be. Standin' off, keepin' his mouth shut, and lettin' yu' find your own trail out. If he tried to show it to yu', yu'd likely hit him. But shucks! Circumstances have showed me the trail this time, you bet!" And the puncher's face, which had been sombre, grew lively, and he laid a friendly hand on my knee.

"The trail's pretty simple," said I.

"You bet! But it's sure a queer world. Tell yu'," said Lin, with the air of having made a discovery, "when a man gets down to bed-rock affairs in this life he's got to do his travellin' alone, same as he does his dyin'. I expect even married men has thoughts and hopes they don't tell their wives."

"Never was married," said I.

"Well—no more was I. Let's go to bed." And Lin

shook my hand, and gave me a singular, rather melancholy smile.

At Salt Lake City, which Ogden was glad to include in his Western holiday, we found both Mormon and Gentile ready to give us odds against rain—only I noticed that those of true faith were less free. Indeed, the Mormon, the Quaker, and most sects of an isolated doctrine have a nice prudence in money. During our brief stay we visited the sights: floating in the lake, listening to pins drop in the gallery of the Tabernacle, seeing frescos of saints in robes speaking from heaven to Joseph Smith in the Sunday clothes of a modern farm-hand, and in the street we heard at a distance a strenuous domestic talk between the new—or perhaps I should say the original—husband and wife.

"She's corralled Sidney's cash!" said the delighted Lin. "He can't bet nothing on this shower."

And then, after all, this time—it didn't rain!

Stripped of money both ways, Cheyenne, having most fortunately purchased a return ticket, sought its home. The perplexed rain-maker went somewhere else, without his assistant. Lusk's exulting wife, having the money, retained him with her.

"Good luck to yu', Sidney!" said Lin, speaking to him for the first time since Cheyenne. "I feel a heap better since I've saw yu' married." He paid no attention to the biscuit-shooter, or the horrible language that she threw after him.

Jode also felt "a heap better." Legitimate science had triumphed. To-day, most of Cheyenne believes with Jode that it was all a coincidence. South Carolina had bet on her principles, and won from Lin the few dollars that I had lent the puncher.

"And what will you do now?" I said to Lin.

"Join the beef round-up. Balaam's payin' forty dollars. I guess that'll keep a single man."

CHAPTER IV

A Journey in Search
of Christmas

THE GOVERNOR descended the steps of the Capitol slowly and with pauses, lifting a list frequently to his eye. He had intermittently pencilled it between stages of the forenoon's public business, and his gait grew absent as he recurred now to his jottings in their accumulation, with a slight pain at their number, and the definite fear that they would be more in seasons to come. They were the names of his friends' children to whom his excellent heart moved him to give Christmas presents. He had put off this regenerating evil until the latest day, as was his custom, and now he was setting forth to do the whole thing at a blow, entirely planless among the guns and rocking-horses that would presently surround him. As he reached the highway he heard himself familiarly addressed from a distance, and, turning, saw four sons of the alkali jogging into town from the plain. One who had shouted to him galloped out from the others, rounded the Capitol's enclosure, and, approaching with radiant countenance, leaned to reach the hand of the Governor, and once again greeted him with a hilarious "Hello, Doc!"

Governor Barker, M.D., seeing Mr. McLean unexpectedly after several years, hailed the horseman with frank and lively pleasure, and, inquiring who might be the other riders behind, was told that they were Shorty, Chalkeye, and Dollar Bill, come for Christmas. "And dandies to hit town with," Mr. McLean added. "Red-hot."

"I am acquainted with them," assented his Excellency.

"We've been ridin' trail for twelve weeks," the cow-puncher continued, "makin' our beds down anywheres, and eatin' the same old chuck every day. So we've shook fried beef and heifer's delight, and we're goin' to feed high."

Then Mr. McLean overflowed with talk and pungent confidences, for the holidays already rioted in his spirit, and his tongue was loosed over their coming rites.

"We've soured on scenery," he finished, in his drastic idiom. "We're sick of moonlight and cow-dung, and we're heeled for a big time."

"Call on me," remarked the Governor, cheerily, "when you're ready for bromides and sulphates."

"I ain't box-headed no more," protested Mr. McLean; "I've got maturity, Doc, since I seen yu' at the rain-making, and I'm a heap older than them hospital days when I bust my leg on yu'. Three or four glasses and quit. That's my rule."

"That your rule, too?" inquired the Governor of Shorty, Chalkeye, and Dollar Bill. These gentlemen of the saddle were sitting quite expressionless upon their horses.

"We ain't talkin', we're waitin'," observed Chalkeye; and the three cynics smiled amiably.

"Well, Doc, see yu' again," said Mr. McLean. He

turned to accompany his brother cow-punchers, but in that particular moment Fate descended or came up from whatever place she dwells in and entered the body of the unsuspecting Governor.

"What's your hurry?" said Fate, speaking in the official's hearty manner. "Come along with me."

"Can't do it. Where're yu' goin'?"

"Christmasing," replied Fate.

"Well, I've got to feed my horse. Christmasing, yu' say?"

"Yes; I'm buying toys."

"Toys! You? What for?"

"Oh, some kids."

"Yourn?" screeched Lin, precipitately.

His Excellency the jovial Governor opened his teeth in pleasure at this, for he was a bachelor, and there were fifteen upon his list, which he held up for the edification of the hasty McLean. "Not mine, I'm happy to say. My friends keep marrying and settling, and their kids call me uncle, and climb around and bother, and I forget their names, and think it's a girl, and the mother gets mad. Why, if I didn't remember these little folks at Christmas they'd be wondering— not the kids, they just break your toys and don't notice; but the mother would wonder—'What's the matter with Dr. Barker? Has Governor Barker gone back on us?'—that's where the strain comes!" he broke off, facing Mr. McLean with another spacious laugh.

But the cow-puncher had ceased to smile, and now, while Barker ran on exuberantly, McLean's wide-open eyes rested upon him, singular and intent, and in their hazel depths the last gleam of jocularity went out.

"That's where the strain comes, you see. Two sets of acquaintances. Grateful patients and loyal voters, and I've got to keep solid with both outfits, especially the wives and mothers. They're the people. So it's drums, and dolls, and sheep on wheels, and games, and monkeys on a stick, and the saleslady shows you a mechanical bear, and it costs too much, and you forget whether the Judge's second girl is Nellie or Susie, and—well, I'm just in for my annual circus this afternoon! You're in luck. Christmas don't trouble a chap fixed like you."

Lin McLean prolonged the sentence like a distant echo.

"A chap fixed like you!" The cow-puncher said it slowly to himself. "No, sure." He seemed to be watching Shorty, and Chalkeye, and Dollar Bill going down the road. "That's a new idea—Christmas," he murmured, for it was one of his oldest, and he was recalling the Christmas when he wore his first long trousers.

"Comes once a year pretty regular," remarked the prosperous Governor. "Seems often when you pay the bill."

"I haven't made a Christmas gift," pursued the cow-puncher, dreamily, "not for—for—Lord! it's a hundred years, I guess. I don't know anybody that has any right to look for such a thing from me." This was indeed a new idea, and it did not stop the chill that was spreading in his heart.

"Gee whiz!" said Barker, briskly, "there goes twelve o'clock. I've got to make a start. Sorry you can't come and help me. Good-bye!"

His Excellency left the rider sitting motionless, and forgot him at once in his own preoccupation. He hastened upon his journey to the shops with the list, not in his pocket, but held firmly, like a plank in the imminence of shipwreck. The Nellies and Susies pervaded his mind, and he struggled with the presentiment that in a day or two he would recall some omitted and wretchedly important child. Quick hoof-beats made him look up, and Mr. McLean passed like a wind. The Governor absently watched him go, and saw the pony hunch and stiffen in the check of his speed when Lin overtook his companions. Down there in the distance they took a side street, and Barker rejoicingly remembered one more name and wrote it as he walked. In a few minutes he had come to the shops, and met face to face with Mr. McLean.

"The boys are seein' after my horse," Lin rapidly began, "and I've got to meet 'em sharp at one. We're twelve weeks shy on a square meal, yu' see, and this first has been a date from 'way back. I'd like to—" Here Mr. McLean cleared his throat, and his speech went less smoothly. "Doc, I'd like just for a while to watch yu' gettin'—them monkeys, yu' know."

The Governor expressed his agreeable surprise at this change of mind, and was glad of McLean's company and judgment during the impending selections. A picture of a cow-puncher and himself discussing a couple of dolls rose nimbly in Barker's mental eye, and it was with an imperfect honesty that he said, "You'll help me a heap."

And Lin, quite sincere, replied, "Thank yu'."

So together these two went Christmasing in the throng. Wyoming's Chief Executive knocked elbows with the spurred and jingling waif, one man as good as another in that raw, hopeful, full-blooded cattle era, which now the sobered West remembers as the days of its fond youth. For one man has been as good as another in three places—Paradise before the Fall; the Rocky Mountains before the wire fence; and the Declaration of Independence. And then this Governor, beside being young, almost as young as Lin McLean or the Chief Justice (who lately had celebrated his thirty-second birthday), had in his doctoring days at Drybone known the cow-puncher with that familiarity which lasts a lifetime without breeding contempt; accordingly he now laid a hand on

Lin's tall shoulder and drew him among the petticoats and toys.

Christmas filled the windows and Christmas stirred in mankind. Cheyenne, not over-zealous in doctrine or litanies, and with the opinion that a world in the hand is worth two in the bush, nevertheless was flocking together, neighbor to think of neighbor, and every one to remember the children; a sacred assembly, after all, gathered to rehearse unwittingly the articles of its belief, the Creed and Doctrine of the Child. Lin saw them hurry and smile among the paper fairies; they questioned and hesitated, crowded and made decisions, failed utterly to find the right thing, forgot and hastened back, suffered all the various desperations of the eleventh hour, and turned homeward, dropping their parcels with that undimmed good-will that once a year makes gracious the universal human face. This brotherhood swam and beamed before the cow-puncher's brooding eyes, and in his ears the greeting of the season sang. Children escaped from their mothers and ran chirping behind the counters to touch and meddle in places forbidden. Friends dashed against each other with rabbits and magic lanterns, greeted in haste, and were gone, amid the sound of musical boxes.

Through this tinkle and bleating of little machinery the murmur of the human heart drifted in and out of McLean's hearing; fragments of home talk, tendernesses, economies, intimate first names, and dinner hours, and whether it was joy or sadness, it was in common; the world seemed knit in a single skein of home ties. Two or three came by whose purses must have been slender, and whose purchases were humble and chosen after much nice adjustment; and when one plain man dropped a word about both ends meeting, and the woman with him laid a hand on his arm, saying that his children must not feel this year was different, Lin made a step toward them.

There were hours and spots where he could readily have descended upon them at that, played the rôle of clinking affluence, waved thanks aside with competent blasphemy, and tossing off some infamous whiskey, cantered away in the full self-conscious strut of the frontier. But here was not the moment; the abashed cow-puncher could make no such parade in this place. The people brushed by him back and forth, busy upon their errands, and aware of him scarcely more than if he had been a spirit looking on from the helpless dead; and so, while these weaving needs and kindnesses of man were within arm's touch of him, he was locked outside with his impulses. Barker had, in the natural press of customers, long parted from him, to become immersed in choosing and rejecting; and now, with a fair part of his mission accomplished, he was ready to go on to the next place, and turned to beckon McLean. He found him obliterated in a corner beside a life-sized image of Santa Claus, standing as still as the frosty saint.

"He looks livelier than you do," said the hearty Governor. " 'Fraid it's been slow waiting."

"No," replied the cow-puncher, thoughtfully. "No, I guess not."

This uncertainty was expressed with such gentleness that Barker roared. "You never did lie to me," he said, "long as I've known you. Well, never mind. I've got some real advice to ask you now."

At this Mr. McLean's face grew more alert. "Say Doc," said he, "what do yu' want for Christmas that nobody's likely to give yu'?"

"A big practice—big enough to interfere with my politics."

"What else? Things and truck, I mean."

"Oh—nothing I'll get. People don't give things much to fellows like me."

"Don't they? Don't they?"

"Why, you and Santa Claus weren't putting up any scheme on my stocking?"

"Well—"

"I believe you're in earnest!" cried his Excellency. "That's simply rich!" Here was a thing to relish! The Frontier comes to town "heeled for a big time," finds that presents are all the rage, and must immediately give somebody something. Oh, childlike, miscellaneous Frontier! So thought the good-hearted Governor; and it seems a venial misconception. "My dear fellow," he added, meaning as well as possible, "I don't want you to spend your money on me."

"I've got plenty all right," said Lin, shortly.

"Plenty's not the point. I'll take as many drinks as you please with you. You didn't expect anything from me?"

"That ain't—that don't—"

"There! Of course you didn't. Then, what are you getting proud about? Here's our shop." They stepped in from the street to new crowds and counters. "Now," pursued the Governor, "this is for a very particular friend of mine. Here they are. Now, which of those do you like best?"

They were sets of Tennyson in cases holding little volumes equal in number, but the binding various, and Mr. McLean reached his decision after one look. "That," said he, and laid a large muscular hand upon the Laureate. The young lady behind the counter spoke out acidly, and Lin pulled the abject hand away. His taste, however, happened to be sound, or, at least, it was at one with the Governor's; but now they learned that there was a distressing variance in the matter of price.

The Governor stared at the delicate article of his choice. "I know that Tennyson is what she—is what's wanted," he muttered; and, feeling himself nudged, looked around and saw Lin's extended fist. This gesture he took for a facetious sympathy, and, dolorously grasping the hand, found himself holding a lump of bills. Sheer amazement relaxed him, and the cow-puncher's matted wealth tumbled on the floor in sight of all people. Barker picked it up and gave it back. "No, no, no!" he said, mirthful over his own inclination to be annoyed; "you can't do that. I'm just as much obliged, Lin," he added.

"Just as a loan, Doc—some of it. I'm grass-bellied with spot-cash."

A giggle behind the counter disturbed them both, but the sharp young lady was only dusting. The Governor at once paid haughtily for Tennyson's expensive works, and the cow-puncher pushed his discountenanced savings back into his clothes. Making haste to leave the book department of this shop, they regained a mutual ease, and the Governor became waggish over Lin's concern at being too rich. He suggested to him the list of delinquent taxpayers and the latest census from which to select indigent persons. He had patients, too, whose inveterate pennilessness he could swear cheerfully to—"since you want to bolt from your own money," he remarked.

"Yes, I'm a green horse," assented Mr. McLean, gallantly; "ain't used to the looks of a twenty-dollar bill, and I shy at 'em."

From his face—that jocular mask—one might have counted him the most serene and careless of vagrants, and in his words only the ordinary voice of banter spoke to the Governor. A good woman, it may well be, would have guessed before this the sensitive soul in the blundering body; but Barker saw just the familiar, whimsical, happy-go-lucky McLean of old days, and so he went gayly and innocently on, treading upon holy ground. "I've got it!" he exclaimed; "give your wife something."

The ruddy cow-puncher grinned. He had passed through the world of woman with but few delays, rejoicing in informal and transient entanglements, and he welcomed the turn which the conversation seemed now to be taking. "If you'll give me her name and address," said he, with the future entirely in his mind.

"Why, Laramie!" and the Governor feigned surprise.

"Say, Doc," said Lin, uneasily, "none of 'em 'ain't married me since I saw yu' last."

"Then she hasn't written from Laramie," said the hilarious Governor; and Mr. McLean understood and winced in his spirit deep down. "Gee whiz!" went on Barker, "I'll never forget you and Lusk that day!"

But the mask fell now. "You're talking of his wife, not mine," said the cow-puncher very quietly, and smiling no more; "and, Doc, I'm going to say a word to yu', for I know yu've always been my good friend. I'll never forget that day myself—but I don't want to be reminded of it."

"I'm a fool, Lin," said the Governor, generous instantly. "I never supposed—"

"I know yu' didn't, Doc. It ain't you that's the fool. And in a way—in a way—" Lin's speech ended among his crowding memories, and Barker, seeing how wistful his face had turned, waited. "But I ain't quite the same fool I was before that happened to me," the cow-puncher resumed, "though maybe my actions don't show to be wiser. I know that there was better luck than a man like me had any call to look for."

The sobered Barker said, simply, "Yes, Lin." He was put to thinking by these words from the unsuspected inner man.

Out in the Bow Leg country Lin McLean had met a woman with thick, red cheeks, calling herself by a maiden name; and this was his whole knowledge of her when he put her one morning astride a Mexican saddle and took her fifty miles to a magistrate and made her his lawful wife to the best of his ability and belief. His sage-brush intimates were confident he

would never have done it but for a rival. Racing the
rival and beating him had swept Mr. McLean past his
own intentions, and the marriage was an inadver-
tence. "He jest bumped into it before he could pull
up," they explained; and this casualty, resulting from
Mr. McLean's sporting blood, had entertained several
hundred square miles of alkali. For the new-made
husband the joke soon died. In the immediate weeks
that came upon him he tasted a bitterness worse
than in all his life before, and learned also how
deep the woman, when once she begins, can sink beneath the man in baseness. That was a knowledge of
which he had lived innocent until this time. But he
carried his outward self serenely, so that citizens in
Cheyenne who saw the cow-puncher with his bride
argued shrewdly that men of that sort liked women
of that sort; and before the strain had broken his en-
durance an unexpected first husband, named Lusk,
had appeared on Sunday in the street, prosperous,
forgiving, and exceedingly drunk. To the arms of Lusk
she went back in the public street, deserting McLean
in the presence of Cheyenne; and when Cheyenne
saw this, and learned how she had been Mrs. Lusk
for eight long, if intermittent, years, Cheyenne
laughed loudly. Lin McLean laughed, too, and went
about his business, ready to swagger at the necessary moment, and with the necessary kind of joke always ready to shield his hurt spirit. And soon, of
course, the matter grew stale, seldom raked up in the
Bow Leg country where Lin had been at work; so
lately he had begun to remember other things beside
the smouldering humiliation.

"Is she with him?" he asked Barker, and musingly
listened while Barker told him. The Governor had
thought to make it a racy story, with the moral that
the joke was now on Lusk; but that inner man had
spoken and revealed the cow-puncher to him in a
new and complicated light; hence he quieted the pro-

posed lively cadence and vocabulary of his anecdote about the house of Lusk, but instead of narrating how Mrs. beat Mr. on Mondays, Wednesdays, and Fridays, and Mr. took his turn the odd days, thus getting one ahead of his lady, while the kid Lusk had outlined his opinion of the family by recently skipping to parts unknown, Barker detailed these incidents more gravely, adding that Laramie believed Mrs. Lusk addicted to opium.

"I don't guess I'll leave my card on 'em," said McLean, grimly, "if I strike Laramie."

"You don't mind my saying I think you're well out of that scrape?" Barker ventured.

"Shucks, no! That's all right, Doc. Only—yu' see now. A man gets tired pretending—onced in a while."

Time had gone while they were in talk, and it was now half after one and Mr. McLean late for that long-plotted first square meal. So the friends shook hands, wishing each other Merry Christmas, and the cowpuncher hastened toward his chosen companions through the stirring cheerfulness of the season. His play-hour had made a dull beginning among the toys. He had come upon people engaged in a pleasant game, and waited, shy and well disposed, for some bidding to join, but they had gone on playing with each other and left him out. And now he went along in a sort of hurry to escape from that loneliness where his human promptings had been lodged with him useless. Here was Cheyenne, full of holiday for sale, and he with his pockets full of money to buy; and when he thought of Shorty, and Chalkeye, and Dollar Bill, those dandies to hit a town with, he stepped out with a brisk, false hope. It was with a mental hurrah and a foretaste of a good time coming that he put on his town clothes, after shaving and admiring himself, and sat down to the square meal. He ate away and drank with a robust imitation of enjoyment that took in even himself at first. But the sorrowful process of his spirit went on, for all he could do. As he groped for the contentment which he saw around him he began to receive the jokes with counterfeit mirth. Memories took the place of anticipation, and through their moody shiftings he began to feel a distaste for the company of his friends and a shrinking from their lively voices. He blamed them for this at once. He was surprised to think he had never recognized before how light a weight was Shorty; and here was Chalkeye, who knew better, talking religion after two glasses. Presently this attack of noticing his friends' shortcomings mastered him, and his mind, according to its wont, changed at a stroke. "I'm celebrating no Christmas with this crowd," said the inner man; and when they had next remembered Lin McLean in their hilarity he was gone.

Governor Barker, finishing his purchases at half-past three, went to meet a friend come from Evanston. Mr. McLean was at the railway station, buying a ticket for Denver.

"Denver!" exclaimed the amazed Governor.

"That's what I said," stated Mr. McLean, doggedly.

"Gee whiz!" went his Excellency. "What are you going to do there?"

"Get good and drunk."

"Can't you find enough whiskey in Cheyenne?"

"I'm drinking champagne this trip."

The cow-puncher went out on the platform and got aboard, and the train moved off. Barker had walked out too in his surprise, and as he stared after the last car, Mr. McLean waved his wide hat defiantly and went inside the door.

"And he says he's got maturity," Barker muttered. "I've known him since seventy-nine, and he's kept about eight years old right along." The Governor was cross, and sorry, and presently crosser. His jokes about Lin's marriage came back to him and put him in a rage with the departed fool. "Yes, about eight. Or six," said his Excellency, justifying himself by the past. For he had first known Lin, the boy of nineteen, supreme in length of limb and recklessness, breaking horses and feeling for an early mustache. Next, when the mustache was nearly accomplished, he had mended the boy's badly broken thigh at Drybone. His skill (and Lin's utter health) had wrought so swift a healing that the surgeon overflowed with the pride of science, and over the bandages would explain the human body technically to his wild-eyed and flattered patient. Thus young Lin heard all about tibia, and comminuted, and other glorious new words, and when sleepless would rehearse them. Then, with the bone so nearly knit that the patient might leave the ward on crutches to sit each morning in Barker's room as a privilege, the disobedient child of twenty-one had slipped out of the hospital and hobbled hastily to the hog ranch, where whiskey and variety waited for a languishing convalescent. Here he grew gay, and was soon carried back with the leg refractured. Yet Barker's surgical rage was disarmed, the patient was so forlorn over his doctor's professional chagrin.

"I suppose it ain't no better this morning, Doc?" he had said, humbly, after a new week of bed and weights.

"Your right leg's going to be shorter. That's all."

"Oh, gosh! I've been and spoiled your comminuted fee-mur! Ain't I a son-of-a-gun?"

You could not chide such a boy as this; and in time's due course he had walked jauntily out into the world with legs of equal length after all, and in his stride the slightest halt possible. And Doctor Barker had missed the child's conversation. To-day his mustache was a perfected thing, and he in the late end of his twenties.

"He'll wake up about noon to-morrow in a dive,

without a cent," said Barker. "Then he'll come back
on a freight and begin over again."

At the Denver station Lin McLean passed through
the shoutings and omnibuses, and came to the beginning of Seventeenth Street, where is the first saloon.
A customer was ordering Hot Scotch; and because he
liked the smell and had not thought of the mixture
for a number of years, Lin took Hot Scotch. Coming
out upon the pavement, he looked across and saw a
saloon opposite with brighter globes and windows
more prosperous. That should have been his choice;
lemon peel would undoubtedly be fresher over there;
and over he went at once, to begin the whole thing
properly. In such frozen weather no drink could be
more timely, and he sat, to enjoy without haste its
mellow fitness. Once again on the pavement, he
looked along the street toward up-town beneath the
crisp, cold electric lights, and three little bootblacks
gathered where he stood and cried "Shine? Shine?"
at him. Remembering that you took the third turn to
the right to get the best dinner in Denver, Lin hit on
the skilful plan of stopping at all Hot Scotches between; but the next occurred within a few yards, and
it was across the street. This one being attained and
appreciated, he found that he must cross back again
or skip number four. At this rate he would not be dining in time to see much of the theatre, and he
stopped to consider. It was a German place he had
just quitted, and a huge light poured out on him from
its window, which the proprietor's father-land sentiment had made into a show. Lights shone among a
well-set pine forest, where beery, jovial gnomes sat
on roots and reached upward to Santa Claus; he,
grinning, fat, and Teutonic, held in his right hand forever a foaming glass, and forever in his left a string
of sausages that dangled down among the gnomes.
With his American back to this, the cow-puncher,
wearing the same serious, absent face he had not

changed since he ran away from himself at Cheyenne, considered carefully the Hot Scotch question, and which side of the road to take and stick to, while the little bootblacks found him once more and cried, "Shine? Shine?" monotonous as snow-birds. He settled to stay over here with the south-side Scotches, and the little one-note song reaching his attention, he suddenly shoved his foot at the nearest boy, who lightly sprang away.

"Dare you to touch him!" piped a snow-bird, dangerously. They were in short trousers, and the eldest enemy, it may be, was ten.

"Don't hit me," said Mr. McLean. "I'm innocent."

"Well, you leave him be," said one.

"What's he layin' to kick you for, Billy? 'Tain't yer pop, is it?"

"Naw!" said Billy, in scorn. "Father never kicked me. Don't know who he is."

"He's a special!" shrilled the leading bird, sensationally. "He's got a badge, and he's goin' to arrest yer."

Two of them hopped instantly to the safe middle of the street, and scattered with practised strategy; but Billy stood his ground. "Dare you to arrest me!" said he.

"What'll you give me not to?" inquired Lin, and he put his hands in his pockets, arms akimbo.

"Nothing; I've done nothing," announced Billy, firmly. But even in the last syllable his voice suddenly failed, a terror filled his eyes, and he, too, sped into the middle of the street.

"What's he claim you lifted?" inquired the leader, with eagerness. "Tell him you haven't been inside a store to-day. We can prove it!" they screamed to the special officer.

"Say," said the slow-spoken Lin from the pavement, "you're poor judges of a badge, you fellows."

His tone pleased them where they stood, wide apart from each other.

Mr. McLean also remained stationary in the bluish illumination of the window. "Why, if any policeman was caught wearin' this here," said he, following his sprightly invention, "he'd get arrested himself.

This struck them extremely. They began to draw together, Billy lingering the last.

"If it's your idea," pursued Mr. McLean, alluringly, as the three took cautious steps nearer the curb, "that blue, clasped hands in a circle of red stars gives the bearer the right to put folks in the jug— why, I'll get somebody else to black my boots for a dollar."

The three made a swift rush, fell on simultaneous knees, and clattering their boxes down, began to spit in an industrious circle.

"Easy!" wheedled Mr. McLean, and they looked up at him, staring and fascinated. "Not having three feet," said the cow-puncher, always grave and slow, "I can only give two this here job."

"He's got a big pistol and a belt!" exulted the leader, who had precociously felt beneath Lin's coat.

"You're a smart boy," said Lin, considering him, "and yu' find a man out right away. Now you stand off and tell me all about myself while they fix the boots—and a dollar goes to the quickest through."

Young Billy and his tow-headed competitor flattened down, each to a boot, with all their might, while the leader ruefully contemplated Mr. McLean.

"That's a Colt .45 you've got," ventured he.

"Right again. Some day, maybe, you'll be wearing one of your own, if the angels don't pull yu' before you're ripe."

"I'm through!" sang out Towhead, rising in haste.

Small Billy was struggling still, but leaped at that, the two heads bobbing to a level together; and Mr.

McLean, looking down, saw that the arrangement had not been a good one for the boots.

"Will you kindly referee," said he, forgivingly, to the leader, "and decide which of them smears is the awfulest?"

But the leader looked the other way and played upon a mouth-organ.

"Well, that saves me money," said Mr. McLean, jingling his pockets. "I guess you've both won." He handed each of them a dollar. "Now," he continued, "I just dassent show these boots uptown; so this time it's a dollar for the best shine."

The two went palpitating at their brushes again, and the leader played his mouth-organ with brilliant unconcern. Lin, tall and brooding, leaned against the jutting sill of the window, a figure somehow plainly strange in town, while through the bright plate-glass Santa Claus, holding out his beer and sausages, perpetually beamed.

Billy was laboring gallantly, but it was labor, the cow-puncher perceived, and Billy no seasoned expert. "See here," said Lin, stooping, "I'll show yu' how it's done. He's playin' that toon crosseyed enough to steer anybody crooked. There. Keep your blacking soft, and work with a dry brush."

"Lemme," said Billy. "I've got to learn." So he finished the boot his own way with wiry determination, breathing and repolishing; and this event was also adjudged a dead heat, with results gratifying to both parties. So here was their work done, and more money in their pockets than from all the other boots and shoes of this day; and Towhead and Billy did not wish for further trade, but to spend this handsome fortune as soon as might be. Yet they delayed in the brightness of the window, drawn by curiosity near this new kind of man whose voice held them and whose remarks dropped them into constant uncertainty. Even the omitted leader had been unable to go away and nurse his pride alone.

"Is that a secret society?" inquired Towhead, lifting a finger at the badge.

Mr. McLean nodded. "Turrible," said he.

"You're a Wells & Fargo detective," asserted the leader.

"Play your harp," said Lin.

"Are you a—a desperaydo?" whispered Towhead.

"Oh, my!" observed Mr. McLean, sadly; "what has our Jack been readin'?"

"He's a cattle-man!" cried Billy. "I seen his heels."

"That's you!" said the discovered puncher, with approval. "You'll do. But I bet you can't tell me what we wearers of this badge have sworn to do this night."

At this they craned their necks and glared at him.

"We—are—sworn—don't yu' jump, now, and give me away—sworn—to—blow off three bootblacks to a dinner."

"Ah, pshaw!" They backed away, bristling with distrust.

"That's the oath, fellows. Yu' may as well make your minds up—*for I have it to do!*"

"Dare you to! Ah!"

"And after dinner it's the Opera-house, to see 'The Children of Captain Crant'!"

They screamed shrilly at him, keeping off beyond the curb.

"I can't waste my time on such smart boys," said Mr. McLean, rising lazily to his full height from the window-sill. "I am goin' somewhere to find boys that ain't so turrible quick stampeded by a roast turkey."

He began to lounge slowly away, serious as he had been throughout, and they, stopping their noise short, swiftly picked up their boxes, and followed him. Some change in the current of electricity that fed the window disturbed its sparkling light, so that Santa Claus, with his arms stretched out behind the

departing cow-puncher, seemed to be smiling more
broadly from the midst of his flickering brilliance.

On their way to turkey, the host and his guests exchanged but few remarks. He was full of good-will,
and threw off a comment or two that would have led
to conversation under almost any circumstances
save these; but the minds of the guests were too dis-
tracted by this whole state of things for them to be
capable of more than keeping after Mr. McLean in silence, at a wary interval, and with their mouths, during most of the journey, open. The badge, the pistol,
their patron's talk, and the unusual dollars, wakened
wide their bent for the unexpected, their street affin-
ity for the spur of the moment; they believed slimly
in the turkey part of it, but what this man might do
next, to be there when he did it, and not to be
trapped, kept their wits jumping deliciously; so when
they saw him stop, they stopped instantly too, ten
feet out of reach. This was Denver's most civilized
restaurant—that one which Mr. McLean had remembered, with foreign dishes and private rooms, where
he had promised himself, among other things, champagne. Mr. McLean had never been inside it, but
heard a tale from a friend; and now he caught a sudden sight of people among geraniums, with plumes
and white shirt-fronts, very elegant. It must have
been several minutes that he stood contemplating
the entrance and the luxurious couples who went in.

"Plumb French!" he observed at length; and then,
"Shucks!" in a key less confident, while his guests ten
feet away watched him narrowly. "They're eatin'
patty de parley-voo in there," he muttered, and the
three bootblacks came beside him. "Say, fellows,"
said Lin, confidingly, "I wasn't raised good enough
for them dude dishes. What do yu' say! I'm after a
place where yu' can mention oyster stoo without
givin' anybody a fit. What do yu' say, boys?"

That lighted the divine spark of brotherhood!

"Ah, you come along with us—we'll take yer! You don't want to go in there. We'll show yer the boss place in Market Street. We won't lose yer." So, shouting together in their shrill little city trebles, they clustered about him, and one pulled at his coat to start him. He started obediently, and walked in their charge, they leading the way.

"Christmas is comin' now, sure," said Lin, grinning to himself. "It ain't exactly what I figured on." It was the first time he had laughed since Cheyenne, and he brushed a hand over his eyes, that were dim with the new warmth in his heart.

Believing at length in him and his turkey, the alert street faces, so suspicious of the unknown, looked at him with ready intimacy as they went along; and soon, in the friendly desire to make him acquainted with Denver, the three were patronizing him. Only Billy, perhaps, now and then stole at him a doubtful look.

The large Country Mouse listened solemnly to his three Town Mice, who presently introduced him to the place in Market Street. It was not boss, precisely, and Denver knows better neighborhoods; but the turkey and the oyster stew were there, with catsup and vegetables in season, and several choices of pie. Here the Country Mouse became again efficient; and to witness his liberal mastery of ordering and imagine his pocket and its wealth, which they had heard and partly seen, renewed in the guests a transient awe. As they dined, however, and found the host as frankly ravenous as themselves, this reticence evaporated, and they all grew fluent with oaths and opinions. At one or two words, indeed, Mr. McLean stared and had a slight sense of blushing.

"Have a cigarette?" said the leader, over his pie.

"Thank yu'," said Lin. "I won't smoke, if yu'll excuse me." He had devised a wholesome meal, with water to drink.

"Chewin's no good at meals," continued the boy. "Don't you use tobaccer?"

"Onced in a while."

The leader spat brightly. "He 'ain't learned yet," said he, slanting his elbows at Billy and sliding a match over his rump. "But beer, now—I never seen anything in it." He and Towhead soon left Billy and his callow profanities behind, and engaged in a town conversation that silenced him, and set him listening with all his admiring young might. Nor did Mr. McLean join in the talk, but sat embarrassed by this knowledge, which seemed about as much as he knew himself.

"I'll be goshed," he thought, "if I'd caught on to half that when I was streakin' around in short pants! Maybe they grow up quicker now." But now the Country Mouse perceived Billy's eager and attentive apprenticeship. "Hello, boys!" he said, "that theatre's got a big start on us."

They had all forgotten he had said anything about theatre; and other topics left their impatient minds, while the Country Mouse paid the bill and asked to be guided to the Opera-house. "This man here will look out for your blackin' and truck, and let yu' have it in the morning."

They were very late. The spectacle had advanced far into passages of the highest thrill, and Denver's eyes were riveted upon a ship and some icebergs. The party found its seats during several beautiful lime-light effects, and that remarkable fly-buzzing of violins which is pronounced so helpful in times of peril and sentiment. The children of Captain Grant had been tracking their father all over the equator and other scenic spots, and now the north pole was about to impale them. The Captain's youngest child, perceiving a hummock rushing at them with a sudden motion, loudly shouted, "Sister, the ice is closing in!" and she replied, chastely, "Then let us pray." It was a superb tableau: the ice split, and the sun rose and joggled at once to the zenith. The act-drop fell, and male Denver, wrung to its religious deeps, went out to the rum-shop.

Of course Mr. McLean and his party did not do this. The party had applauded exceedingly the defeat of the elements, and the leader, with Towhead, discussed the probable chances of the ship's getting farther south in the next act. Until lately Billy's doubt of the cow-puncher had lingered; but during this intermission whatever had been holding out in him seemed won, and in his eyes, that he turned stealthily upon his unconscious, quiet neighbor, shone the beginnings of hero-worship.

"Don't you think this is splendid?" said he.

"Splendid," Lin replied, a trifle remotely.

"Don't you like it when they all get balled up and get out that way?"

"Humming," said Lin.

"Don't you guess it's just girls, though, that do that?"

"What, young fellow?"

"Why, all that prayer-saying an' stuff."

"I guess it must be."

"She said to do it when the ice scared her, an' of course a man had to do what she wanted him."

"Sure."

"Well, do you believe they'd 'a' done it if she hadn't been on that boat, an' clung around an' cried an' everything, an' made her friends feel bad?"

"I hardly expect they would," replied the honest Lin, and then, suddenly mindful of Billy, "except there wasn't nothin' else they could think of," he added, wishing to speak favorably of the custom.

"Why, that chunk of ice weren't so awful big anyhow. I'd 'a' shoved her off with a pole. Wouldn't you?"

"Butted her like a ram," exclaimed Mr. McLean.

"Well, I don't say my prayers any more. I told Mr. Perkins I wasn't a-going to, an' he—I think he is a flubdub anyway."

"I'll bet he is!" said Lin, sympathetically. He was scarcely a prudent guardian.

"I told him straight, an' he looked at me an' down he flops on his knees. An' he made 'em all flop, but I told him I didn't care for them putting up any camp-meeting over me; an' he says, 'I'll lick you,' an' I says, 'Dare you to!' I told him mother kep' a-licking me for nothing, an' I'd not pray for her, not in Sunday-school or anywheres else. Do you pray much?"

"No," replied Lin, uneasily.

"There! I told him a man didn't, an' he said then a man went to hell. 'You lie; father ain't going to hell,' I says, and you'd ought to heard the first class laugh right out loud, girls an' boys. An' he was that mad! But I didn't care. I came here with fifty cents."

"Yu' must have felt like a millionaire."

"Ah, I felt all right! I bought papers an' sold 'em, an' got more an' saved, an' got my box an' blacking outfit. I weren't going to be licked by her just because she felt like it, an' she feeling like it most any time. Lemme see your pistol."

"You wait," said Lin. "After this show is through I'll put it on you."

"Will you, honest? Belt an' everything? Did you ever shoot a bear?"

"Lord! lots."

"Honest? Silver-tips?"

"Silver-tips, cinnamon, black; and I roped a cub onced."

"O-h! I never shot a bear."

"You'd ought to try it."

"I'm a-going to. I'm a-going to camp out in the mountains. I'd like to see you when you camp. I'd like to camp with you. Mightn't I some time?" Billy had drawn nearer to Lin, and was looking up at him adoringly.

"You bet!" said Lin; and though he did not, perhaps, entirely mean this, it was with a curiously softened face that he began to look at Billy. As with dogs and his horse, so always he played with what children he met—the few in his sage-brush world; but this was ceasing to be quite play for him, and his hand went to the boy's shoulder.

"Father took me camping with him once, the time mother was off. Father gets awful drunk, too. I've quit Laramie for good."

Lin sat up, and his hand gripped the boy. "Laramie!" said he, almost shouting it. "Yu'—yu'—is your name Lusk?"

But the boy had shrunk from him instantly. "You're not going to take me home?" he piteously wailed.

"Heaven and heavens!" murmured Lin McLean. "So you're her kid!"

He relaxed again, down in his chair, his legs stretched their straight length below the chair in front. He was waked from his bewilderment by a brushing under him, and there was young Billy diving for escape to the aisle, like the cornered city mouse that he was. Lin nipped that poor little attempt and had the limp Billy seated inside again before the two in discussion beyond had seen anything. He had said not a word to the boy, and now watched his unhappy eyes seizing upon the various exits and dispositions of the theatre; nor could he imagine anything to tell him that should restore the perished confidence. "Why did yu' lead him off?" he asked himself unexpectedly, and found that he did not seem to know; but as he watched the restless and estranged runaway he grew more and more sorrowful. "I just hate him to think that of me," he reflected. The curtain rose, and he saw Billy make up his mind to wait until they should all be going out in the crowd. While the children of Captain Grant grew hotter and hotter upon their father's geographic trail, Lin sat saying to himself a number of contradictions. "He's nothing to me; what's any of them to me?" Driven to bay by his bewilderment, he restated the facts of the past. "Why, she'd deserted him and Lusk before she'd ever laid eyes on me. I needn't to bother myself. He wasn't never even my step-kid." The past, however, brought no guidance. "Lord, what's the thing to do about this? If I had any home— This is a stinkin' world in some respects," said Mr. McLean, aloud, unknowingly. The lady in the chair beneath which the cowpuncher had his legs nudged her husband. They took it for emotion over the sad fortune of Captain Grant, and their backs shook. Presently each turned, and saw the singular man with untamed, wide-open eyes glowering at the stage, and both backs shook again.

Once more his hand was laid on Billy. "Say!"

The boy glanced at him, and quickly away.

"Look at me, and listen."

Billy swervingly obeyed.

"I ain't after yu', and never was. This here's your business, not mine. Are yu' listenin' good?"

The boy made a nod, and Lin proceeded, whispering: "You've got no call to believe what I say to yu'— yu've been lied to, I guess, pretty often. So I'll not stop yu' runnin' and hidin', and I'll never give it away I saw yu', but yu' keep doin' what yu' please. I'll just go now. I've saw all I want, but you and your friends stay with it till it quits. If yu' happen to wish to speak to me about that pistol or bears, yu' come around to Smith's Palace—that's the boss hotel here, ain't it?— and if yu' don't come too late I'll not be gone to bed. But this time of night I'm liable to get sleepy. Tell your friends good-bye for me, and be good to yourself. I've appreciated your company."

Mr. McLean entered Smith's Palace, and, engaging a room with two beds in it, did a little delicate lying by means of the truth. "It's a lost boy—a runaway," he told the clerk. "He'll not be extra clean, I expect, if he does come. Maybe he'll give me the slip, and I'll have a job cut out to-morrow. I'll thank yu' to put my money in your safe."

The clerk placed himself at the disposal of the secret service, and Lin walked up and down, looking at the railroad photographs for some ten minutes, when Master Billy peered in from the street.

"Hello!" said Mr. McLean, casually, and returned to a fine picture of Pike's Peak.

Billy observed him for a space, and, receiving no further attention, came stepping along. "I'm not a-going back to Laramie," he stated, warningly.

"I wouldn't," said Lin. "It ain't half the town Denver is. Well, good-night. Sorry yu' couldn't call sooner—I'm dead sleepy."

"O-h!" Billy stood blank. "I wish I'd shook the darned old show. Say, lemme black your boots in the morning?"

"Not sure my train don't go too early."

"I'm up! I'm up! I get around to all of 'em."

"Where do yu' sleep?"

"Sleeping with the engine-man now. Why can't you put that on me to-night?"

"Goin' up-stairs. This gentleman wouldn't let you go up-stairs."

But the earnestly petitioned clerk consented, and Billy was the first to hasten into the room. He stood rapturous while Lin buckled the belt round his scanty stomach, and ingeniously buttoned the suspenders outside the accoutrement to retard its immediate descent to earth.

"Did it ever kill a man?" asked Billy, touching the six-shooter.

"No. It 'ain't never had to do that, but I expect maybe it's stopped some killin' me."

"Oh, leave me wear it just a minute! Do you collect

arrow-heads? I think they're bully. There's the finest one you ever seen." He brought out the relic, tightly wrapped in paper, several pieces. "I foun' it myself, camping with father. It was sticking in a crack right on top of a rock, but nobody'd seen it till I came along." Ain't it fine?"

Mr. McLean pronounced it a gem.

"Father an' me found a lot, an' they made mother mad laying around, an' she throwed 'em out. She takes stuff from Kelley's."

"Who's Kelley?"

"He keeps the drug-store at Laramie. Mother gets awful funny. That's how she was when I came home. For I told Mr. Perkins he lied, an' I ran then. An' I knowed well enough she'd lick me when she got through her spell—an' father can't stop her, an' I—ah, I was sick of it! She's lamed me up twice beating me—an' Perkins wanting me to say 'God bless my mother!' a-getting up and a-going to bed—he's a flub-dub! An' so I cleared out. But I'd just as leaves said for God to bless father—an' you. I'll do it now if you say it's any sense."

Mr. McLean sat down in a chair. "Don't yu' do it now," said he.

"You wouldn't like mother," Billy continued. "You can keep that." He came to Lin and placed the arrow-head in his hands, standing beside him. "Do you like birds' eggs? I collect them. I got twenty-five kinds—sage-hen, an' blue grouse, an' willow-grouse, an' lots more kinds harder—but I couldn't bring all them from Laramie. I brought the magpie's, though. D'you care to see a magpie egg? Well, you stay to-morrow an' I'll show you that an' some other things I got the engine-man lets me keep there, for there's boys that would steal an egg. An' I could take you where we could fire that pistol. Bet you don't know what that is!"

He brought out a small tin box shaped like a thimble, in which were things that rattled.

Mr. McLean gave it up.

"That's kinni-kinnic seed. You can have that, for I got some more with the engine-man."

Lin received this second token also, and thanked the giver for it. His first feeling had been to prevent the boy's parting with his treasures, but something that came not from the polish of manners and experience made him know that he should take them. Billy talked away, laying bare his little soul; the street boy that was not quite come made place for the child that was not quite gone, and unimportant words and confidences dropped from him disjointed as he climbed to the knee of Mr. McLean, and inadvertently took that cow-puncher for some sort of parent he had not hitherto met. It lasted but a short while, however, for he went to sleep in the middle of a sentence, with his head upon Lin's breast. The man held him perfectly still, because he had not the faintest notion that Billy would be impossible to disturb. At length he spoke to him, suggesting that bed might prove more comfortable; and, finding how it was, rose and undressed the boy and laid him between the sheets. The arms and legs seemed aware of the moves required of them, and stirred conveniently; and directly the head was upon the pillow the whole small frame burrowed down, without the opening of an eye or a change in the breathing. Lin stood some time by the bedside, with his eyes on the long, curling lashes and the curly hair. Then he glanced craftily at the door of the room, and at himself in the looking-glass. He stooped and kissed Billy on the forehead, and, rising from that, gave himself a hang-dog stare in the mirror, and soon in his own bed was sleeping the sound sleep of health.

He was faintly roused by the church bells, and lay still, lingering with his sleep, his eyes closed, and his

thoughts unshaped. As he became slowly aware of
the morning, the ringing and the light reached him,
and he waked wholly, and, still lying quiet, considered the strange room filled with the bells and the
sun of the winter's day. "Where have I struck now?"
he inquired; and as last night returned abruptly upon
his mind, he raised himself on his arm.

There sat Responsibility in a chair, washed clean
and dressed, watching him.

"You're awful late," said Responsibility. "But I
weren't a-going without telling you good-bye."

"Go?" exclaimed Lin. "Go where? Yu' surely ain't
leavin' me to eat breakfast alone?" The cow-puncher
made his voice very plaintive. Set Responsibility free
after all his trouble to catch him? This was more than
he could do!

"I've got to go. If I'd thought you'd want for me to
stay—why, you said you was a-going by the early
train!"

"But the durned thing's got away on me," said Lin,
smiling sweetly from the bed.

"If I hadn't a-promised them—"

"Who?"

"Sidney Ellis and Pete Goode. Why, you know
them; you grubbed with them."

"Shucks!"

"We're a-going to have fun to-day."

"Oh!"

"For it's Christmas, an' we've bought some good cigars, an' Pete says he'll learn me sure. O' course I've
smoked some, you know. But I'd just as leaves stayed
with you if I'd only knowed sooner. I wish you lived
here. Did you smoke whole big cigars when you was
beginning?"

"Do you like flapjacks and maple syrup?" inquired
the artful McLean. "That's what I'm figuring on inside
twenty minutes."

"Twenty minutes! If they'd wait—"

"See here, Bill. They've quit expecting yu', don't yu' think? I'd ought to waked, yu' see, but I slep' and slep', and kep' yu' from meetin' your engagements, yu' see—for you couldn't go, of course. A man couldn't treat a man that way now, could he?"

"Course he couldn't," said Billy, brightening.

"And they wouldn't wait, yu' see. They wouldn't fool away Christmas, that only comes onced a year, kickin' their heels and sayin' 'Where's Billy?' They'd say, 'Bill has sure made other arrangements, which he'll explain to us at his leesyure.' And they'd skip with the cigars."

The advocate paused, effectively, and from his bolster regarded Billy with a convincing eye.

"That's so," said Billy.

"And where would yu' be then, Bill? In the street, out of friends, out of Christmas, and left both ways, no tobaccer and no flapjacks. Now Bill, what do yu' say to us putting up a Christmas deal together? Just you and me?"

"I'd like that," said Billy. "Is it all day?"

"I was thinkin' of all day," said Lin. "I'll not make yu' do anything yu'd rather not."

"Ah, they can smoke without me," said Billy, with sudden acrimony. "I'll see 'em to-morro'."

"That's you!" cried Mr. McLean. "Now, Bill, you hustle down and tell them to keep a table for us. I'll get my clothes on and follow yu'."

The boy went, and Mr. McLean procured hot water and dressed himself, tying his scarf with great care. "Wished I'd a clean shirt," said he. "But I don't look very bad. Shavin' yesterday afternoon was a good move." He picked up the arrow-head and the kinni-kinnic, and was particular to store them in his safest pocket. "I ain't sure whether you're crazy or not," said he to the man in the looking-glass. "I 'ain't never been sure." And he slammed the door and went down-stairs.

He found young Bill on guard over a table for four, with all the chairs tilted against it as warning to strangers. No one sat at any other table or came into the room, for it was late, and the place quite emptied of breakfasters, and the several entertained waiters had gathered behind Billy's important-looking back. Lin provided a thorough meal, and Billy pronounced the flannel cakes superior to flapjacks, which were not upon the bill of fare.

"I'd like to see you often," said he. "I'll come and see you if you don't live too far."

"That's the trouble," said the cow-puncher. "I do. Awful far." He stared out of the window.

"Well, I might come some time. I wish you'd write me a letter. Can you write?"

"What's that? Can I write? Oh yes."

"I can write, an' I can read too. I've been to school in Sidney, Nebraska, an' Magaw, Kansas, an' Salt Lake—that's the finest town except Denver."

Billy fell into that cheerful strain of comment which, unreplied to, yet goes on contented and self-sustaining, while Mr. McLean gave amiable signs of assent; but chiefly looked out of the window; and when the now interested waiter said respectfully that he desired to close the room, they went out to the office, where the money was got out of the safe and the bill paid.

The streets were full of the bright sun, and seemingly at Denver's gates stood the mountains sparkling; an air crisp and pleasant wafted from their peaks; no smoke hung among the roofs, and the sky spread wide over the city without a stain; it was holiday up among the chimneys and tall buildings, and down among the quiet ground-stories below as well; and presently from their scattered pinnacles through the town the bells broke out against the jocund silence of the morning.

"Don't you like music?" inquired Billy.

"Yes," said Lin.

Ladies with their husbands and children were passing and meeting, orderly yet gayer than if it were only Sunday, and the salutations of Christmas came now and again to the cow-puncher's ears; but to-day, possessor of his own share in this, Lin looked at every one with a sort of friendly challenge, and young Billy talked along beside him.

"Don't you think we could go in here?" Billy asked. A church door was open, and the rich organ sounded through to the pavement. "They've good music here, an' they keep it up without much talking between. I've been in lots of times."

They went in and sat to hear the music. Better than the organ, it seemed to them, were the harmonious voices raised from somewhere outside, like unexpected visitants; and the pair sat in their back seat, too deep in listening to the processional hymn to think of rising in decent imitation of those around them. The crystal melody of the refrain especially reached their understandings, and when for the fourth time "Shout the glad tidings, exultingly sing," pealed forth and ceased, both the delighted faces fell.

"Don't you wish there was more?" Billy whispered.

"Wish there was a hundred verses," answered Lin.

But canticles and responses followed, with so little talking between them they were held spell-bound, seldom thinking to rise or kneel. Lin's eyes roved over the church, dwelling upon the pillars in their evergreen, the flowers and leafy wreaths, the texts of white and gold. " 'Peace, good-will towards men,' " he read. "That's so. Peace and good-will. Yes, that's so. I expect they got that somewheres in the Bible. It's awful good, and you'd never think of it yourself."

There was a touch on his arm, and a woman handed a book to him. "This is the hymn we have now," she whispered, gently; and Lin, blushing scarlet, took it passively without a word. He and Billy stood up and held the book together, dutifully reading the words:

> "It came upon the midnight clear,
>   That glorious song of old,
> From angels bending near the earth
>   To touch their harps of gold;
> Peace on the earth—"

This tune was more beautiful than all, and Lin lost himself in it, until he found Billy recalling him with a finger upon the words, the concluding ones:

> "And the whole world sent back the song
>   Which now the angels sing."

The music rose and descended to its lovely and simple end; and, for a second time in Denver, Lin brushed a hand across his eyes. He turned his face from his neighbor, frowning crossly; and since the heart has reasons which Reason does not know, he seemed to himself a fool; but when the service was over and he came out, he repeated again, " 'Peace and good-will.' When I run on to the Bishop of Wyoming I'll tell him if he'll preach on them words I'll be there."

"Couldn't we shoot your pistol now?" asked Billy.

"Sure, boy. Ain't yu' hungry, though?"

"No. I wish we were away off up there. Don't you?"

"The mountains? They look pretty, so white! A heap better 'n houses. Why, we'll go there! There's trains to Golden. We'll shoot around among the foothills."

To Golden they immediately went, and after a meal there, wandered in the open country until the cartridges were gone, the sun was low, and Billy was walked off his young heel—a truth he learned complete in one horrid moment, and battled to conceal.

"Lame!" he echoed, angrily. "I ain't."

"Shucks!" said Lin, after the next ten steps. "You are, and both feet."

"Tell you, there's stones here, an' I'm just a-skipping them."

Lin, briefly, took the boy in his arms and carried him to Golden. "I'm played out myself," he said, sitting in the hotel and looking lugubriously at Billy on a bed. "And I ain't fit to have charge of a hog." He came and put his hand on the boy's head.

"I'm not sick," said the cripple. "I tell you I'm bully. You wait an' see me eat dinner."

But Lin had hot water and cold water and salt, and was an hour upon his knees bathing the hot feet. And then Billy could not eat dinner!

There was a doctor in Golden; but in spite of his light prescription and most reasonable observations, Mr. McLean passed a foolish night of vigil, while Billy slept, quite well at first, and, as the hours passed, better and better. In the morning he was entirely brisk, though stiff.

"I couldn't work quick to-day," he said. "But I guess one day won't lose me my trade."

"How d' yu' mean?" asked Lin.

"Why, I've got regulars, you know. Sidney Ellis an' Pete Goode has theirs, an' we don't cut each other. I've got Mr. Daniels an' Mr. Fisher an' lots, an' if you lived in Denver I'd shine your boots every day for nothing. I wished you lived in Denver."

"Shine my boots? Yu'll never! And yu' don't black Daniels or Fisher, or any of the outfit."

"Why, I'm doing first-rate," said Billy, surprised at the swearing into which Mr. McLean now burst. "An' I ain't big enough to get to make money at any other job."

"I want to see that engine-man," muttered Lin. "I don't like your smokin' friend."

"Pete Goode? Why, he's awful smart. Don't you think he's smart?"

"Smart's nothin'," observed Mr. McLean.

"Pete has learned me and Sidney a lot," pursued Billy, engagingly.

"I'll bet he has!" growled the cow-puncher; and again Billy was taken aback at his language.

It was not so simple, this case. To the perturbed mind of Mr. McLean it grew less simple during that day at Golden, while Billy recovered, and talked, and ate his innocent meals. The cow-puncher was far too wise to think for a single moment of restoring the runaway to his debauched and shiftless parents. Possessed of some imagination, he went through a scene in which he appeared at the Lusk threshold with Billy and forgiveness, and intruded upon a conjugal assault and battery. "Shucks!" said he. "The kid would be off again inside a week. And I don't want him there, anyway."

Denver, upon the following day, saw the little boot-black again at his corner, with his trade not lost; but near him stood a tall, singular man, with hazel eyes and a sulky expression. And citizens during that week noticed, as a new sight in the streets, the tall man and the little boy walking together. Sometimes they would be in shops. The boy seemed as happy as possible, talking constantly, while the man seldom said a word, and his face was serious.

Upon New-year's Eve Governor Barker was overtaken by Mr. McLean riding a horse up Hill Street, Cheyenne.

"Hello!" said Barker, staring humorously through his glasses. "Have a good drunk?"

"Changed my mind," said Lin, grinning. "Proves I've got one. Struck Christmas all right, though."

"Who's you friend?" inquired his Excellency.

"This is Mister Billy Lusk. Him and me have agreed that towns ain't nice to live in. If Judge Henry's foreman and his wife won't board him at Sunk Creek—why, I'll fix it somehow."

The cow-puncher and his Responsibility rode on together toward the open plain.

"Suffering Moses!" remarked his Excellency.

CHAPTER V

Separ's Vigilante

WE HAD fallen half asleep, my pony and I, as we went jogging and jogging through the long sunny afternoon. Our hills of yesterday were a pale-blue coast sunk almost away behind us, and ahead our goal lay shining, a little island of houses in this quiet mid-ocean of sage-brush. For two hours it had looked as clear and near as now, rising into sight across the huge dead calm and sinking while we travelled our undulating, imperceptible miles. The train had come and gone invisibly, except for its slow pillar of smoke I had watched move westward against Wyoming's stainless sky. Though I was still far off, the water-tank and other buildings stood out plain and complete to my eyes, like children's blocks arranged and forgotten on the floor. So I rode along, hypnotized by the sameness of the lazy, splendid plain, and almost unaware of the distant rider, till, suddenly, he was close and hailing me.

"They've caved!" he shouted.

"Who?" I cried, thus awakened.

"Ah, the fool company," said he, quieting his voice as he drew near. "They've shed their haughtiness," he added, confidingly, as if I must know all about it.

"Where did they learn that wisdom?" I asked, not knowing in the least.

"Experience," he called over his shoulder (for already we had met and passed); "nothing like experience for sweating the fat off the brain."

He yelled me a brotherly good-bye, and I am sorry never to have known more of him, for I incline to value any stranger so joyous. But now I waked the pony and trotted briskly, surmising as to the company and its haughtiness. I had been viewing my destination across the sage-brush for so spun-out a time that (as constantly in Wyoming journeys) the emotion of arrival had evaporated long before the event, and I welcomed employment for my otherwise high-and-dry mind. Probably he meant the railroad company; certainly something large had happened. Even as I dismounted at the platform another hilarious cow-puncher came out of the station, and, at once remarking, "They're going to leave us alone," sprang on his horse and galloped to the corrals down the line, where some cattle were being loaded into a train. I went inside for my mail, and here were four more cow-punchers playing with the agent. They had got a letter away from him, and he wore his daily look of anxiety to appreciate the jests of these rollicking people. "Read it!" they said to me; and I did read the private document, and learned that the railroad was going to waive its right to enforce law and order here, and would trust to Separ's good feeling. "Nothing more," the letter ran, "will be done about the initial outrage or the subsequent vandalisms. We shall pass over our wasted outlay in the hope that a policy of friendship will prove our genuine desire to benefit that section."

" 'Initial outrage,' " quoted one of the agent's large playmates. "Ain't they furgivin'?"

"Well," said I, "you would have some name for it yourself if you sent a deputy sheriff to look after your rights, and he came back tied to the cow-catcher!"

The man smiled luxuriously over this memory. "We didn't hurt him none. Just returned him to his home. Hear about the label Honey Wiggin pinned on to him? 'Send us along one dozen as per sample.' Honey's quaint! Yes," he drawled, judicially, "I'd be mad at that. But if you're making peace with a man because it's convenient, why, your words must be pleasanter than if you really felt pleasant." He took the paper from me, and read, sardonically: " 'Subsequent vandalisms ... wasted outlay.' I suppose they run this station from charity to the cattle. Saves the poor things walking so far to the other railroad. 'Policy of friendship ... genuine desire'—oh, mouth-wash!" And, shaking his bold, clever head, he daintily flattened the letter upon the head of the agent. "Tubercle," said he (this was their name for the agent, who had told all of us about his lungs), "it ain't your fault we saw their fine letter. They just intended you should give it out how they wouldn't bother us any more, and then we'd act square. The boys'll sit up late over this joke."

Then they tramped to their horses and rode away. The spokesman had hit the vital point unerringly; for cow-punchers are shrewdly alive to frankness, and it often draws out the best that is in them; but its opposite affects them unfavorably; and I needing sleep, sighed to think of their late sitting up over that joke. I walked to the board box painted "Hotel Brunswick"—"hotel" in small italics and "Brunswick" in enormous capitals, the N and the S wrong side up.

Here sat a girl outside the door, alone. Her face was broad, wholesome, and strong, and her eyes alert and sweet. As I came she met me with a chal-

lenging glance of good-will. Those women who journeyed along the line in the wake of payday to traffic
with the men employed a stare well known; but this
straight look seemed like the greeting of some pleasant young cowboy. In surprise I forgot to be civil, and
stepped foolishly by her to see about supper and
lodging.

At the threshold I perceived all lodging bespoken.
On each of the four beds lay a coat or pistol or other
article of dress, and I must lodge myself. There were
my saddle-blankets—rather wet; or Lin McLean might
ride in to-night on his way to Riverside; or perhaps
down at the corrals I could find some other acquaintance whose habit of washing I trusted and whose
bed I might share. Failing these expedients, several
empties stood idle upon a siding, and the box-like
darkness of these freight-cars was timely. Nights
were short now. Camping out, the dawn by three
o'clock would flow like silver through the universe,
and, sinking through my blankets, remorselessly per-
vade my buried hair and brain. But with clean straw
in the bottom of an empty, I could sleep my fill until
five or six. I decided for the empty, and opened the
supper-room door, where the table was set for more
than enough to include me; but the smell of the butter that awaited us drove me out of the Hotel Brunswick to spend the remaining minutes in the air.

"I was expecting you," said the girl. "Well, if I
haven't frightened him!" She laughed so delightfully
that I recovered and laughed too. "Why," she explained, "I just knew you'd not stay in there. Which
side are you going to butter *your* bread this evening?"

"You had smelt it?" said I, still cloudy with surprise. "Yes. Unquestionably. Very rancid." She
glanced oddly at me, and, with less fellowship in her
tone, said, "I was going to warn you—" when suddenly, down at the corrals, the boys began to shoot

at large. "Oh, dear!" she cried, starting up. "There's trouble."

"Not trouble," I assured her. "Too many are firing at once to be in earnest. And you would be safe here."

"Me? A lady without escort? Well, I should reckon so! Leastways, we are respected where I was raised. I was anxious for the gentlemen ovah yondah. Shawhan, K. C. branch of the Louavull an' Nashvull, is my home." The words "Louisville and Nashville" spoke creamily of Blue-grass.

"Unescorted all that way!" I exclaimed.

"Isn't it awful?" said she, tilting her head with a laugh, and showing the pistol she carried. "But we've always been awful in Kentucky. Now I suppose New York would never speak to poor me as it passed by?" And she eyed me with capable, good-humored satire.

"Why New York?" I demanded. "Guess again."

"Well," she debated, "well, cowboy clothes and city language—he's English!" she burst out; and then she turned suddenly red, and whispered to herself, reprovingly, "If I'm not acting rude!"

"Oh!" said I, rather familiarly.

"It was, sir; and please to excuse me. If you had started joking so free with me, I'd have been insulted. When I saw you—the hat and everything—I took you— You see I've always been that used to talking to—to folks around!" Her bright face saddened, memories evidently rose before her, and her eyes grew distant.

I wished to say, "Treat me as 'folks around,'" but this tall country girl had put us on other terms. On discovering I was not "folks around," she had taken refuge in deriding me, but swiftly feeling no solid ground there, she drew a firm, clear woman's line between us. Plainly she was a comrade of men, in her buoyant innocence secure, yet by no means in the dark as to them.

"Yes, unescorted two thousand miles," she resumed, "and never as far as twenty from home till last Tuesday. I expect you'll have to be scandalized, for I'd do it right over again to-morrow."

"You've got me all wrong," said I. "I'm not English; I'm not New York. I am good American, and not bounded by my own farm either. No sectional line, or Mason and Dixon, or Missouri River tattoos me. But you, when you say United States, you mean United Kentucky!"

"Did you ever!" said she, staring at what was Greek to her—as it is to most Americans. "And so if you had a sister back East, and she and you were all there was of you any more, and she hadn't seen you since—not since you first took to staying out nights, and she started to visit you, you'd not tell her 'Fie for shame'?"

"I'd travel my money's length to meet her!" said I.

A wave of pain crossed her face. "Nate didn't know," she said then, lightly. "You see, Nate's only a boy, and regular thoughtless about writing."

Ah! So this Nate never wrote, and his sister loved and championed him! Many such stray Nates and Bobs and Bills galloped over Wyoming, lost and forgiven.

"I'm starting for him in the Buffalo stage," continued the girl.

"Then I'll have your company on a weary road," said I; for my journey was now to that part of the cattle country.

"To Buffalo?" she said, quickly. "Then maybe you—maybe— My brother is Nate Buckner." She paused. "Then you're not acquainted with him?"

"I may have seen him," I answered, slowly. "But faces and names out here come and go."

I knew him well enough. He was in jail, convicted of forgery last week, waiting to go to the penitentiary for five years. And even this wild border community that hated law courts and punishments had not been sorry; for he had cheated his friends too often, and the wide charity of the sage-brush does not cover that sin. Beneath his pretty looks and daring skill with horses they had found vanity and a cold, false heart; but his sister could not. Here she was, come to find him after lonely years, and to this one soul that loved him in the world how was I to tell the desolation and the disgrace? I was glad to hear her ask me if the stage went soon after supper.

"Now isn't that a bother?" said she, when I answered that it did not start till morning. She glanced with rueful gayety at the hotel. "Never mind," she continued, briskly; "I'm used to things. I'll just sit up somewhere. Maybe the agent will let me stay in the office. You're sure all that shooting's only jollification?"

"Certain," I said. "But I'll go and see."

"They always will have their fun," said she. "But I hate to have a poor boy get hurt—even him deserving it!"

"They use pistols instead of fire-crackers," said I. "But you must never sleep in that office. I'll see what we can do."

"Why, you're real kind!" she exclaimed, heartily. And I departed, wondering what I ought to do.

Perhaps I should have told you before that Separ was a place once—a sort of place; but you will relish now, I am convinced, the pithy fable of its name. Midway between two sections of this still unfinished line that, rail after rail and mile upon mile, crawled over the earth's face visibly during the constructing hours of each new day, lay a camp. To this point these unjoined pieces were heading, and here at length they met. Camp Separation it had been fitly called; but how should the American railway man afford time to say that? Separation was pretty and apt, but needless; and with the sloughing of two syllables came the brief, businesslike result—Separ. Chicago, 1137½ miles. It was labelled on a board, large almost as the hut station. A Y-switch, two sidings, the fat water-tank and steam-pump, and a section-house with three trees before it composed the north side. South of the track were no trees. There was one long siding by the corrals and cattle-chute, there were a hovel where plug tobacco and canned goods were for sale, a shed where you might get your horse shod, a wire fence that at shipping times enclosed bales of pressed hay, the hotel, the stage stable, and the little station—some seven shanties all told. Between them were spaces of dust, the immediate plains engulfed them, and through their midst ran the far-vanishing railroad, to which they hung like beads on a great string from horizon to horizon. A great east-and-west string, one end in the rosy sun at morning, and one in the crimson sun at night. Beyond each sky-line lay cities and ports where the world went on out of sight and hearing. This lone steel thread had been stretched across the continent because it was the day of haste and hope, when dollars seemed many and hard times were few; and from the Yellowstone to the Rio Grande similar threads were stretching, and little Separs by dispersed hundreds hung on them, as it were in space eternal. Can you wonder that vigorous young men with pistols should, when they came to such a place, shoot them off to let loose their unbounded joy of living?

And yet it was not this merely that began the custom, but an error of the agent's. The new station was scarce created when one morning Honey Wiggin with the Virginian had galloped innocently in from the round-up to telegraph for some additional cars.

"I'm dead on to you!" squealed the official, dropping flat at the sight of them; and bang went his gun at them. They, most naturally, thought it was a maniac, and ran for their lives among the supports of the water-tank, while he remained anchored with his weapon, crouched behind the railing that fenced him and his apparatus from the laity; and some fifteen strategic minutes passed before all parties had crawled forth to an understanding, and the message was written and paid for and comfortably despatched. The agent was an honest creature, but of tame habits, sent for the sake of his imperfect lungs to this otherwise inappropriate air. He had lived chiefly in mid-West towns, a serious reader of our comic weeklies; hence the apparition of Wiggin and the Virginian had reminded him sickeningly of bandits. He had express money in the safe, he explained to them, and this was a hard old country, wasn't it? and did they like good whiskey?

They drank his whiskey, but it was not well to have mentioned that about the bandits. Both were aware that when shaved and washed of their round-up grime they could look very engaging. The two cowpunchers rode out, not angry, but grieved that a man come here to dwell among them should be so tactless.

"If we don't get him used to us," observed the Virginian, "he and his pop-gun will be guttin' some blameless man."

Forthwith the cattle country proceeded to get the agent used to it. The news went over the sage-brush from Belle Fourche to Sweetwater, and playful, howling horsemen made it their custom to go rioting with pistols round the ticket-office, educating the agent. His lungs improved, and he came dimly to smile at this life which he did not understand. But the company discerned no humor whatever in having its water-tank perforated, which happened twice; and sheriffs and deputies and other symptoms of authority began to invest Separ. Now what should authority do upon these free plains, this wilderness of do-as-you-please, where mere breathing the air was like inebriation? The large, headlong children who swept in from the sage-brush and out again meant nothing that they called harm until they found themselves resisted. Then presently happened that affair of the cow-catcher; and later a too-zealous marshal, come about a mail-car they had side-tracked and held with fiddles, drink, and petticoats, met his death accidentally, at which they were sincerely sorry for about five minutes. They valued their own lives as little, and that lifts them forever from baseness at least. So the company, concluding such things must be endured for a while yet, wrote their letter, and you have seen how wrong the letter went. All it would do would be from now on to fasten upon Separ its code of recklessness; to make shooting the water-tank (for example) part of a gentleman's deportment when he showed himself in town.

It was not now the season of heavy shipping; tonight their work would be early finished, and then they were likely to play after their manner. To arrive in such a place on her way to her brother, the felon in jail, made the girl's journey seem doubly forlorn to me as I wandered down to the corrals.

A small, bold voice hailed me. "Hello, you!" it said; and here was Billy Lusk, aged nine, in boots and overalls, importantly useless with a stick, helping the men prod the steers at the chute.

"Thought you were at school," said I.

"Ah, school's quit," returned Billy, and changed the subject. "Say, Lin's hunting you. He's a-going to eat at the hotel. I'm grubbing with the outfit." And Billy resumed his specious activity.

Mr. McLean was in the ticket-office, where the newspaper had transiently reminded him of politics. "Wall Street," he was explaining to the agent, "has been lunched on by them Ross-childs, and they're moving on. Feeding along to Chicago. We want—"

Here he noticed me and, dragging his gauntlet off, shook my hand with his lusty grasp.

"Your eldest son just said you were in haste to find me," I remarked.

"Lose you, he meant. The kid gets his words twisted."

"Didn't know you were a father, Mr. McLean," simpered the agent.

Lin fixed his eye on the man. "And you don't know it now," said he. Then he removed his eye. "Let's grub," he added to me. My friend did not walk to the hotel, but slowly round and about, with a face overcast. "Billy is a good kid," he said at length, and, stopping, began to kick small mounds in the dust. Politics floated lightly over him, but here was a matter dwelling with him, heavy and real. "He's dead stuck on being a cow-puncher," he presently said.

"Some day—" I began.

"He don't want to wait that long," Lin said, and smiled affectionately. "And, anyhow, what is 'some day'? Some day we punchers will not be here. The living will be scattered, and the dead—well, they'll be all right. Have yu' studied the wire fence? It's spreading to catch us like nets do the salmon in the Columbia River. No more salmon, no more cow-punchers," stated Mr. McLean, sententiously; and his words made me sad, though I know that progress cannot spare land and water for such things. "But Billy," Lin resumed, "has agreed to school again when it starts up in the fall. He takes his medicine because I want him to." Affection crept anew over the cow-puncher's face. "He can learn books with the quickest when he wants, that Bear Creek school-marm says. But he'd ought to have a regular mother till—till I can do for him, yu' know. It's onwholesome him seeing and hearing the boys—and me, and me when I forget!— but shucks! how can I fix it? Billy was sure enough

dropped and deserted. But when I found him the little calf could run and notice like everything!"

"I should hate your contract, Lin," said I. "Adopting's
a touch-and-go business even when a man has a
home."

"I'll fill the contract, you bet! I wish the little son-
of-a-gun was mine. I'm a heap more natural to him
than that pair of drunkards that got him. He likes me:
I think he does. I've had to lick him now and then,
but Lord! his badness is all right—not sneaky. I'll take
him hunting next month, and then the foreman's wife
at Sunk Creek boards him till school. Only when they
move, Judge Henry'll make his Virginia man
foreman—and he's got no woman to look after Billy,
yu' see."

"He's asking one hard enough," said I, digressing.

"Oh yes; asking! Talk of adopting—" said Mr.
McLean, and his wide-open, hazel eyes looked away
as he coughed uneasily. Then abruptly looking at me
again, he said: "Don't you get off any more truck
about eldest son and that, will yu', friend? The boys
are joshing me now—not that I care for what might
easy enough be so, but there's Billy. Maybe he'd not
mind, but maybe he would after a while; and I am
kind o' set on—well—he didn't have a good time till
he shook that home of his, and I'm going to make
this old bitch of a world pay him what she owes him,
if I can. Now you'll drop joshing, won't yu'?" His forehead was moist over getting the thing said and laying
bare so much of his soul.

"And so the world owes us a good time, Lin?"
said I.

He laughed shortly. "She must have been dead
broke, then, quite a while, you bet! Oh no. Maybe I
used to travel on that basis. But see here" (Lin laid
his hand on my shoulder), "if you can't expect a
good time for yourself *in* reason, you can sure make
the kids happy *out* o' reason, can't yu'?"

I fairly opened my mouth at him.

"Oh yes," he said, laughing in that short way again (and he took his hand off my shoulder); "I've been thinking a wonderful lot since we met last. I guess I know some things yu' haven't got to yet yourself— Why, there's a girl!"

"That there is!" said I. "And certainly the world owes her a better—"

"She's a fine-looker," interrupted Mr. McLean, paying me no further attention. Here the decrepit, straw-hatted proprietor of the Hotel Brunswick stuck his beard out of the door and uttered "Supper!" with a shrill croak, at which the girl rose.

"Come!" said Lin, "let's hurry!"

But I hooked my fingers in his belt and in spite of his plaintive oaths at my losing him the best seat at the table, told him in three words the sister's devoted journey.

"Nate Buckner!" he exclaimed. "Him with a decent sister!"

"It's the other way round," said I. "Her with him for a brother!"

"He goes to the penitentiary this week," said Lin. "He had no more cash to stake his lawyer with, and the lawyer lost interest in him. So his sister could have waited for her convict away back at Joliet, and saved time and money. How did she act when yu' told her?"

"I've not told her."

"Not? Too kind o' not your business? Well, well! You'd ought to know better 'n me. Only it don't seem right to let her—no, sir; it's not right, either. Put it her brother was dead (and Mrs. Fligg's husband would like dearly to make him dead), you'd not let her come slap up against the news unwarned. You would tell her he was sick, and start her gently."

"Death's different," said I.

"Shucks! And she's to find him caged, and waiting

for stripes and a shaved head? How d' yu' know she mightn't hate that worse 'n if he'd been just shot like a man in a husband scrape, instead of jailed like a skunk for thieving? No, sir, she mustn't. Think of how it'll be. Quick as the stage pulls up front o' the Buffalo post-office, plump she'll be down ahead of the mailsacks, inquiring after her brother, and all that crowd around staring. Why, we can't let her do that; she can't do that. If you don't feel so interfering, I'm good for this job myself." And Mr. McLean took the lead and marched jingling in to supper.

The seat he had coveted was vacant. On either side the girl were empty chairs, two or three; for with that clean, shy respect of the frontier that divines and evades a good woman, the dusty company had sat itself at a distance, and Mr. McLean's best seat was open to him. Yet he had veered away to the other side of the table, and his usually roving eye attempted no gallantry. He ate sedately, and it was not until after long weeks and many happenings that Miss Buckner told Lin she had known he was looking at her through the whole of this meal. The straw-hatted proprietor came and went, bearing beefsteak hammered flat to make it tender. The girl seemed the one happy person among us; for supper was going forward with the invariable alkali etiquette, all faces brooding and feeding amid a disheartening silence as of guilt or bereavement that springs from I have never been quite sure what—perhaps reversion to the native animal absorbed in his meat, perhaps a little from every guest's uneasiness lest he drink his coffee wrong or stumble in the accepted uses of the fork. Indeed, a diffident, uncleansed youth nearest Miss Buckner presently wiped his mouth upon the cloth; and Mr. McLean, knowing better than that, eyed him for this conduct in the presence of a lady. The lively strength of the butter must, I think, have reached all in the room; at any rate, the table-cloth

lad, troubled by Mr. McLean's eye, now relieved the
general silence by observing, chattily:

"Say, friends, that butter ain't in no trance."

"If it's too rich for you," croaked the enraged proprietor, "use axle-dope."

The company continued gravely feeding, while I
struggled to preserve the decorum of sadness, and
Miss Buckner's face was also unsteady. But sternness
mantled in the countenance of Mr. McLean, until the
harmless boy, embarrassed to pieces, offered the un-
tasted smelling-dish to Lin, to me, helped himself,
and finally thrust the plate at the girl, saying, in his
Texas idiom,

"Have butter."

He spoke in the shell voice of adolescence, and on
"butter" cracked an octave up into the treble. Miss
Buckner was speechless, and could only shake her
head at the plate.

Mr. McLean, however, thought she was offended.
"She wouldn't choose for none," he said to the
youth, with appalling calm. "Thank yu' most to
death."

"I guess," fluted poor Texas, in a dove falsetto, "it
would go slicker rubbed outside than swallered."

At this Miss Buckner broke from the table and fled
out of the house.

"You don't seem to know anything," observed Mr.
McLean. "What toy-shop did you escape from?"

"Wind him up! Wind him up!" said the proprietor,
sticking his head in from the kitchen.

"Ah, what's the matter with this outfit?" screamed
the boy, furiously. "Can't yu' leave a man eat? Can't
yu' leave him be? You make me sick!" And he
flounced out with his young boots.

All the while the company fed on unmoved. Presently one remarked.

"Who's hiring him?"

"The C. Y. outfit," said another.

"Half-circle L.," a third corrected.

"I seen one like him onced," said the first, taking his hat from beneath his chair. "Up in the Black Hills he was. Eighteen seventy-nine. Gosh!" And he wandered out upon his business. One by one the others also silently dispersed.

Upon going out, Lin and I found the boy pacing up and down, eagerly in talk with Miss Buckner. She had made friends with him, and he was now smoothed down and deeply absorbed, being led by her to tell her about himself. But on Lin's approach his face clouded, and he made off for the corrals, displaying a sullen back, while I was presenting Mr. McLean to the lady.

Overtaken by his cow-puncher shyness, Lin was greeting her with ungainly ceremony, when she began at once, "You'll excuse me, but I just had to have my laugh."

"That's all right, m'm," said he; "don't mention it."

"For that boy, you know—"

"I'll fix him, m'm. He'll not insult yu' no more. I'll speak to him.

"Now, please don't! Why—why—you were every bit as bad!" Miss Buckner pealed out, joyously. "It was the two of you. Oh dear!"

Mr. McLean looked crestfallen. "I had no—I didn't go to—"

"Why, there was no harm! To see him mean so well and you mean so well, and—I know I ought to behave better!"

"No, yu' oughtn't!" said Lin, with sudden ardor; and then, in a voice of deprecation, "You'll think us plumb ignorant."

"You know enough to be kind to folks," said she.

"We'd like to."

"It's the only thing makes the world go round!" she declared, with an emotion that I had heard in her tone once or twice already. But she caught herself up, and said gayly to me, "And where's that house you were going to build for a lone girl to sleep in?"

"I'm afraid the foundations aren't laid yet," said I.

"Now you gentlemen needn't bother about me."

"We'll have to, m'm. You ain't used to Separ."

"Oh, I am no—tenderfoot, don't you call them?" She whipped out her pistol, and held it at the cowpuncher, laughing.

This would have given no pleasure to me; but over Lin's features went a glow of delight, and he stood gazing at the pointed weapon and the girl behind it. "My!" he said, at length, almost in a whisper, "she's got the drop on me!"

"I reckon I'd be afraid to shoot that one of yours," said Miss Buckner. "But this hits a target real good and straight at fifteen yards." And she handed it to him for inspection.

He received it, hugely grinning, and turned it over and over. "My!" he murmured again. "Why, shucks!" He looked at Miss Buckner with stark rapture, caressing the polished revolver at the same time with a fond, unconscious thumb. "You hold it just as steady as I could," he said with pride, and added, insinuatingly, "I could learn yu' the professional drop in a morning. This here is a little dandy gun."

"You'd not trade, though," said she, "for all your flattery."

"Will yu' trade?" pounced Lin. "Won't yu'?"

"Now, Mr. McLean, I am afraid you're thoughtless. How could a girl like me ever hold that awful .45 Colt steady?"

"She knows the brands, too!" cried Lin, in ecstasy. "See here," he remarked to me with a manner that smacked of command, "we're losing time right now. You go and tell the agent to hustle and fix his room up for a lady, and I'll bring her along."

I found the agent willing, of course, to sleep on the floor of the office. The toy station was also his home.

The front compartment held the ticket and telegraph and mail and express chattels, and the railing, and room for the public to stand; through a door you then passed to the sitting, dining, and sleeping box; and through another to a cooking-stove in a pigeon-hole. Here flourished the agent and his lungs, and here the company's strict orders bade him sleep in charge; so I helped him put his room to rights. But we need not have hurried ourselves. Mr. McLean was so long in bringing the lady that I went out and found him walking and talking with her, while fifty yards away skulked poor Texas, alone. This boy's name was, like himself, of the somewhat unexpected order, being Manassas Donohoe.

As I came towards the new friends they did not appear to be joking, and on seeing me Miss Buckner said to Lin, "Did he know?"

Lin hesitated.

"You did know!" she exclaimed but lost her resentment at once, and continued, very quietly and with a friendly tone, "I reckon you don't like to have to tell folks bad news."

It was I that now hesitated.

"Not to a strange girl, anyway!" said she. "Well, now I have good news to tell you. You would not have given me any shock if you had said you knew about poor Nate, for that's the reason—Of course those things can't be secrets! Why, he's only twenty, sir! How should he know about this world? He hadn't learned the first little thing when he left home five years ago. And I am twenty-three—old enough to be Nate's grandmother, he's that young and thoughtless. He couldn't ever realize bad companions when they came around. See that!" She showed me a paper, taking it out like a precious thing, as indeed it was; for it was a pardon signed by Governor Barker. "And the Governor has let me carry it to Nate myself. He won't know a thing about it till I tell him. The Governor was real kind, and we will never forget him. I reckon Nate must have a mustache by now?" said she to Lin.

"Yes," Lin answered, gruffly, looking away from her, "he has got a mustache all right."

"He'll be glad to see you," said I, for something to say.

"Of course he will! How many hours did you say we will be?" she asked Lin, turning from me again; for Mr. McLean had not been losing time. It was plain that between these two had arisen a freemasonry from which I was already shut out. Her woman's heart had answered his right impulse to tell her about her brother, and I had been found wanting!

So now she listened over again to the hours of stage jolting that "we" had before us, and that lay between her and Nate. "We" would be four—herself, Lin, myself, and the boy Billy. Was Billy the one at supper? Oh no; just Billy Lusk, of Laramie. "He's a kid I'm taking up the country," Lin explained. "Ain't you most tuckered-out?"

"Oh, me!" she confessed, with a laugh and a sigh.

There again! She had put aside my solicitude lightly, but was willing Lin should know her fatigue. Yet, fatigue and all, she would not sleep in the agent's room. At sight of it and the close quarters she drew back into the outer office, so prompted by that inner, unsuspected strictness she had shown me before.

"Come out!" she cried, laughing. "Indeed, I thank you. But I can't have you sleep on this hard floor out here. No politeness, now! Thank you ever so much. I'm used to roughing it pretty near as well as if I was—a cowboy!" And she glanced at Lin. "They're calling forty-seven," she added to the agent.

"That's me," he said, coming out to the telegraph instrument. "So you're one of us?"

"I didn't know forty-seven meant Separ," said I. "How in the world do you know that?"

"I didn't. I heard forty-seven, forty-seven, forty-

seven, start and go right along, so I guessed they
wanted him, and he couldn't hear them from this
room."

"Can yu' do astronomy and Spanish too?" inquired
the proud and smiling McLean.

"Why, it's nothing! I've been day operator back
home. Why is a deputy coming through on a special
engine?"

"Please don't say it out loud!" quavered the agent,
as the machine clicked its news.

"Yu' needn't be scared of a girl," said Lin. "Another
sheriff! So they're not quit bothering us yet."

However, this meddling was not the company's,
but the county's; a sheriff sent to arrest, on a charge
of murder, a man named Trampas, said to be at the
Sand Hill Ranch. That was near Rawhide, two stations beyond, and the engine might not stop at Separ,
even to water. So here was no molesting of Separ's
liberties.

"All the same," Lin said, for pistols now and then
still sounded at the corrals, "the boys'll not understand that till it's explained, and they may act way-
ward first. I'd feel easier if you slept here," he urged
to the girl. But she would not. "Well, then, we must
rustle some other private place for you. How's the
section-house?"

"Rank," said the agent, "since those Italians used
it. The pump engineer has been scouring, but he's
scared to bunk there yet himself."

"Too bad you couldn't try my plan of a freight-car!"
said I.

"An empty?" she cried. "Is there a clean one?"

"You've sure never done that?" Lin burst out.

"So you're scandalized," said she, punishing him
instantly. "I reckon it does take a decent girl to shock
you." And while she stood laughing at him with robust irony, poor Lin began to stammer that he meant

no offence. "Why, to be sure you didn't!" said she. "But I do enjoy you real thoroughly."

"Well, m'm," protested the wincing cow-puncher, driven back to addressing her as "ma'am," "we ain't used—"

"Don't tangle yourself up worse, Mr. McLean. No more am I 'used.' I have never slept in an empty in my life. And why is that? Just because I've never had to. And there's the difference between you boys and us. You do lots of things you don't like, and tell us. And we put up with lots of things we don't like, but we never let you find out. I know you meant no offence," she continued, heartily, softening towards her crushed protector, "because you're a gentleman. And lands! I'm not complaining about an empty. That will be rich—if I can have the door shut."

Upon this she went out to view the cars, Mr. McLean hovering behind her with a devoted, uneasy countenance, and frequently muttering "Shucks!" while the agent and I followed with a lamp, for the dark was come. With our help she mounted into the first car, and then into the next, taking the lamp. And while she scanned the floor and corners, and slid the door back and forth, Lin whispered in my ear: "Her name's Jessamine. She told me. "Don't yu' like that name?" So I answered him, "Yes, very much," thinking that some larger flower—but still a flower—might have been more apt.

"Nobody seems to have slept in these," said she, stepping down; and on learning that even the tramp avoided Separ when he could, she exclaimed, "What lodging could be handier than this! Only it would be so cute if you had a Louavull an' Nashvull car," said she. " 'Twould seem like my old Kentucky home!" And laughing rather sweetly at her joke, she held the lamp up to read the car's lettering. " 'D. and R. G.' Oh that's a way-off stranger! I reckon they're all strange." She went along the train with her lamp. "Yes, 'B. and

M.' and 'S. C. and P.' Oh, this is rich! Nate will laugh when he hears. I'll choose 'C., B. and Q.' That's a little nearer my country. What time does the stage start? Porter, please wake 'C., B. and Q.' at six, sharp," said she to Lin.

From this point of the evening on, I think of our doings—their doings—with a sort of unchanging homesickness. Nothing like them can ever happen again, I know; for it's all gone—settled, sobered and gone. And whatever wholesomer prose of good fortune waits in our cup, how I thank my luck for this swallow of frontier poetry which I came in time for!

To arrange some sort of bed for her was the next thing, and we made a good shake-down—clean straw and blankets and a pillow, and the agent would have brought sheets; but though she would not have these, she did not resist—what do you suppose?—a looking-glass for next morning! And we got a bucket of water and her valise. It was all one to her, she said, in what car Lin and I put up; and let it be next door, by all means, if it pleased him to think he could watch over her safety better so; and she shut herself in, bidding us good-night. We began spreading straw and blankets for ourselves, when a whistle sounded far and long, and its tone rose in pitch as it came.

"I'll get him to run right to the corrals," said the agent, "so the sheriff can tell the boys he's not after them."

"That'll convince 'em he is," said Lin. "Stop him here, or let him go through."

But we were not to steer the course that events took now. The rails of the main line beside us brightened in wavering parallels as the headlight grew down upon us, and in this same moment the shoutings at the corrals chorused in a wild, hilarious threat. The burden of the coming engine heavily throbbed in the air and along the steel, and met and mixed with the hard, light beating of hoofs. The sounds approached together like a sort of charge, and I stepped between the freight-cars, where I heard Lin ordering the girl inside to lie down flat, and could see the agent running about in the dust, flapping his arms to signal with as much coherence as a chicken with its head off. I had very short space for wonder or alarm. The edge of one of my freight-cars glowed suddenly with the imminent headlight, and galloping shots invaded the place. The horsemen flew by, over-reaching, and leaning back and lugging against their impetus. They passed in a tangled swirl, and their dust coiled up thick from the dark ground and lumi-nously unfolded across the glare of the sharp-halted locomotive. Then they wheeled, and clustered around it where it stood by our cars, its air-brake pumping deep breaths, and the internal steam hum-ming through its bowels; and I came out in time to see Billy Lusk climb its front with callow, enterprising shouts. That was child's play; and the universal yell now raised by the horsemen was their child's play too; but the whole thing could so precipitately reel into the fatal that my thoughts stopped. I could only look when I saw that they had somehow recognized the man on the engine for a sheriff. Two had sprung from their horses and were making boisterously to-ward the cab, while Lin McLean, neither boisterous nor joking, was going to the cab from my side, with his pistol drawn, to keep the peace. The engineer sat with a neutral hand on the lever, the fireman had run along the top of the coal in the tender and de-scended and crouched somewhere, and the sheriff, cool, and with a good-natured eye upon all parties, was just beginning to explain his errand, when some rider from the crowd cut him short with an invitation to get down and have a drink. At the word of ribald endearment by which he named the sheriff, a passing fierceness hardened the officer's face, and the new yell they gave was less playful. Waiting no more explanations, they swarmed against the locomotive, and McLean pulled himself up on the step. The loud talking fell at a stroke to let business go on, and in this silence came the noise of a sliding-door. At that I looked, and they all looked, and stood harmless, like children surprised. For there on the threshold of the freight-car, with the interior darkness behind her, and touched by the headlight's diverging rays, stood Jessamine Buckner.

"Will you gentlemen do me a favor?" said she. "Strangers, maybe, have no right to ask favors, but I reckon you'll let that pass this time. For I'm real sleepy!" She smiled as she brought this out. "I've been four days and nights on the cars, and to-morrow I've got to stage to Buffalo. You see I'll not be here to spoil your fun to-morrow night, and I want boys to be boys just as much as ever they can. Won't you put it off till to-morrow night?"

In their amazement they found no spokesman; but I saw Lin busy among them, and that some word was passing through their groups. After the brief interval of stand-still they began silently to get on their horses, while the looming engine glowed and pumped its breath, and the sheriff and engineer remained as they were.

"Good-night, lady," said a voice among the moving horsemen, but the others kept their abashed native silence; and thus they slowly filed away to the corrals. The figures, in their loose shirts and leathern chaps, passed from the dimness for a moment through the cone of light in front of the locomotive, so that the metal about them made here and there a faint, vanishing glint; and here and there in the departing column a bold, half-laughing face turned for a look at the girl in the doorway, and then was gone again into the dimness.

The sheriff in the cab took off his hat to Miss Buckner, remarking that she should belong to the force; and as the bell rang and the engine moved, off popped young Billy Lusk from his cow-catcher. With an exclamation of horror she sprang down, and Mr. McLean appeared, and, with all a parent's fright and rage, held the boy by the arm grotesquely as the sheriff steamed by.

"I ain't a-going to chase it," said young Billy, struggling.

"I've a mind to cowhide you," said Lin.

But Miss Buckner interposed. "Oh, well," said she, "next time; if he does it next time. It's so late to-night! You'll not frighten us that way again if he lets you off?" she asked Billy.

"No," said Billy, looking at her with interest. "Father 'd have cowhided me anyway, I guess," he added, meditatively.

"Do you call him father?"

"Ah, father's at Laramie," said Billy, with disgust. "He'd not stop for your asking. Lin don't bother me much."

"You quit talking and step up there!" ordered his guardian. "Well, m'm, I guess yu' can sleep good now in there."

"If it was only an 'L. and N.' I'd not have a thing against it! Good-night, Mr. McLean; good-night, young Mr.—"

"I'm Billy Lusk. I can ride Chalkeye's pinto that bucked Honey Wiggin."

"I am sure you can ride finely, Mr. Lusk. Maybe you and I can take a ride together. Pleasant dreams!"

She nodded and smiled to him, and slid her door to; and Billy considered it, remarking: "I like her. What makes her live in a car?"

But he was drowsing while I told him; and I lifted him up to Lin, who took him in his own blankets, where he fell immediately asleep. One distant whistle showed how far the late engine had gone from us. We left our car open, and I lay enjoying the cool air. Thus was I drifting off, when I grew aware of a figure in the door. It was Lin, standing in his stockings and not much else, with his pistol. He listened, and then leaped down, light as a cat. I heard some repressed talking, and lay in expectancy; but back he came, noiseless in his stockings, and as he slid into bed I asked what the matter was. He had found the Texas boy, Manassas Donohoe, by the girl's car, with no worse intention than keeping a watch on it. "So I gave him to understand," said Lin, "that I had no objection to him amusing himself playing picket-line, but that I guessed I was enough guard, and he would find sleep healthier for his system." After this I went to sleep wholly; but, waking once in the night, thought I heard some one outside, and learned in the morning from Lin that the boy had not gone until the time came for him to join his outfit at the corrals. And I was surprised that Lin, the usually good-hearted, should find nothing but mirth in the idea of this unknown, unthanked young sentinel. "Sleeping's a heap better for them kind till they get their growth," was his single observation.

But when Separ had dwindled to toys behind us in the journeying stage I told Miss Jessamine, and although she laughed too, it was with a note that young Texas would have liked to hear; and she hoped she might see him upon her return, to thank him.

"Any Jack can walk around all night," said Mr. McLean, disparagingly.

"Well, then, and I know a Jack who didn't," observed the young lady.

This speech caused her admirer to be full of explanations; so that when she saw how readily she could perplex him, and yet how capable and untiring he was about her comfort, helping her out or tucking her in at the stations where we had a meal or changed horses, she enjoyed the hours very much, in spite of their growing awkwardness.

But oh, the sparkling, unbashful Lin! Sometimes he sat himself beside her to be close, and then he would move opposite, the better to behold her.

Never, except one long after (when sorrow manfully borne had still further refined his clay), have I heard Lin's voice or seen his look so winning. No doubt many a male bird cares nothing what neighbor bird overhears his spring song from the top of the open tree, but I extremely doubt if his lady-love, even if she be a frank, bouncing robin, does not prefer to listen from some thicket, and not upon the public lawn. Jessamine grew silent and almost peevish; and from discourse upon man and woman she hopped, she skipped, she flew. When Lin looked at his watch and counted the diminished hours between her and Buffalo, she smiled to herself; but from mention of her brother she shrank, glancing swiftly at me and my well-assumed slumber. And it was with indignation and self-pity that I climbed out in the hot sun at last beside the driver and small Billy.

"I know this road," piped Billy, on the box. "I camped here with father when mother was off that time. You can take a left-hand trail by those cottonwoods and strike the mountains."

So I inquired what game he had then shot.

"Ah, just a sage-hen. Lin's a-going to let me shoot a bear, you know. What made Lin marry mother when father was around?"

The driver gave me a look over Billy's head, and I gave him one; and I instructed Billy that people supposed his father was dead. I withheld that his mother gave herself out as Miss Peck in the days when Lin met her on Bear Creek.

The formidable nine-year-old pondered. "The geography says they used to have a lot of wives at Salt

Lake City. Is there a place where a woman can have a lot of husbands?"

"It don't especially depend on the place," remarked the driver to me.

"Because," Billy went on, "Bert Taylor told me in recess that mother 'd had a lot, and I told him he lied, and the other boys they laughed, and I blacked Bert's eye on him, and I'd have blacked the others too, only Miss Wood came out. I wouldn't tell her what Bert said, and Bert wouldn't, and Sophy Armstrong told her. Bert's father found out, and he come round, and I thought he was a-going to lick me about the eye, and he licked Bert! Say, am I Lin's, honest?"

"No, Billy, you're not" I said.

"Wish I was. They couldn't get me back to Laramie then; but, oh, bother! I'd not go for 'em! I'd like to see 'em try! Lin wouldn't leave me go. You ain't married, are you? No more is Lin now, I guess. A good many are, but I wouldn't want to. I don't think anything of 'em. I've seen mother take 'pothecary stuff on the sly. She's whaled me worse than Lin ever does. I guess he wouldn't want to be mother's husband again; and if he does," said Billy, his voice suddenly vindictive, "I'll quit him and skip."

"No danger, Bill," said I.

"How would the nice lady inside please you?" inquired the driver.

"Ah, pshaw! she ain't after Lin!" sang out Billy, loud and scornful. "She's after her brother. She's all right, though," he added, approvingly.

At this all talk stopped short inside, reviving in a casual, scanty manner; while unconscious Billy Lusk, tired of the one subject, now spoke cheerfully of birds' eggs.

Who knows the child-soul, young in days, yet old as Adam and the hills? That school-yard slur about his mother was as dim to his understanding as to the offender's, yet mysterious nature had bid him go to

instant war! How foreseeing in Lin to choke the un-
founded jest about his relation to Billy Lusk, in hopes
to save the boy's ever awakening to the facts of his
mother's life! "Though," said the driver, an easy-going
cynic, "folks with lots of fathers will find heaps of
brothers in this country!" But presently he let Billy
hold the reins, and at the next station carefully lifted
him down and up. "I've knowed that woman, too," he
whispered to me. "Sidney, Nebraska. Lusk was off
half the time. We laughed when she fooled Lin into
marryin' her. Come to think," he mused, as twilight
deepened around our clanking stage, and small Billy
slept sound between us, "there's scarcely a thing in
life you get a laugh out of that don't make soberness
for somebody."

Soberness had now visited the pair behind us;
even Lin's lively talk had quieted, and his tones were
low and few. But though Miss Jessamine at our next
change of horses "hoped" I would come inside, I
knew she did not hope very earnestly, and outside I
remained until Buffalo.

Journeying done, her face revealed the strain beneath her brave brightness, and the haunting care
she could no longer keep from her eyes. The imminence of the jail and the meeting had made her
cheeks white and her countenance seem actually
smaller; and when, reminding me that we should
meet again soon, she gave me her hand, it was ice-
cold. I think she was afraid Lin might offer to go with
her. But his heart understood the lonely sacredness
of her next half-hour, and the cow-puncher, standing
aside for her to pass, lifted his hat wistfully and
spoke never a word. For a moment he looked after
her with sombre emotion; but the court-house and
prison stood near and in sight, and, as plain as if he
had said so, I saw him suddenly feel she should not
be stared at going up those steps; it must be all
alone, the pain and the joy of that reprieve! He

turned away with me, and after a few silent steps said, "Wasted! all wasted!"

"Let us hope—" I began.

"You're not a fool," he broke in, roughly. "You don't hope anything."

"He'll start life elsewhere," said I.

"Elsewhere! Yes, keep starting till all the elsewheres know him like Powder River knows him. But she! I have had to sit and hear her tell and tell about him; all about back in Kentucky playin' around the farm, and how she raised him after the old folks died. Then he got bigger and made her sell their farm, and she told how it was right he should turn it into money and get his half. I did not dare say a word, for she'd have just bit my head off, and—and that would sure hurt me now!" Lin brought up with a comical chuckle. "And she went to work, and he cleared out, and no more seen or heard of him. That's for five years, and she'd given up tracing him, when one morning she reads in the paper about how her long-lost brother is convicted for forgery. That's the way she knows he's not dead, and she takes her savings off her railroad salary and starts for him. She was that hasty she thought it was Buffalo, New York, till she got in the cars and read the paper over again. But she had to go as far as Cincinnati, either way. She was paid every cent of the money he stole." We had come to the bridge, and Lin jerked a stone into the quick little river. "She's awful strict in some ways. Thought Buffalo must be a wicked place because of the shops bein' open Sunday. Now if that was all Buffalo's wickedness! And she thinks divorce is mostly sin. But her heart is a shield for Nate. Her face is as beautiful as her actions," he added.

"Well," said I, "and would you make such a villain your brother-in-law?"

He whirled round and took both my shoulders. "Come walking!" he urged. "I must talk some." So we followed the stream out of town towards the mountains. "I came awful near asking her in the stage," said he.

"Goodness, Lin! give yourself time!"

"Time can't increase my feelings."

"Hers, man, hers! How many hours have you known her?"

"Hours and hours! You're talking foolishness! What have they got to do with it? And she will listen to me. I can tell she will. I *know* I can be so she'll listen, and it will go all right, for I'll ask so hard. And everything'll come out straight. Yu' see, I've not been spending to speak of since Billy's on my hands, and now I'll fix up my cabin and finish my fencing and my ditch—and she's going to like Box Elder Creek better than Shawhan. She's the first I've ever loved."

"Then I'd like to ask—" I cried out.

"Ask away!" he exclaimed, inattentively, in his enthusiasm.

"When you—" but I stopped, perceiving it impossible. It was, of course, not the many transient passions on which he had squandered his substance, but the one where faith also had seemed to unite. Had he not married once, innocent of the woman's being already a wife? But I stopped, for to trench here was not for me or any one. And my pause strangely flashed on him something of that I had in my mind.

"No," he said, his eyes steady and serious upon me, "don't you ask about the things you're meaning." Then his face grew radiant and rather stern. "Do you suppose I don't know she's too good for me? And that some bygones can't ever by bygones? But if you," he said, "never come to look away up to a woman from away down, and mean to win her just the same as if you did deserve her, why, you'll make a turruble mess of the whole business!"

When we walked in silence for a long while, he

lighted again with the blossoming dawn of his sentiment. I thought of the coarse yet taking vagabond of
twenty I had once chanced upon, and hunted and
camped with since through the years. Decidedly he
was not that boy to-day! It is not true that all of us rise
through adversity, any more than that all plants need
shadow. Some starve out of the sunshine; and I have
seen misery deaden once kind people to everything
but self—almost the saddest sight in the world! But
Lin's character had not stood well the ordeal of happiness, and for him certainly harsh days and responsibility had been needed to ripen the spirit. Yes, Jessamine
Buckner would have been much too good for him before that humiliation of his marriage, and this care of
young Billy with which he had loaded himself. "Lin,"
said I, "I will drink your health and luck."

"I'm healthy enough," said he; and we came back to
the main street and into the main saloon.

"How d'ye, boys?" said some one, and there was
Nate Buckner. "It's on me to-day," he continued, shov-
ing whiskey along the bar; and I saw he was a little
drunk. "I'm setting 'em up," he continued. "Why? Why,
because"—he looked around for appreciation—
"because it's not every son-of-a-gun in Wyoming gets
pardoned by Governor Barker. I'm important, I want
you to understand," he pursued to the cold bystand-
ers. "They'll have a picture of me in the Cheyenne paper. 'The Bronco-buster of Powder River!' They can't
do without me! If any son-of-a-gun here thinks he
knows how to break a colt," he shouted, looking
around with the irrelevant fierceness of drink—and
then his challenge ebbed vacantly in laughter as the
subject blurred in his mind. "You're not drinking, Lin,"
said he.

"No," said McLean, "I'm not."

"Sworn off again? Well, water never did agree with
me."

"Yu' never gave water the chance," retorted the

cow-puncher, and we left the place without my having drunk his health.

It was a grim beginning, this brag attempt to laugh his reputation down, with the jail door scarce closed behind him. "Folks are not going to like that," said Lin, as we walked across the bridge again to the hotel. Yet the sister, left alone here after an hour at most of her brother's company, would pretend it was a matter of course. Nate was not in, she told us at once. He had business to attend to and friends to see; he must get back to Riverside and down in that country where colts were waiting for him. He was the only one the E. K. outfit would allow to handle their young stock. Did we know that? And she was going to stay with a Mrs. Pierce down there for a while, near where Nate would be working. All this she told us; but when he did not return to dine with her on this first day, I think she found it hard to sustain her wilful cheeriness. Lin offered to take her driving to see the military post and dress parade at retreat, and Cloud's Peak, and Buffalo's various sights; but she made excuses and retired to her room. Nate, however, was at tea, shaven clean, with good clothes, and well conducted. His tone and manner to Jessamine were confidential and caressing, and offended Mr. McLean, so that I observed to him that it was scarcely reasonable to be jealous.

"Oh, no jealousy!" said he. "But he comes in and kisses her, and he kisses her good-night, and us strangers looking on! It's such oncontrollable affection, yu' see, after never writing for five years. I expect she must have some of her savings left."

It is true that the sister gave the brother money more than once; and as our ways lay together, I had chances to see them both, and to wonder if her joy at being with him once again was going to last. On the road to Riverside I certainly heard Jessamine beg him to return home with her; and he ridiculed such a notion. What proper life for a live man was that dead

place back East? he asked her. I thought he might have
expressed some regret that they must dwell so far
apart, or some intention to visit her now and then; but
he said nothing of the sort, though he spoke volubly of
himself and his prospects. I suppose this spectacle of
brother and sister had rubbed Lin the wrong way too
much, for he held himself and Billy aloof, joining me
on the road but once, and then merely to give me the
news that people here wanted no more of Nate
Buckner; he would be run out of the country, and respect for the sister was all that meanwhile saved him.
But Buckner, like so many spared criminals, seemed
brazenly unaware he was disgraced, and went hailing
loudly any riders or drivers we met, while beside him
his sister sat close and straight, her stanch affection
and support for the world to see. For all she let appear, she might have been bringing him back from
some gallant heroism achieved; and as I rode along the
travesty seemed more and more pitiful, the outcome
darker and darker.

At all times is Riverside beautiful, but most beautiful
when the sun draws down through the openings of the
hills. From each one a stream comes flowing clearly
out into the plain, and fields spread green along the
margins. It was beneath the long-slanted radiance of
evening that we saw Blue Creek and felt its coolness
rise among the shifting veils of light. The red bluff eastward, the tall natural fortress, lost its stern masonry of
shapes, and loomed a soft towering enchantment of violet and amber and saffron in the changing rays. The
cattle stood quiet about the levels, and horses were
moving among the restless colts. These the brother
bade his sister look at, for with them was his glory;
and I heard him boasting of his skill—truthful boasting,
to be sure. Had he been honest in his dealings, the
good-will that man's courage and dashing appearance
beget in men would have brought him more employment than he could have undertaken. He told Jessa-

mine his way of breaking a horse that few would dare, and she listened eagerly. "Do you remember when I used to hold the pony for you to get on?" she said. "You always would scare me, Nate!" And he replied, fluently, Yes, yes; did she see that horse there, near the fence? He was a four-year-old, an outlaw, and she would find no one had tried getting on his back since he had been absent. This was the first question he asked on reaching the cabin, where various neighbors were waiting the mail-rider; and, finding he was right, he turned in pride to Jessamine.

"They don't know how to handle that horse," said he. "I told you so. Give me a rope."

Did she notice the cold greeting Nate received? I think not. Not only was their welcome to her the kinder, but any one is glad to witness bold riding, and this chance made a stir which the sister may have taken for cordiality. But Lin gave me a look; for it was the same here as it had been in the Buffalo saloon.

"The trick is easy enough," said Nate, arriving with his outlaw, and liking an audience. "You don't want a bridle, but a rope hackamore like this—Spanish style. Then let them run as hard as they want, and on a sudden reach down your arm and catch the hackamore short, close up by the mouth, and jerk them round quick and heavy at full speed. They quit their fooling after one or two doses. Now watch your outlaw!"

He went into the saddle so swift and secure that the animal, amazed, trembled stock-still, then sprang headlong. It stopped, vicious and knowing, and plunged in a rage, but could do nothing with the man, and bolted again, and away in a straight blind line over the meadow, when the rider leaned forward to his trick. The horse veered in a jagged swerve, rolled over and over with its twisted impetus, and up on its feet and on without a stop, the man still seated and upright in the saddle. How we cheered to see it! But the figure now tilted strangely, and something awful and nameless came over us and chilled our noise to silence. The horse, dazed and tamed by the fall, brought its burden towards us, a wobbling thing, falling by small shakes backward, until the head sank on the horse's rump.

"Come away," said Lin McLean to Jessamine; and at his voice she obeyed and went, leaning on his arm.

Jessamine sat by her brother until he died, twelve hours afterwards, having spoken and known nothing. The whole weight of the horse had crushed him internally. He must have become almost instantly unconscious, being held in the saddle by his spurs, which had caught in the hair cinch; it may be that our loud cheer was the last thing of this world that he knew. The injuries to his body made impossible any taking him home, which his sister at first wished to do. "Why, I came here to bring him home," she said, with a smile and tone like cheerfulness in wax. Her calm, the unearthly ease with which she spoke to any comer (and she was surrounded with rough kindness), embarrassed the listeners; she saw her calamity clear as they did, but was sleep-walking in it. It was Lin gave her what she needed—the repose of his strong, silent presence. He spoke no sympathy and no advice, nor even did he argue with her about the burial; he perceived somehow that she did not really hear what was said to her, and that these first griefless, sensible words came from some mechanism of the nerves; so he kept himself near her, and let her tell her story as she would. Once I heard him say to her, with the same authority of that first "come away": "Now you've had enough of the talking. Come for a walk." Enough of the talking—as if it were a treatment! How did he think of that? Jessamine, at any rate, again obeyed him, and I saw the two going quietly about in the meadows and along the curving brook; and that night she slept well. On one only point did the cow-puncher consult me.

"They figured to put Nate on top of that bald mound," said he. "But she has talked about the flowers and shade where the old folks lie, and where she wants him to be alongside of them. I've not let her look at him to-day, for—well, she might get the way he looks now on her memory. But I'd like to show you my idea before going further."

Lin had indeed chosen a beautiful place, and so I told him at the first sight of it.

"That's all I wanted to know," said he. "I'll fix the rest."

I believe he never once told Jessamine the body could not travel so far as Kentucky. I think he let her live and talk and grieve from hour to hour, and then led her that afternoon to the nook of sunlight and sheltering trees, and won her consent to it thus; for there was Nate laid, and there she went to sit, alone. Lin did not go with her on those walks.

But now something new was on the fellow's mind. He was plainly occupied with it, whatever else he was doing, and he had some active cattle-work. On my asking him if Jessamine Buckner had decided when to return east, he inquired of me, angrily, what was there in Kentucky she could not have in Wyoming? Consequently, though I surmised what he must be debating, I felt myself invited to keep out of his confidence, and I did so. My advice to him would have been ill received, and—as was soon to be made plain—would have done his delicacy injustice. Next, one morning he and Billy were gone. My first thought was that he had rejoined Jessamine at Mrs. Pierce's, where she was, and left me away over here on Bear Creek, where we had come for part of a week.

But stuck in my hat-band I found a pencilled farewell.

Now Mr. McLean constructed perhaps three letters in the year—painful, serious events—like an interview with some important person with whom your speech must decorously flow. No matter to whom he was writing, it froze all nature stiff in each word he achieved; and his bald business diction and wild archaic penmanship made documents that I value among my choicest correspondence; this one, especially:

> *"Wensday four a. m.*

"DEAR SIR   this is to Inform you that i have gone to Separ on important bisness where i expect to meet you on your arrival at same point. You will confer a favor and oblidge undersigned by Informing Miss J. Buckner of date (if soon) you fix for returning per stage to Separ as Miss J. Buckner may prefer company for the trip being long and poor accommodations.

> "Yours &c.   L. McLEAN."

This seemed to point but one way; and (uncharitable though it sound) that this girl, so close upon bereavement, should be able to give herself to a lover was distasteful to me.

But, most extraordinary, Lin had gone away without a word to her, and she was left as plainly in the dark as myself. After her first frank surprise at learning of his departure, his name did not come again from her lips, at any rate to me. Good Mrs. Pierce dropped a word one day as to her opinion of men who deceive women into expecting something from them.

"Let us talk straight," said I. "Do you mean that Miss Buckner says that, or that you say it?"

"Why, the poor thing says nothing!" exclaimed the lady. "It's like a man to think she would. And I'll not say anything, either, for you're all just the same, except when you're worse; and that Lin McLean is going to know what I think of him next time we meet."

He did. On that occasion the kind old dame told

him he was the best boy in the country, and stood on her toes and kissed him. But meanwhile we did not know why he had gone, and Jessamine (though he was never subtle or cruel enough to plan such a thing) missed him, and thus in her loneliness had the chance to learn how much he had been to her.

Though pressed to stay indefinitely beneath Mrs. Pierce's hospitable roof, the girl, after lingering awhile, and going often to that nook in the hill by Riverside, took her departure. She was restless, yet clung to the neighborhood. It was with a wrench that she fixed her going when I told her of my own journey back to the railroad. In Buffalo she walked to the court-house and stood a moment as if bidding this site of one life-memory farewell, and from the stage she watched and watched the receding town and mountains. "It's awful to be leaving him!" she said. "Excuse me for acting so in front of you." With the poignant emptiness overcoming her in new guise, she blamed herself for not waiting in Illinois until he had been sent to Joliet, for then, so near home, he must have gone with her.

How could I tell her that Nate's death was the best end that could have come to him? But I said: "You know you don't think it was your fault. You know you would do the same again." She listened to me, but her eyes had no interest in them. "He never knew pain," I pursued, "and he died doing the thing he liked best in the world. He was happy and enjoying himself, and you gave him that. It's bad only for you. Some would talk religion, but I can't."

"Yes," she answered, "I can think of him so glad to be free. Thank you for saying that about religion. Do you think it's wicked not to want it—to hate it sometimes? I hope it's not. Thank you, truly."

During our journey she summoned her cheerfulness, and all that she said was wholesome. In the robust, coarse soundness of her fibre, the wounds of grief would heal and leave no sickness—perhaps no higher sensitiveness to human sufferings than her broad native kindness already held. We touched upon religion again, and my views shocked her Kentucky notions, for I told her Kentucky locked its religion in an iron cage called Sunday, which made it very savage and fond of biting strangers. Now and again I would run upon that vein of deep-seated prejudice that was in her character like some fine wire. In short, our disagreements brought us to terms more familiar than we had reached hitherto. But when at last Separ came, where was I? There stood Mr. McLean waiting, and at the suddenness of him she had no time to remember herself, but stepped out of the stage with such a smile that the ardent cowpuncher flushed and beamed.

"So I went away without telling you good-bye!" he began, not wisely. "Mrs. Pierce has been circulating war talk about me, you bet!"

The maiden in Jessamine spoke instantly. "Indeed? There was no special obligation for you to call on me, or her to notice if you didn't."

"Oh!" said Lin, crestfallen. "Yu' sure don't mean that?"

She looked at him, and was compelled to melt. "No, neighbor, I don't mean it."

"Neighbor!" he exclaimed; and again, "Neighbor," much pleased. "Now it would sound kind o' pleasant if you'd call me that for a steady thing."

"It would sound kind of odd, Mr. McLean, thank you."

"Blamed if I understand her," cried Lin. "Blamed if I do. But you're going to understand me sure quick!" He rushed inside the station, spoke sharply to the agent, and returned in the same tremor of elation that had pushed him to forwardness with his girl, and with which he seemed near bursting. "I've been here three days to meet you. There's a letter, and I

expect I know what's in it. Tubercle has got it here."
He took it from the less hasty agent and thrust it in
Jessamine's hand. "You needn't to fear. Please open
it; it's good news this time, you bet!" He watched it in
her hand as the boy of eight watches the string of a
Christmas parcel he wishes his father would cut in-
stead of so carefully untie. "Open it," he urged again.
"Keeping me waiting this way!"

"What in the world does all this mean?" cried Jessamine, stopping short at the first sentence.

"Read," said Lin.

"You've done this!" she exclaimed.

"Read, read!"

So she read, with big eyes. It was an official letter
of the railroad, written by the division superintendent at Edgeford. It hoped Miss Buckner might feel
like taking the position of agent at Separ. If she was
willing to consider this, would she stop over at
Edgeford, on her way east, and talk with the superintendent? In case the duties were more than she had
been accustomed to on the Louisville and Nashville,
she could continue east with the loss of only a day.
The superintendent believed the salary could be arranged satisfactorily. Enclosed please to find an order for a free ride to Edgeford.

Jessamine turned her wondering eyes on Lin. "You
did do this," she repeated, but this time with extraordinary quietness.

"Yes," said he. "And I am plumb proud of it."

She gave a rich laugh of pleasure and amusement;
a long laugh, and stopped. "Did anybody ever!" she
said.

"We can call each other neighbors now, yu' see,"
said the cow-puncher.

"Oh no! oh no!" Jessamine declared. "Though how
am I ever to thank you?"

"By not argufying," Lin answered.

"Oh no, no! I can do no such thing. Don't you see I can't? I believe you are crazy."

"I've been waiting to hear yu' say that," said the complacent McLean. "I'm not argufying. We'll eat supper now. The east-bound is due in an hour, and I expect you'll be wanting to go on it."

"And I expect I'll go, too," said the girl.

"I'll be plumb proud to have yu'," the cow-puncher assented.

"I'm going to get my ticket to Chicago right now," said Jessamine, again laughing, sunny and defiant.

"You bet you are!" said the incorrigible McLean. He let her go into the station serenely. "You can't get used to new ideas in a minute," he remarked to me. "I've figured on all that, of course. But that's why," he broke out, impetuously, "I quit you on Bear Creek so sudden. 'When she goes back away home,' I'd been saying to myself every day, 'what'll you do then, Lin McLean?' Well, I knew I'd go to Kentucky too. Just knew I'd have to, yu' see, and it was inconvenient, turrible inconvenient—Billy here and my ranch, and the beef round-up comin'—but how could I let her go and forget me? Take up, maybe, with some Blue-grass son-of-a-gun back there? And I hated the fix I was in till that morning, getting up, I was joshin' the Virginia man that's after Miss Wood. I'd been sayin' no educated lady would think of a man who talked with an accent like his. 'It's repo'ted you have a Southern rival yourself,' says he, joshin' back. So I said I guessed the rival would find life uneasy. 'He does,' says he. 'Any man with his voice broke in two halves, and one down in his stomach and one up among the angels, is goin' to feel uneasy. But Texas talks a heap about his lady vigilante in the freight-car.' 'Vigilante!' I said; and I must have jumped, for they all asked where the lightning had struck. And in fifteen minutes after writing you I'd hit the trail for Separ. Oh, I figured things out on that ride!" (Mr. McLean here clapped me on

the back.) "Got to Separ. Got the sheriff's address—
the sheriff that saw her that night they held up the
locomotive. Got him to meet me at Edgeford and
make a big talk to the superintendent. Made a big
talk myself. I said, 'Put that girl in charge of Separ,
and the boys'll quit shooting your water-tank. But Tubercle can't influence 'em.' 'Tubercle?' says the superintendent. 'What's that?' And when I told him it
was the agent, he flapped his two hands down on the
chair arms each side of him and went to rockin' up
and down. I said the agent was just a temptation to
the boys to be gay right along, and they'd keep
a-shooting. 'You can choose between Tubercle and
your tank,' I said; 'but you've got to move one of 'em
from Separ if yu' want peace.' The sheriff backed me
up good, too. He said a man couldn't do much with
Separ the way it was now; but a decent woman
would be respected there, and the only question was
if she could conduct the business. So I spoke up
about Shawhan, and when the whole idea began to
soak into that superintendent his eyeballs jingled
and he looked as wise as a work-ox. 'I'll see her,' says
he. And he's going to see her."

"Well," said I, "you deserve success after thinking
of a thing like that! You're wholly wasted punching
cattle. But she's going to Chicago. By eleven o'clock
she will have passed by your superintendent."

"Why, so she will!" said Lin, affecting surprise.

He baffled me, and he baffled Jessamine. Indeed,
his eagerness with her parcels, his assistance in
checking her trunk, his cheerful examination of
check and ticket to be sure they read over the same
route, plainly failed to gratify her. Her firmness about
going was sincere, but she had looked for more dis-
suasion; and this sprightly abettal of her departure
seemed to leave something vacant in the ceremonies.
She fell singularly taciturn during supper at the Hotel
Brunswick, and presently observed,

"I hope I shall see Mr. Donohoe."

"Texas?" said Lin. "I expect they'll have tucked him in bed by now up at the ranch. The little fellow is growing yet."

"He can walk round a freight-car all night," said Miss Buckner, stoutly. "I've always wanted to thank him for looking after me."

Mr. McLean smiled elaborately at his plate.

"Well, if he's not actually thinking he'll tease me!" cried out Jessamine. "Though he claims not to be foolish like Mr. Donohoe. Why, Mr. McLean, you surely must have been young once! See if you can't remember!"

"Shucks!" began Lin.

But her laughter routed him. "Maybe you didn't notice you were young," she said. "But don't you reckon perhaps the men around did? Why, maybe even the girls kind o' did!"

"She's hard to beat, ain't she?" inquired Lin, admiringly, of me.

In my opinion she was. She had her wish, too, about Texas; for we found him waiting on the railroad platform, dressed in his best, to say good-bye. The friendly things she told him left him shuffling and repeating that it was a mistake to go, a big mistake; but when she said the butter was not good enough, his laugh cracked joyously up into the treble. The train's arrival brought quick sadness to her face, but she made herself bright again with a special farewell for each acquaintance.

"Don't you ride any more cow-catchers," she warned Billy Lusk, "or I'll have to come back and look after you."

"You said you and me were going for a ride, and we ain't," shouted the long-memoried nine-year-old.

"You will," murmured Mr. McLean, oracularly.

As the train's pace quickened he did not step off, and Miss Buckner cried "Jump!"

"Too late," said he, placidly. Then he called to me, "I'm hard to beat, too!" So the train took them both away, as I might have guessed was his intention all along.

"Is that marriage again?" said Billy, anxiously. "He wouldn't tell me nothing."

"He's just seeing Miss Buckner as far as Edgeford," said the agent. "Be back to-morrow."

"Then I don't see why he wouldn't take me along," Billy complained. And Separ laughed.

But the lover was not back to-morrow. He was capable of anything, gossip remarked, and took up new themes. The sun rose and set, the two trains made their daily slight event and gathering; the water-tank, glaring bulkily in the sun, beaconed unmolested; and the agent's natural sleep was unbroken by pistols, for the cow-boys did not happen to be in town. Separ lay a clot of torpor that I was glad to leave behind me for a while. But news is a strange, permeating substance, and it began to be sifted through the air that Tubercle was going to God's country. That is how they phrased it in cow-camp, meaning not the next world, but the Eastern States.

"It's certainly a shame him leaving after we've got him so good and used to us," said the Virginian.

"We can't tell him good-bye," said Honey Wiggin. "Separ'll be slow."

"We can give his successor a right hearty welcome," the Virginian suggested.

"That's you!" said Honey. "Schemin' mischief away ahead. You're the leadin' devil in this country, and just because yu' wear a faithful-looking face you're tryin' to fool a poor school-marm."

"Yes," drawled the Southerner, "that's what I'm aiming to do."

So now they were curious about the successor, planning their hearty welcome for that official, and were encouraged in this by Mr. McLean. He reap-

peared in the neighborhood with a manner and conversation highly casual.

"Bring your new wife?" they inquired.

"No; she preferred Kentucky," Lin said.

"Bring the old one?"

"No; she preferred Laramie."

"Kentucky's a right smart way to chase after a
girl," said the Virginian.

"Sure!" said Mr. McLean. "I quit at Edgeford."

He met their few remarks so smoothly that they
got no joy from him; and being asked had he seen
the new agent, he answered yes, that Tubercle had
gone Wednesday, and his successor did not seem to
be much of a man.

But to me Lin had nothing to say until noon camp
was scattering from its lunch to work, when he
passed close, and whispered, "You'll see her to-
morrow if you go in with the outfit." Then, looking
round to make sure we were alone in the sage-brush,
he drew from his pocket, cherishingly, a little shining
pistol. "Hers," said he, simply.

I looked at him.

"We've exchanged," he said.

He turned the token in his hand, caressing it as on
that first night when Jessamine had taken his heart
captive.

"My idea," he added, unable to lift his eyes from
the treasure. "See this, too."

I looked, and there was the word "Neighbor" en-
graved on it.

"Her idea," said he.

"A good one!" I murmured.

"It's on both, yu' know. We had it put on the day
she settled to accept the superintendent's proposi-
tion." Here Lin fired his small exchanged weapon at a
cotton-wood, striking low. "She can beat that with
mine!" he exclaimed, proud and tender. "She took
four days deciding at Edgeford, and I learned her to

hit the ace of clubs." He showed me the cards they had practised upon during those four days of indecision; he had them in a book as if they were pressed flowers. "They won't get crumpled that way," said he; and he further showed me a tintype. "She's got the other at Separ," he finished.

I shook his hand with all my might. Yes, he was worthy of her! Yes, he deserved this smooth course his love was running! And I shook his hand again. To tonic her grief, Jessamine had longed for some activity, some work, and he had shown her Wyoming might hold this for her as well as Kentucky. "But how in the world," I asked him, "did you persuade her to stop over at Edgeford at all?"

"Yu' mustn't forget," said the lover (and he blushed), "that I had her four hours alone on the train."

But his face that evening round the fire, when they talked of their next day's welcome to the new agent, became comedy of the highest; and he was so desperately canny in the moments he chose for silence or for comment! He had not been sure of their ignorance until he arrived, and it was a joke with him too deep for laughter. He had a special eye upon the Virginian, his mate in such a tale of mischiefs, and now he led him on. He suggested to the Southerner that caution might be wise; this change at Separ was perhaps some new trick of the company's.

"We mostly take their tricks," observed the Virginian.

"Yes," said Lin, nodding sagely at the fire, "that's so, too."

Yet not he, not any one, could have foreseen the mortifying harmlessness of the outcome. They swept down upon Separ like all the hordes of legend—more egregiously, perhaps, because they were play-acting, and no serious horde would go on so. Our final hundred yards of speed and copious howling brought all

dwellers in Separ out to gaze and disappear like
rabbits—all save the new agent in the station. Nobody ran out or in there, and the horde whirled up to
the tiny, defenceless building and leaped to earth—
except Lin and me; we sat watching. The innocent
door stood open wide to any cool breeze or invasion,
and Honey Wiggin tramped in foremost, hat lowering
over eyes and pistol prominent. He stopped rooted,
staring, and his mouth came open slowly; his hand
went feeling up for his hat, and came down with it by
degrees as by degrees his grin spread. Then in a
milky voice, he said: "Why, excuse me, ma'am! Good-
morning."

There answered a clear, long, rippling, ample
laugh. It came out of the open door into the heat; it
made the sun-baked air merry; it seemed to welcome
and mock; it genially hovered about us in the dusty
quiet of Separ; for there was no other sound anywhere at all in the place, and the great plain
stretched away silent all round it. The bulging water-
tank shone overhead in bland, ironic safety.

The horde stood blank; then it shifted its legs,
looked sideways at itself, and in a hesitating clump
reached the door, shambled in, and removed its foolish hat.

"Good-morning, gentlemen," said Jessamine
Buckner, seated behind her railing; and various
voices endeavored to reply conventionally.

"If you have any letters, ma'am," said the Virginian,
more inventive, "I'll take them. Letters for Judge Henry's." He knew the judge's office was seventy miles
from here.

"Any for the C. Y.?" muttered another, likewise
knowing better.

It was a happy, if simple, thought, and most of
them inquired for the mail. Jessamine sought carefully, making them repeat their names, which some

did guiltily: they foresaw how soon the lady would find out no letters ever came for these names!

There was not letter for any one present.

"I'm sorry, truly," said Jessamine behind the railing. "For you seemed real anxious to get news. Better luck next time! And if I make mistakes, please everybody set me straight, for of course I don't understand things yet."

"Yes, m'm."

"Good-day, m'm."

"Thank yu', m'm."

They got themselves out of the station and into their saddles.

"No, she don't understand things yet," soliloquized the Virginian. "Oh dear, no." He turned his slow, dark eyes upon us. "You Lin McLean," said he, in his gentle voice, "you have cert'nly fooled me plumb through this mawnin'."

Then the horde rode out of town, chastened and orderly till it was quite small across the sage-brush, when reaction seized it. It sped suddenly and vanished in dust with far, hilarious cries; and here were Lin and I, and here towered the water-tank, shining and shining.

Thus did Separ's vigilante take possession and vindicate Lin's knowledge of his kind. It was not three days until the Virginian, that lynx observer, fixed his grave eyes upon McLean. " 'Neighbor' is as cute a name for a six-shooter as ever I heard," said he. "But she'll never have need of your gun in Separ—only to shoot up peaceful playin'-cyards while she hearkens to your courtin'."

That was his way of congratulation to a brother lover. "Plumb strange," he said to me one morning after an hour of riding in silence, "how a man will win two women while another man gets aged waitin' for one."

"Your hair seems black as ever," said I.

"My hopes ain't so glossy any more," he answered. "Lin has done better this second trip."

"Mrs. Lusk don't count," said I.

"I reckon she counted mighty plentiful when he thought he'd got her clamped to him by lawful marriage. But Lin's lucky." And the Virginian fell silent again.

Lucky Lin bestirred him over his work, his plans, his ranch on Box Elder that was one day to be a home for his lady. He came and went, seeing his idea triumph and his girl respected. Not only was she a girl, but a good shot too. And as if she and her small, neat home were a sort of possession, the cow-punchers would boast of her to strangers. They would have dealt heavily now with the wretch who should trifle with the water-tank. When camp came within visiting distance, you would see one or another shaving and parting his hair. They wrote unnecessary letters, and brought them to mail as excuses for an afternoon call. Honey Wiggin, more original, would look in the door with his grin, and hold up an ace of clubs. "I thought maybe yu' could spare a minute for a shootin'-match," he would insinuate; and Separ now heard no more objectionable shooting than this. Texas brought her presents of game—antelope, sage-chickens—but, shyness intervening, he left them outside the door, and entering, dressed in all the "Sunday" that he had, would sit dumbly in the lady's presence. I remember his emerging from one of these placid interviews straight into the hands of his tormentors.

"If she don't notice your clothes, Texas," said the Virginian, "just mention them to her."

"Now yer've done offended her," shrilled Manassas Donohoe. "She heard that."

"She'll hear you singin' sooprano," said Honey Wiggin. "It's good this country has reformed, or they'd have you warblin' in some dance-hall and corrupt your morals."

"You sca'cely can corrupt the morals of a soprano man," observed the Virginian. "Go and play with Billy till you can talk hass."

But it was the boldest adults that Billy chose for playmates. Texas he found immature. Moreover, when next he came, he desired play with no one. Summer was done. September's full moon was several nights ago; he had gone on his hunt with Lin, and now spelling-books were at hand. But more than this clouded his mind; he had been brought to say good-bye to Jessamine Buckner, who had scarcely seen him, and to give her a wolverene-skin, a hunting trophy. "She can have it," he told me. "I like her." Then he stole a look at his guardian. "If they get married and send me back to mother," said he, "I'll run away sure." So school and this old dread haunted the child, while for the man, Lin the lucky, who suspected nothing of it, time was ever bringing love nearer to his hearth. His Jessamine had visited Box Elder, and even said she wanted chickens there; since when Mr. McLean might occasionally have been seen at his cabin, worrying over barn-yard fowls, feeding and cursing them with equal care. Spring would see him married, he told me.

"This time right!" he exclaimed. "And I want her to know Billy some more before he goes to Bear Creek."

"Ah, Bear Creek!" said Billy, acidly. "Why can't I stay home?"

"Home sounds kind o' slick," said Lin to me. "Don't it, now? 'Home' is closer than 'neighbor,' you bet! Billy, put the horses in the corral, and ask Miss Buckner if we can come and see her after supper. If you're good, maybe she'll take yu' for a ride to-morrow. And, kid, ask her about Laramie."

Again suspicion quivered over Billy's face, and he dragged his horses angrily to the corral.

Lin nudged me, laughing. "I can rile him every time about Laramie," said he, affectionately. "I wouldn't have believed the kid set so much store by me. Nor I didn't need to ask Jessamine to love him for my sake. What do yu' suppose? Before I'd got far as thinking of Billy at all—right after Edgeford, when my head was just a whirl of joy—Jessamine says to me one day, 'Read that.' It was Governor Barker writin' to her about her brother and her sorrow." Lin paused. "And about me. I can't never tell you—but he said a heap I didn't deserve. And he told her about me picking up Billy in Denver streets that time, and doing for him because his own home was not a good one. Governor Barker wrote Jessamine all that; and she said, 'Why did you never tell me?' And I said it wasn't anything to tell. And she just said to me, 'It shall be as if he was your son and I was his mother.' And that's the first regular kiss she ever gave me I didn't have to take myself. God bless her! God bless her!"

As we ate our supper, young Billy burst out of brooding silence: "I didn't ask her about Laramie. So there!"

"Well, well, kid," said the cow-puncher, patting his head, "yu' needn't to, I guess."

But Billy's eye remained sullen and jealous. He paid slight attention to the picture-book of soldiers and war that Jessamine gave him when we went over to the station. She had her own books, some flowers in pots, a rocking-chair, and a cosey lamp that shone on her bright face and dark dress. We drew stools from the office desks, and Billy perched silently on one.

"Scanty room for company!" Jessamine said. "But we must make out this way—till we have another way." She smiled on Lin, and Billy's face darkened. "Do you know," she pursued to me, "with all those chickens Mr. McLean tells me about, never a one has he thought to bring here."

"Livin' or dead do you want 'em?" inquired Lin.

"Oh, I'll not bother you. Mr. Donohoe says he will—"

"Texas? Chickens? Him? Then he'll have to steal 'em!" And we all laughed together.

"You won't make me go back to Laramie, will you?" spoke Billy, suddenly, from his stool.

"I'd like to see anybody try to make you!" exclaimed Jessamine. "Who says any such thing?"

"Lin did," said Billy.

Jessamine looked at her lover reproachfully. "What a way to tease him!" she said. "And you so kind. Why, you've hurt his feelings!"

"I never thought," said Lin the boisterous. "I wouldn't have."

"Come sit here, Billy," said Jessamine. "Whenever he teases, you tell me, and we'll make him behave."

"Honest?" persisted Billy.

"Shake hands on it," said Jessamine.

" 'Cause I'll go to school. But I won't go back to Laramie for no one. And you're a-going to be Lin's wife, honest?"

"Honest! Honest!" And Jessamine, laughing, grew red beside her lamp.

"Then I guess mother can't never come back to Lin, either," stated Billy, relieved.

Jessamine let fall the child's hand.

" 'Cause she liked him onced, and he liked her."

Jessamine gazed at Lin.

"It's simple," said the cow-puncher. "It's all right."

But Jessamine sat by her lamp, very pale.

"It's all right," repeated Lin in the silence, shifting his foot and looking down. "Once I made a fool of myself. Worse than usual."

"Billy?" whispered Jessamine. "Then you—But his name is Lusk!"

"Course it is," said Billy. "Father and mother are living in Laramie."

"It's all straight," said the cow-puncher. "I never saw her till three years ago. I haven't anything to hide, only—only—only it don't come easy to tell."

I rose. "Miss Buckner," said I, "he will tell you. But he will not tell you he paid dearly for what was no fault of his. It has been no secret. It is only something his friends and his enemies have forgotten."

But all the while I was speaking this, Jessamine's eyes were fixed on Lin, and her face remained white.

I left the girl and the man and the little boy together, and crossed to the hotel. But its air was foul, and I got my roll of camp blankets to sleep in the clean night, if sleeping-time should come; meanwhile I walked about in the silence. To have taken a wife once in good faith, ignorant she was another's, left no stain, raised no barrier. I could have told Jessamine the same old story myself—or almost; but what had it to do with her at all? Why need she know? Reasoning thus, yet with something left uncleared by reason that I could not state, I watched the moon edge into sight, heavy and rich-hued, a melon-slice of glow, seemingly near, like a great lantern tilted over the plain. The smell of the sage-brush flavored the air; the hush of Wyoming folded distant and near things; and all Separ but those three inside the lighted window were in bed. Dark windows were everywhere else, and looming above rose the water-tank, a dull mass in the night, and forever somehow to me a Sphinx emblem, the vision I instantly see when I think of Separ. Soon I heard a door creaking. It was Billy, coming alone, and on seeing me he walked up and spoke in a half-awed voice.

"She's a-crying," said he.

I withheld from questions, and as he kept along by my side he said: "I'm sorry. Do you think she's mad

with Lin for what he's told her? She just sat, and
when she started crying he made me go away."

"I don't believe she's mad," I told Billy; and I sat
down on my blanket, he beside me, talking while the
moon grew small as it rose over the plain, and the
light steadily shone in Jessamine's window. Soon
young Billy fell asleep, and I looked at him, thinking
how in a way it was he who had brought this trouble
on the man who had saved him and loved him. But
that man had no such untender thoughts. Once more
the door opened, and it was he who came this time,
alone also. She did not follow him and stand to watch
him from the threshold, though he forgot to close the
door, and, coming over to me, stood looking down.

"What?" I said at length.

I don't know that he heard me. He stooped over
Billy and shook him gently. "Wake, son," said he.
"You and I must get to our camp now."

"Now?" said Billy. "Can't we wait till morning?"

"No, son. We can't wait here any more. Go and get
the horses and put the saddles on." As Billy obeyed,
Lin looked at the lighted window. "She is in there,"
he said. "She's in there. So near." He looked, and
turned to the hotel, from which he brought his chaps
and spurs and put them on. "I understand her
words," he continued. "Her words, the meaning of
them. But not what she means, I guess. It will take
studyin' over. Why, she don't blame me!" he suddenly
said, speaking to me instead of to himself.

"Lin," I answered, "she has only just heard this,
you see. Wait awhile."

"That's not the trouble. She knows what kind of
man I have been, and she forgives that just the way
she did her brother. And she knows how I didn't in-
tentionally conceal anything. Billy hasn't been
around, and she never realized about his mother and
me. We've talked awful open, but that was not pleasant to speak of, and the whole country knew it so

long—and I never thought! She don't blame me. She says she understands; but she says I have a wife livin'."

"That is nonsense," I declared.

"Yu' mustn't say that," said he. "She don't claim she's a wife, either. She just shakes her head when I asked her why she feels so. It must be different to you and me from the way it seems to her. I don't see her view; maybe I never can see it; but she's made me feel she has it, and that she's honest, and loves me true—" His voice broke for a moment. "She said she'd wait."

"You can't have a marriage broken that was never tied," I said. "But perhaps Governor Barker or Judge Henry—"

"No," said the cow-puncher. "Law couldn't fool her. She's thinking of something back of law. She said she'd wait—always. And when I took it in that this was all over and done, and when I thought of my ranch and the chickens—well, I couldn't think of things at all, and I came and walked Billy to clear out and quit."

"What did you tell her?" I asked.

"Tell her? Nothin', I guess. I don't remember getting out of the room. Why, here's actually her pistol, and she's got mine!"

"Man, man!" said I, "go back and tell her to keep it, and that you'll wait too—always!"

"Would yu'?"

"Look!" I pointed to Jessamine standing in the door.

I saw his face as he turned to her, and I walked toward Billy and the horses. Presently I heard steps on the wooden station, and from its black, brief shadow the two came walking, Lin and his sweetheart, into the moonlight. They were not speaking, but merely walked together in the clear radiance, hand in hand, like two children. I saw that she was weeping, and that beneath the tyranny of her resolution her whole loving, ample nature was wrung. But the strange, narrow fibre in her would not yield! I saw them go to the horses, and Jessamine stood while Billy and Lin mounted. Then quickly the cow-puncher sprang down again and folded her in his arms.

"Lin, dear Lin! dear neighbor!" she sobbed. She could not withhold this last good-bye.

I do not think he spoke. In a moment the horses started and were gone, flying, rushing away into the great plain, until sight and sound of them were lost, and only the sage-brush was there, bathed in the high, bright moon. The last thing I remember as I lay in my blankets was Jessamine's window still lighted, and the water-tank, clear-lined and black, standing over Separ.

CHAPTER VI

Destiny At Drybone

I

CHILDREN HAVE many special endowments, and of these
the chiefest is to ask questions that their elders must
skirmish to evade. Married people and aunts and un-
cles commonly discover this, but mere instinct does
not guide one to it. A maiden of twenty-three will not
necessarily divine it. Now except in one unhappy
hour of stress and surprise, Miss Jessamine Buckner
had been more than equal to life thus far. But never
yet had she been shut up a whole day in one room
with a boy of nine. Had this experience been hers,
perhaps she would not have written to Mr. McLean
the friendly and singular letter in which she hoped
he was well, and said that she was very well, and how
was dear little Billy? She was glad Mr. McLean
had stayed away. That was just like his honorable nature, and what she expected of him. And she was
perfectly happy at Separ, and "yours sincerely and always, 'Neighbor.'" Postscript. Talking of Billy
Lusk—if Lin was busy with gathering the cattle, why

not send Billy down to stop quietly with her. She would make him a bed in the ticket-office, and there she would be to see after him all the time. She knew Lin did not like his adopted child to be too much in cow-camp with the men. She would adopt him, too, for just as long as convenient to Lin—until the school opened on Bear Creek, if Lin so wished. Jessamine wrote a good deal about how much better care any woman can take of a boy of Billy's age than any man knows. The stage-coach brought the answer to this remarkably soon—young Billy with a trunk and a letter of twelve pages in pencil and ink—the only writing of this length ever done by Mr. McLean.

"I can write a lot quicker than Lin," said Billy, upon arriving. "He was fussing at that away late by the fire in camp, an' waked me up crawling in our bed. An' then he had to finish it next night when he went over to the cabin for my clothes."

"You don't say!" said Jessamine. And Billy suffered her to kiss him again.

When not otherwise occupied Jessamine took the letter out of its locked box and read it, or looked at it. Thus the first days had gone finely at Separ, the weather being beautiful and Billy much out-of-doors. But sometimes the weather changes in Wyoming; and now it was that Miss Jessamine learned the talents of childhood.

Soon after breakfast this stormy morning Billy observed the twelve pages being taken out of their box, and spoke from his sudden brain. "Honey Wiggin says Lin's losing his grip about girls," he remarked. "He says you couldn't 'a' downed him onced. You'd 'a' had to marry him. Honeys says Lin 'ain't worked it like he done in old times."

"Now I shouldn't wonder if he was right," said Jessamine, buoyantly. "And that being the case, I'm going to set to work at your things till it clears, and then we'll go for our ride."

"Yes," said Billy. "When does a man get too old to marry?"

"I'm only a girl, you see. I don't know."

"Yes. Honey said he wouldn't 'a' thought Lin was that old. But I guess he must be thirty."

"Old!" exclaimed Jessamine. And she looked at a photograph upon her table.

"But Lin 'ain't been married very much," pursued Billy. "Mother's the only one they speak of. You don't have to stay married always, do you?"

"It's better to," said Jessamine.

"Ah, I don't think so," said Billy, with disparagement. "You ought to see mother and father. I wish you would leave Lin marry you, though," said the boy, coming to her with an impulse of affection. "Why won't you if he don't mind?"

She continued to parry him, but this was not a very smooth start for eight in the morning. Moments of lull there were, when the telegraph called her to the front room, and Billy's young mind shifted to inquires about the cipher alphabet. And she gained at least an hour teaching him to read various words by the sound. At dinner, too, he was refreshingly silent. But such silences are unsafe, and the weather was still bad. Four o'clock found them much where they had been at eight.

"Please tell me why you won't leave Lin marry you." He was at the window, kicking the wall.

"That's nine times since dinner," she replied, with tireless good humor. "Now if you ask me twelve—"

"You'll tell?" said the boy, swiftly.

She broke into a laugh. "No. I'll go riding and you'll stay at home. When I was little and would ask things beyond me, they only gave me three times."

"I've got two more, anyway. Ha-ha!"

"Better save 'em up, though."

"What did they do to you? Ah, I don't want to go a-riding. It's nasty all over." He stared out at the day against which Separ's doors had been tight closed since morning. Eight hours of furious wind had raised the dust like a sea. "I wish the old train would come," observed Billy, continuing to kick the wall. "I wish I was going somewheres." Smoky, level, and hot, the south wind leapt into Separ across five hundred unbroken miles. The plain was blanketed in a tawny eclipse. Each minute the near buildings became invisible in a turbulent herd of clouds. Above this travelling blur of the soil the top of the water-tank alone rose bulging into the clear sun. The sand spirals would lick like flames along the bulk of the lofty tub, and soar skyward. It was not shipping season. The freight-cars stood idle in a long line. No cattle huddled in the corrals. No strangers moved in town. No cow-ponies dozed in front of the saloon. Their riders were distant in ranch and camp. Human noise was extinct in Separ. Beneath the thunder of the sultry blasts the place lay dead in its flapping shroud of dust. "Why won't you tell me?" droned Billy. For some time he had been returning, like a mosquito brushed away.

"That's ten times," said Jessamine, promptly.

"Oh, goodness! Pretty soon I'll not be glad I came. I'm about twiced as less glad now."

"Well," said Jessamine, "there's a man coming to-day to mend the government telegraph-line between Drybone and McKinney. Maybe he would take you back as far as Box Elder, if you want to go very much. Shall I ask him?"

Billy was disappointed at this cordial seconding of his mood. He did not make a direct rejoinder. "I guess I'll go outside now," said he, with a threat in his tone.

She continued mending his stockings. Finished ones lay rolled at one side of her chair, and upon the other were more waiting her attention.

"And I'm going to turn back hand-springs on top of *all* the freight-cars," he stated, more loudly.

She indulged again in merriment, laughing sweetly at him, and without restraint.

"And I'm sick of what you all keep a-saying to me!" he shouted. "Just as if I was a baby."

"Why, Billy, who ever said you were a baby?"

"All of you do. Honey, and Lin, and you, now, and everybody. What makes you say 'that's nine times, Billy; oh, Billy, that's ten times,' if you don't mean I'm a baby? And you laugh me off, just like they do, and just like I was a regular baby. You won't tell me—"

"Billy, listen. Did nobody ever ask you something you did not want to tell them?"

"That's not a bit the same, because—because—because I treat 'em square and because it's not their business. But every time I ask anybody 'most anything, they say I'm not old enough to understand; and I'll be ten soon. And it is my business when it's about the kind of a mother I'm a-going to have. Suppose I quit acting square, an' told 'em, when they bothered me, they weren't young enough to understand! Wish I had. Guess I will, too, and watch 'em step around." For a moment his mind dwelt upon this, and he whistled a revengeful strain.

"Goodness, Billy!" said Jessamine, at the sight of the next stocking. "The whole heel is scorched off."

He eyed the ruin with indifference. "Ah, that was last month when I and Lin shot the bear in the swamp willows. He made me dry off my legs. Chuck it away."

"And spoil the pair? No, indeed!"

"Mother always chucked 'em, an' father 'd buy new ones till I skipped from home. Lin kind o' mends 'em."

"Does he?" said Jessamine, softly. And she looked at the photograph.

"Yes. What made you write him for to let me come and bring my stockin's and things?"

"Don't you see, Billy, there is so little work at this station that I'd be looking out of the window all day just the pitiful way you do?"

"Oh!" Billy pondered. "And so I said to Lin," he continued, "why didn't he send down his own clothes, too, an' let you fix 'em all. And Honey Wiggin laughed right in his coffee-cup so it all sploshed out. And the cook he asked me if mother used to mend Lin's clothes. But I guess she chucked 'em like she always did father's and mine. I was with father, you know, when mother was married to Lin that time." He paused again, while his thoughts and fears struggled. "But Lin says I needn't ever go back," he went on, reasoning and confiding to her. "Lin don't like mother any more, I guess." His pondering grew still deeper, and he looked at Jessamine for some while. Then his face wakened with a new theory. "Don't Lin like you any more?" he inquired.

"Oh," cried Jessamine, crimsoning, "yes! Why, he sent you to me!"

"Well, he got hot in camp when I said that about sending his clothes to you. He quit supper pretty soon, and went away off a-walking. And that's another time they said I was too young. But Lin don't come to see you any more."

"Why, I hope he loves me," murmured Jessamine. "Always."

"Well, I hope so too," said Billy, earnestly. "For I like you. When I seen him show you our cabin on Box Elder, and the room he had fixed for you, I was glad you were coming to be my mother. Mother used to be awful. I wouldn't 'a' minded her licking me if she'd done other things. Ah, pshaw! I wasn't going to stand that." Billy now came close to Jessamine. "I do wish you would come and live with me and Lin," said he. "Lin's awful nice."

"Don't I know it?" said Jessamine, tenderly.

" 'Cause I heard you say you were going to marry him," went on Billy. "And I seen him kiss you and you let him that time we went away when you found out about mother. And you're not mad, and he's not, and nothing happens at all, all the same! Won't you tell me, please?"

Jessamine's eyes were glistening, and she took him in her lap. She was not going to tell him that he was too young this time. But whatever things she had shaped to say to the boy were never said.

Through the noise of the gale came the steadier sound of the train, and the girl rose quickly to preside over her ticket-office and duties behind the railing in the front room of the station. The boy ran to the window to watch the great event of Separ's day. The locomotive loomed out from the yellow clots of drift, paused at the water-tank, and then with steam and humming came slowly on by the platform. Slowly its long dust-choked train emerged trundling behind it, and ponderously halted. There was no one to go. No one came to buy a ticket of Jessamine. The conductor looked in on business, but she had no telegraphic orders for him. The express agent jumped off and looked in for pleasure. He received his daily smile and nod of friendly discouragement. Then the light bundle of mail was flung inside the door. Separ had no mail to go out. As she was picking up the letters young Billy passed her like a shadow, and fled out. Two passengers had descended from the train, a man and a large woman. His clothes were loose and careless upon him. He held valises, and stood uncertainly looking about him in the storm. Her firm, heavy body was closely dressed. In her hat was a large, handsome feather. Along between the several cars brakemen leaned out, watched her, and grinned to each other. But her big, hard-shining blue eyes were fixed curiously upon the station where Jessamine was.

"It's all night we may be here, is it?" she said to the man, harshly.

"How am I to help that?" he retorted.

"I'll help it. If this hotel's the sty it used to be, I'll walk to Tommy's. I've not saw him since I left Bear Creek."

She stalked into the hotel, while the man went slowly to the station. He entered, and found Jessamine behind her railing, sorting the slim mail.

"Good-evening," he said. "Excuse me. There was to be a wagon sent here."

"For the telegraph-mender? Yes, sir. It came Tuesday. You're to find the pole-wagon at Drybone."

This news was good, and all that he wished to know. He could drive out and escape a night at the Hotel Brunswick. But he lingered, because Jessamine spoke so pleasantly to him. He had heard of her also.

"Governor Barker has not been around here?" he said.

"Not yet, sir. We understand he is expected through on a hunting trip."

"I suppose there is room for two and a trunk on that wagon?"

"I reckon so, sir." Jessamine glanced at the man, and he took himself out. Most men took themselves out if Jessamine so willed; and it was mostly achieved thus, in amity.

On the platform the man found his wife again.

"Then I needn't to walk to Tommy's," she said. "And we'll eat as we travel. But you'll wait till I'm through with her." She made a gesture toward the station.

"Why—why—what do you want with her? Don't you know who she is?"

"It was me told you who she was, James Lusk. You'll wait till I've been and asked her after Lin

McLean's health, and till I've saw how the likes of her talks to the likes of me."

He made a feeble protest that this would do no one any good.

"Sew yourself up, James Lusk. If it has been your idea I come with yus clear from Laramie to watch yus plant telegraph-poles in the sage-brush, why you're off. I 'ain't heard much o' Lin since the day he learned it was you and not him that was my husband. And I've come back in this country to have a look at my old friends—and" (she laughed loudly and nodded at the station) "my old friends' new friends!"

Thus ordered, the husband wandered away to find his wagon and the horse.

Jessamine, in the office, had finished her station duties and returned to her needle. She sat contemplating the scorched sock of Billy's, and heard a heavy step at the threshold. She turned, and there was the large woman with the feather quietly surveying her. The words which the stranger spoke then were usual enough for a beginning. But there was something of threat in the strong animal countenance, something of laughter ready to break out. Much beauty of its kind had evidently been in the face, and now, as substitute for what was gone, was the brag look of assertion that it was still all there. Many stranded travellers knocked at Jessamine's door, and now, as always, she offered the hospitalities of her neat abode, the only room in Separ fit for a woman. As she spoke, and the guest surveyed and listened, the door blew shut with a crash.

Outside, in a shed, Billy had placed the wagon between himself and his father.

"How you have grown!" the man was saying; and he smiled. "Come, shake hands. I did not think to see you here."

"Dare you touch me!" Billy screamed. "No, I'll never come with you. Lin says I needn't to."

The man passed his hand across his forehead, and leaned against the wheel. "Lord, Lord!" he muttered.

His son warily slid out of the shed and left him leaning there.

II

Lin McLean, bachelor, sat out in front of his cabin, looking at a small bright pistol that lay in his hand. He held it tenderly, cherishing it, and did not cease slowly to polish it. Revery filled his eyes, and in his whole face was sadness unmasked, because only the animals were there to perceive his true feelings. Sunlight and waving shadows moved together upon the green of his pasture, cattle and horses loitered in the opens by the stream. Down Box Elder's course, its valley and golden-chimneyed bluffs widened away into the level and the blue of the greater valley. Upstream the branches and shining, quiet leaves entered the mountains where the rock chimneys narrowed to a gateway, a citadel of shafts and turrets, crimson and gold above the filmy emerald of the trees. Through there the road went up from the cotton-woods into the cool quaking asps and pines, and so across the range and away to Separ. Along the ridge-pole of the new stable, two hundred yards down-stream, sat McLean's turkeys, and cocks and hens walked in front of him here by his cabin and fenced garden. Slow smoke rose from the cabin's chimney into the air, in which were no sounds but the running water and the afternoon chirp of birds. Amid this framework of a home the cow-puncher sat, lonely, inattentive, polishing the treasured weapon as if it were not already long clean. His target stood some twenty steps in front of him—a small cottonwood-tree, its trunk chipped and honeycombed with bullets which he had fired into it each

day for memory's sake. Presently he lifted the pistol
and looked at its name—the word "Neighbor" en-
graved upon it.

"I wonder," said he, aloud, "if she keeps the rust
off mine?" Then he lifted it slowly to his lips and
kissed the word "Neighbor."

The clank of wheels sounded on the road, and he
put the pistol quickly down. Dreaminess vanished
from his face. He looked around alertly, but no one
had seen him. The clanking was still among the trees
a little distance up Box Elder. It approached deliber-
ately, while he watched for the vehicle to emerge
upon the open where his cabin stood; and then they
came, a man and a woman. At sight of her Mr.
McLean half rose, but sat down again. Neither of
them had noticed him, sitting as they were in silence
and the drow.

"It's business, I tell you. I've got to catch Governor
Barker before he—"

The pistol cracked, and a second chicken shuffled
in the dust. "Better stay to supper," drawled McLean.

The man looked up at his wife.

"So yus need me!" she broke out. "Ain't got heart
enough in yer played-out body to stand up to a man.
We'll eat here. Get down."

The husband stepped to the ground. "I didn't supposed you'd want—"

"Ho! want? What's Lin, or you, or anything to me?
Help me out."

Both men came forward. She descended, leaning
heavily upon each, her blue staring eyes fixed upon
the cow-puncher.

"No, yus 'ain't changed," she said. "Same in your
looks and same in your actions. Was you expecting
you could scare me, you, Lin McLean?"

"I just wanted chicken for supper," said he.

Mrs. Lusk gave a hard high laugh. "I'll eat 'em. It's
not I that cares. As for—" She stopped. Her eye had

fallen upon the pistol and the name "Neighbor." "As for you," she continued to Mr. Lusk, "don't you be standing dumb same as the horse."

"Better take him to the stable, Lusk," said McLean.

He picked the chickens up, showed the woman to the best chair in his room, and went into his kitchen to cook supper for three. He gave his guests no further attention, nor did either of them come in where he was, nor did the husband rejoin the wife. He walked slowly up and down in the air, and she sat by herself in the room. Lin's steps as he made ready round the stove and table, and Lusk's slow tread out in the setting sunlight, were the only sounds about the cabin. When the host looked into the door of the next room to announce this his meal was served, the woman sat in her chair no longer, but stood with her back to him by a shelf. She gave a slight start at his summons, and replaced something. He saw that she had been examining "Neighbor," and his face hardened suddenly to fierceness as he looked at her; but he repeated quietly that she had better come in. Thus did the three sit down to their meal. Occasionally a word about handing some dish fell from one or other of them, but nothing more, until Lusk took out his watch and mentioned the hour.

"Yu've not ate especially hearty," said Lin, resting his arms upon the table.

"I'm going," asserted Lusk. "Governor Barker may start out. I've got my interests to look after."

"Why, sure," said Lin. "I can't hope you'll waste all your time on just me."

Lusk rose and looked at his wife. "It'll be ten now before we get to Drybone," said he. And he went down to the stable.

The woman sat still, pressing the crumbs of her bread. "I know you seen me," she said, without looking at him.

"Saw you when?"

"I knowed it. And I seen how you looked at me."
She sat twisting and pressing the crumb. Sometimes
it was round, sometimes it was a cube, now and then
she flattened it to a disk. Mr. McLean seemed to have
nothing that he wished to reply.

"If you claim that pistol is yourn," she said next,
"I'll tell you I know better. If you ask me whose
should it be if not yourn, I would not have to guess
the name. She has talked to me, and me to her."

She was still looking away from him at the bread-
crumb, or she could have seen that McLean's hand
was trembling as he watched her, leaning on his
arms.

"Oh yes, she was willing to talk to me!" The woman
uttered another sudden laugh. "I knowed about
her—all. Things get heard of in this world. Did not all
about you and me come to her knowledge in its own
good time, and it done and gone how many years?
My, my, my!" Her voice grew slow and absent. She
stopped for a moment, and then more rapidly resumed: "It had travelled around about you and her
like it always will travel. It was known how you had
asked her, and how she had told you she would have
you, and then told you she would not when she
learned about you and me. Folks that knowed yus
and folks that never seen yus in their lives had to
have their word about her facing you down you had
another wife, though she knowed the truth about me
being married to Lusk and him livin' the day you
married me, and ten and twenty marriages could not
have tied you and me up, no matter how honest you
swore to no hinderance. Folks said it was plain she
did not want yus. It give me a queer feelin' to see
that girl. It give me a wish to tell her to her face that
she did not love yus and did not know love. Wait—
wait, Lin! Yu' never hit me yet."

"No," said the cow-puncher. "Nor now. I'm not
Lusk."

"Yu' looked so—so bad, Lin. I never seen yu' look so bad in old days. Wait, now, and I must tell it. I wished to laugh in her face and say, 'What do you know about love?' So I walked in. Lin, she does love yus!"

"Yes," breathed McLean.

"She was sittin' back in her room at Separ. Not the ticket-office, but—"

"I know," the cow-puncher said. His eyes were burning.

"It's snug, the way she has it. 'Good-afternoon,' I says. 'Is this Miss Jessamine Buckner?'"

At his sweetheart's name the glow in Lin's eyes seemed to quiver to a flash.

"And she spoke pleasant to me—pleasant and gay-like. But a woman can tell sorrow in a woman's eyes. And she asked me would I rest in her room there, and what was my name. 'They tell me you claim to know it better than I do,' I says. 'They tell me you say it is Mrs. McLean.' She put her hand to her breast, and she keeps lookin' at me without never speaking. 'Maybe I am not so welcome now,' I says. 'One minute,' says she. 'Let me get used to it.' And she sat down.

"Lin, she is a square-lookin' girl. I'll say that for her.

"I never thought to sit down onced myself. I don't know why, but I kep' a-standing, and I took in that room of hers. She had flowers and things around there, and I seen your picture standing on the table, and I seen your six-shooter right by it—and, oh, Lin, hadn't I knowed your face before ever she did, and that gun you used to let me shoot on Bear Creek? It took me that sudden! Why, it rushed over me so I spoke right out different from when I'd meant and what I had ready fixed up to say.

"'Why did you do it?' I says to her, while she was a-sitting. 'How could you act so, and you a woman?'

She just sat, and her sad eyes made me madder at the idea of her. 'You have had real sorrow,' says I, 'if they report correct. You have knowed your share of death, and misery, and hard work, and all. Great God! ain't there things enough that come to yus uncalled for and natural, but you must run around huntin' up more that was leavin' yus alone and givin' yus a chance? I knowed him once. I knowed your Lin McLean. And when that was over, I knowed for the first time how men can be different.' I'm started, Lin, I'm started. Leave me go on, and when I'm through I'll quit. 'Some of 'em, anyway,' I says to her, 'has hearts and self-respect, and ain't hogs clean through.'

" 'I know,' she says, thoughtful-like.

"And at her whispering that way I gets madder.

" 'You know!' I says then. 'What is it that you know? Do you know that you have hurt a good man's heart? For onced I hurt it myself, though different. And hurts in them kind of hearts stays. Some hearts is that luscious and pasty you can stab 'em and it closes up so yu'd never suspicion the place—but Lin McLean! Nor yet don't yus believe his is the kind that breaks—if any kind does that. You may sit till the gray hairs, and you may wall up your womanhood, but if a man has got manhood like him, he will never sit till the gray hairs. Grief over losin' the best will not stop him from searchin' for a second best after a while. He wants a home, and he has got a right to one,' says I to Miss Jessamine. 'You have not walled up Lin McLean,' I says to her. Wait, Lin, wait. Yus needn't to tell me that's a lie. I know a man thinks he's walled up for a while."

"She could have told you it was a lie," said the cow-puncher.

"She did not. 'Let him get a home,' says she. 'I want him to be happy.' 'That flash in your eyes talks different,' says I. 'Sure enough yus wants him to be happy. Sure enough. But not happy along with Miss Second Best.'

"Lin, she looked at me that piercin'!

"And I goes on, for I was wound away up. 'And he will be happy, too,' I says. 'Miss Second-Best will have a talk with him about your picture and little "Neighbor," which he'll not send back to yus, because the hurt in his heart is there. And he will keep 'em out of sight somewheres after his talk with Miss Second Best.' Lin, Lin, I laughed at them words of mine, but I was that wound up I was strange to myself. And she watchin' me that way! And I says to her: 'Miss Second Best will not be the crazy thing to think I am any wife of his standing in her way. He will tell her about me. He will tell how onced he thought he was solid married to me till Lusk came back; and she will drop me out of sight along with the rest that went nameless. They was not oncomprehensible to you, was they? You have learned something by livin', I guess! And Lin—your Lin, not mine, nor never mine in heart for a day so deep as he's yourn right now—he has been gay—gay as any I've knowed. Why, look at that face of his! Could a boy with a face like that help bein' gay? But that don't touch what's the true Lin deep down. Nor will his deep-down love for you hinder him like it will hinder you. Don't you know men and us is different when it comes to passion? We're all one thing then, but they ain't simple. They keep along with lots of other things. I can't make yus know, and I guess it takes a woman like I have been to learn their nature. But you did know he loved you, and you sent him away, and you'll be homeless in yer house when he has done the right thing by himself and found another girl.'

"Lin, all the while I was talkin' all I knowed to her, without knowin' what I'd be sayin' next, for it come that unexpected, she was lookin' at me with them steady eyes. And all she says when I quit was, 'If I saw him I would tell him to find a home.' "

"Didn't she tell yu' she'd made me promise to keep away from seeing her?" asked the cow-puncher.

Mrs. Lusk laughed. "Oh, you innocent!" said she.

"She said if I came she would leave Separ," muttered McLean, brooding.

Again the large woman laughed out, but more harshly.

"I have kept my promise," Lin continued.

"Keep it some more. Sit here rotting in your chair till she goes away. Maybe she's gone."

"What's that?" said Lin. But still she only laughed harshly. "I could be there by to-morrow night," he murmured. Then his face softened. "She would never do such a thing!" he said, to himself.

He had forgotten the woman at the table. While she had told him matters that concerned him he had listened eagerly. Now she was of no more interest than she had been before her story was begun. She looked at his eyes as he sat thinking and dwelling upon his sweetheart. She looked at him, and a longing welled up into her face. A certain youth and heavy beauty relighted the features.

"You are the same, same Lin everyways," she said. "A woman is too many for you still, Lin!" she whispered.

At her summons he looked up from his revery.

"Lin, I would not have treated you so."

The caress that filled her voice was plain. His look met hers as he sat quite still, his arms on the table. Then he took his turn at laughing.

"You!" he said. "At least I've had plenty of education in you."

"Lin, Lin, don't talk that brutal to me to-day. If yus knowed how near I come shooting myself with 'Neighbor.' That would have been funny! I knowed yus wanted to tear that pistol out of my hand be-

cause it was hern. But yus never did such things to
me, fer there's a gentleman in you somewheres, Lin.
And yus didn't never hit me, not even when you
come to know me well. And when I seen you so unexpected again to-night, and you just the same old Lin,
scaring Lusk with shooting them chickens, so comic
and splendid, I could 'a' just killed Lusk sittin' in the
wagon. Say, Lin, what made yus do that, anyway?"

"I can't hardly say," said the cow-puncher. "Only
noticing him so turrible anxious to quit me—well, a
man acts without thinking."

"You always did, Lin. You was always a comical ge-
nius. Lin, them were good times."

"Which times?"

"You know. You can't tell me you have forgot."

"I have not forgot much. What's the sense in this?"

"Yus never loved me!" she exclaimed.

"Shucks!"

"Lin, Lin, is it all over? You know yus loved me on
Bear Creek. Say you did. Only say it was once that
way." And as he sat, she came and put her arms
round his neck. For a moment he did not move, letting himself be held; and then she kissed him. The
plates crashed as he beat and struck her down upon
the table. He was on his feet, cursing himself. As he
went out of the door, she lay where she had fallen beneath his fist, looking after him and smiling.

McLean walked down Box Elder Creek through the
trees toward the stable, where Lusk had gone to put
the horse in the wagon. Once he leaned his hand
against a cotton-wood, and stood still with half-
closed eyes. Then he continued on his way. "Lusk!"
he called, presently, and in a few steps more, "Lusk!"
Then, as he came slowly out of the trees to meet the
husband he began, with quiet evenness, "Your wife
wants to know—" But he stopped. No husband was
there. Wagon and horse were not there. The door
was shut. The bewildered cow-puncher looked up the

stream where the road went, and he looked down. Out of the sky where daylight and stars were faintly shining together sounded the long cries of the night hawks as they sped and swooped to their hunting in the dusk. From among the trees by the stream floated a cooler air, and distant and close by sounded the plashing water. About the meadow where Lin stood his horses fed, quietly crunching. He went to the door, looked in, and shut it again. He walked to his shed and stood contemplating his own wagon alone there. Then he lifted away a piece of trailing vine from the gate of the corral, while the turkeys moved their heads and watched him from the roof. A rope was hanging from the corral, and seeing it, he dropped the vine. He opened the corral gate, and walked quickly back into the middle of the field, where the horses saw him and his rope, and scattered. But he ran and herded them, whirling the rope, and so drove them into the corral, and flung his noose over two. He dragged two saddles—men's saddles—from the stable, and next he was again at his cabin door with the horses saddled. She was sitting quite still by the table where she had sat during the meal, nor did she speak or move when she saw him look in at the door.

"Lusk has gone," said he. "I don't know what he expected you would do, or I would do. But we will catch him before he gets to Drybone."

She looked at him with her dumb stare. "Gone?" she said.

"Get up and ride," said McLean. "You are going to Drybone."

"Drybone?" she echoed. Her voice was toneless and dull.

He made no more explanations to her, but went quickly about the cabin. Soon he had set it in order, the dishes on their shelves, the table clean, the fire in the stove arranged; and all these movements she

followed with a sort of blank mechanical patience. He
made a small bundle for his own journey, tied it behind his saddle, brought her horse beside a stump.
When at his sharp order she came out, he locked his
cabin and hung the key by a window, where travellers could find it and be at home.

She stood looking where her husband had slunk
off. Then she laughed. "It's about his size," she murmured.

Her old lover helped her in silence to mount into
the man's saddle—this they had often done together
in former years—and so they took their way down
the silent road. They had not many miles to go, and
after the first two lay behind them, when the horses
were limbered and had been put to a canter, they
made time quickly. They had soon passed out of the
trees and pastures of Box Elder and came among the
vast low stretches of the greater valley. Not even by
day was the river's course often discernible through
the ridges and cheating sameness of this wilderness;
and beneath this half-darkness of stars and a quarter
moon the sage spread shapeless to the looming
mountains, or to nothing.

"I will ask you one thing," said Lin, after ten miles.

The woman made no sign of attention as she rode
beside him.

"Did I understand that she—Miss Buckner, I
mean—mentioned she might be going away from
Separ?"

"How do I know what you understood?"

"I thought you said—"

"Don't you bother me, Lin McLean." Her laugh rang
out, loud and forlorn—one brief burst that startled
the horses and that must have sounded far across
the sage-brush. "You men are rich," she said.

They rode on, side by side, and saying nothing after that. The Drybone road was a broad trail, a worn
strip of bareness going onward over the endless

shelvings of the plain, visible even in this light; and presently, moving upon its grayness on a hill in front of them, they made out the wagon. They hastened and overtook it.

"Put your carbine down," said McLean to Lusk. "It's not robbers. It's your wife I'm bringing you." He spoke very quietly.

The husband addressed no word to the cow-puncher. "Get in, then," he said to his wife.

"Town's not far now," said Lin. "Maybe you would prefer riding the balance of the way?"

"I'd—" But the note of pity that she felt in McLean's question overcame her, and her utterance choked. She nodded her head, and the three continued slowly climbing the hill together.

From the narrows of the steep, sandy, weather-beaten banks that the road slanted upward through for a while, they came out again upon the immensity of the table-land. Here, abruptly, like an ambush, was the whole unsuspected river close below to their right, as if it had emerged from the earth. With a circling sweep from somewhere out in the gloom it cut in close to the lofty mesa beneath tall clean-graded descents of sand, smooth as a railroad embankment. As they paused on the level to breathe their horses, the wet gulp of its eddies rose to them through the stillness. Upstream they could make out the light of the Drybone bridge, but not the bridge itself; and two lights on the farther bank showed where stood the hog-ranch opposite Drybone. They went on over the table-land and reached the next herald of the town, Drybone's chief historian, the graveyard. Beneath its slanting headboards and wind-shifted sand lay many more people than lived in Drybone. They passed by the fence of this shelterless acre on the hill, and shoutings and high music began to reach them. At the foot of the hill they saw the sparse lights and shapes of the town where ended the gray

strip of road. The many sounds—feet, voices, and
music—grew clearer, unravelling from their muffled
confusion, and the fiddling became a tune that could
be known.

"There's a dance to-night," said the wife to the husband. "Hurry."

He drove as he had been driving. Perhaps he had
not heard her.

"I'm telling you to hurry," she repeated. "My new
dress is in that wagon. There'll be folks to welcome
me here that's older friends than you."

She put her horse to a gallop down the broad road
toward the music and the older friends. The husband
spoke to his horse, cleared his throat and spoke
louder, cleared his throat again and this time his sullen voice carried, and the animal started. So Lusk
went ahead of Lin McLean, following his wife with the
new dress at as good a pace as he might. If he did
not want her company, perhaps to be alone with the
cow-puncher was still less to his mind.

"It ain't only her he's stopped caring for," mused
Lin, as he rode slowly along. "He don't care for himself any more."

III

To-day, Drybone has altogether returned to the
dust. Even in that day its hour could have been
heard beginning to sound, but its inhabitants were
rather deaf. Gamblers, saloon-keepers, murderers,
outlaws male and female, all were so busy with their
cards, their lovers, and their bottles as to make the
place seem young and vigorous; but it was second
childhood which had set in.

Drybone had known a wholesome adventurous
youth, where manly lives and deaths were plenty. It
had been an army post. It had seen horse and foot,

and heard the trumpet. Brave wives had kept house for their captains upon its bluffs. Winter and summer they had made the best of it. When the War Department ordered the captains to catch Indians, the wives bade them God-speed. When the Interior Department ordered the captains to let the Indians go again, still they made the best of it. You must not waste Indians. Indians were a source of revenue to so many people in Washington and elsewhere. But the process of catching Indians, armed with weapons sold them by friends of the Interior Department, was not entirely harmless. Therefore there came to be graves in the Drybone graveyard. The pale weather-washed head-boards told all about it: "Sacred to the memory of Private So-and-So, killed on the Dry Cheyenne, May 6, 1875." Or it would be, "Mrs. So-and-So, found scalped on Sage Creek." But even the financiers at Washington could not wholly preserve the Indian in Drybone's neighborhood. As the cattle by ten thousands came treading with the next step of civilization into this huge domain, the soldiers were taken away. Some of them went West to fight more Indians in Idaho, Oregon, or Arizona. The battles of the others being done, they went East in better coffins to sleep where their mothers or their comrades wanted them. Though wind and rain wrought changes upon the hill, the ready-made graves and boxes which these soldiers left behind proved heirlooms as serviceable in their way as were the tenements that the living had bequeathed to Drybone. Into these empty barracks came to dwell and do business every joy that made the cow-puncher's holiday, and every hunted person who was baffling the sheriff. For the sheriff must stop outside the line of Drybone, as shall presently be made clear. The captain's quarters were a saloon now; professional cards were going in the adjutant's office night and day; and the commissary building made a good dance-hall and hotel. Instead of guard-mounting, you would see a horse-race on the parade-ground, and there was no provost-sergeant to gather up the broken bottles and old boots. Heaps of these choked the rusty fountain. In the tufts of yellow, ragged grass that dotted the place plentifully were lodged many aces and queens and ten-spots, which the Drybone wind had blown wide from the doors out of which they had been thrown when a new pack was called for inside. Among the grass tufts would lie visitors who had applied for beds too late at the dance-hall, frankly sleeping their whiskey off in the morning air.

Above, on the hill, the graveyard quietly chronicled this new epoch of Drybone. So-and-so was seldom killed very far out of town, and of course scalping had disappeared. "Sacred to the memory of Four-ace Johnston, accidently shot, Sep. 4, 1885." Perhaps one is still there unaltered. "Sacred to the memory of Mrs. Ryan's babe. Aged two months." This unique corpse had succeeded in dying with its boots off.

But a succession of graves was not always needed to read the changing tale of the place, and how people died there; one grave would often be enough. The soldiers, of course, had kept treeless Drybone supplied with wood. But in these latter days wood was very scarce. None grew nearer than twenty or thirty miles—none, that is, to make boards of a sufficient width for epitaphs. And twenty miles was naturally far to go to hew a board for a man of whom you knew perhaps nothing but what he said his name was, and to whom you owed nothing, perhaps, but a trifling poker debt. Hence it came to pass that headboards grew into a sort of directory. They were light to lift from one place to another. A single coat of white paint would wipe out the first tenant's name sufficiently to paint over it the next comer's. By this thrifty habit the original boards belonging to the sol-

diers could go round, keeping pace with the new civilian population; and though at first sight you might
be puzzled by the layers of names still visible beneath the white paint, you could be sure that the
clearest and blackest was the one to which the present tenant had answered.

So there on the hill lay the graveyard, steadily writing Drybone's history, and making that history lay
the town at the bottom—one thin line of houses
framing three sides of the old parade-ground. In
these slowly rotting shells people rioted, believing
the golden age was here, the age when everybody
should have money and nobody should be arrested.
For Drybone soil, you see, was still government soil,
not yet handed over to Wyoming; and only government could arrest there, and only for government
crimes. But government had gone, and seldom wor-
ried Drybone! The spot was a postage-stamp of sanc-
tuary pasted in the middle of Wyoming's big map, a
paradise for the Four-ace Johnstons. Only, you must
not steal a horse. That was really wicked, and
brought you instantly to the notice of Drybone's one
official—the coroner! For they did keep a coroner—
Judge Slaghammer. He was perfectly illegal, and lived
next door in Albany County. But that county paid
fees and mileage to keep tally of Drybone's casual-
ties. His wife owned the dance-hall, and between
their industries they made out a living. And all the
citizens made out a living. The happy cow-punchers
on ranches far and near still earned and instantly
spent the high wages still paid them. With their bod-
ies full of youth and their pockets full of gold, they
rode into town by twenties, by fifties, and out again
next morning, penniless always and happy. And then
the Four-ace Johnstons would sit card-playing with
each other till the innocents should come to town
again.

To-night the innocents had certainly come to town,

and Drybone was furnishing to them all its joys. Their many horses stood tied at every post and corner—patient, experienced cow-ponies, well knowing it was an all-night affair. The talk and laughter of the riders was in the saloons; they leaned joking over the bars, they sat behind their cards at the tables, they strolled to the post-trader's to buy presents for their easy sweethearts, their boots were keeping audible time with the fiddle at Mrs. Slaghammer's. From the multitude and vigor of the sounds there, the dance was being done regularly. "Regularly" meant that upon the conclusion of each set the gentleman led his lady to the bar and invited her to choose; and it was also regular that the lady should choose. Beer and whiskey were the alternatives.

Lin McLean's horse took him across the square without guiding from the cow-puncher, who sat absently with his hands folded upon the horn of his saddle. This horse, too, was patient and experienced, and could not know what remote thoughts filled his master's mind. He looked around to see why his master did not get off lightly, as he had done during so many gallant years, and hasten in to the conviviality. But the lonely cow-puncher sat mechanically identifying the horses of acquaintances.

"Toothpick Kid is here," said he, "and Limber Jack, and the Doughie. You'd think he'd stay away after the trouble he—I expect that pinto is Jerky Bill's."

"Go home!" said a hearty voice.

McLean eagerly turned. For the moment his face lighted from its sombreness. "I'd forgot you'd be here," said he. And he sprang to the ground. "It's fine to see you."

"Go home!" repeated the Governor of Wyoming, shaking his ancient friend's hand. "You in Drybone to-night, and claim you're reformed? Fie!"

"Yu' seem to be on hand yourself," said the cow-puncher, bracing to be jocular, if he could.

"Me! I've gone fishing. Don't you read the papers? If we poor governors can't lock up the State House and take a whirl now and then—"

"Doc," interrupted Lin, "it's plumb fine to see yu'!" Again he shook hands.

"Why, yes! we've met here before, you and I." His Excellency the Hon. Amory W. Barker, M.D., stood laughing, familiar and genial, his sound white teeth shining. But behind his round spectacles he scrutinized McLean. For in this second hand-shaking was a fervor that seemed a grasp, a reaching out, for comfort. Barker had passed through Separ. Though an older acquaintance than Billy, he had asked Jessamine fewer and different questions. But he knew what he knew. "Well, Drybone's the same old Drybone," said he. "Sweet-scented hole of iniquity! Let's see how you walk nowadays."

Lin took a few steps.

"Pooh! I said you'd never get over it." And his Excellency beamed with professional pride. In his doctor days Barker had set the boy McLean's leg; and before it was properly knit the boy had escaped from the hospital to revel loose in Drybone on such another night as this. Soon he had been carried back, with the fracture split open again.

"It shows, does it?" said Lin. "Well, it don't usually. Not except when I'm—when I'm—"

"Down?" suggested his Excellency.

"Yes, Doc. Down," the cow-puncher confessed.

Barker looked into his friend's clear hazel eyes. Beneath their dauntless sparkle was something that touched the Governor's good heart. "I've got some whiskey along on the trip—Eastern whiskey," said he. "Come over to my room awhile."

"I used to sleep all night onced," said McLean, as they went. "Then I come to know different. But I'd never have believed just mere thoughts could make yu'—make yu' feel like the steam was only half on. I eat, yu' know!" he stated, suddenly. "And I expect one or two in camp lately have not found my muscle lacking. Feel me, Doc."

Barker dutifully obeyed, and praised the excellent sinews.

Across from the dance-hall the whining of the fiddle came, high and gay; feet blurred the talk of voices, and voices rose above the trampling of feet. Here and there some lurking form stumbled through the dark among the rubbish; and clearest sound of all, the light crack of billiard-balls reached dry and far into the night. Barker contemplated the stars and calm splendid dimness of the plain. " 'Though every prospect pleases, and only man is vile,' " he quoted. "But don't tell the Republican party I said so."

"It's awful true, though, Doc. I'm vile myself. Yu' don't know. Why, *I* didn't know!"

And then they sat down to confidences and whiskey; for so long as the world goes round a man must talk to a man sometimes, and both must drink over it. The cow-puncher unburdened himself to the Governor; and the Governor filled up his friend's glass with the Eastern whiskey, and nodded his spectacles, and listened, and advised, and said he should have done the same, and like the good Governor that he was, never remembered he was Governor at all with political friends here who had begged a word or two. He became just Dr. Barker again, the young hospital surgeon (the hospital that now stood a ruin), and Lin was again his patient—Lin, the sun-burnt free-lance of nineteen, reckless, engaging, disobedient, his leg broken and his heart light, with no Jessamine or conscience to rob his salt of its savor. While he now told his troubles, the quadrilles fiddled away careless as ever, and the crack of the billiard-balls sounded as of old.

"Nobody has told you about this, I expect," said the lover. He brought forth the little pistol, "Neighbor." He did not hand it across to Barker, but walked over to Barker's chair, and stood holding it for the doctor to see. When Barker reached for it to see better, since it was half hidden in the cow-puncher's big hand, Lin yielded it to him, but still stood and soon drew it back. "I take it around," he said, "and when one of those stories comes along, like there's plenty of, that she wants to get rid of me, I just kind o' take a look at 'Neighbor' when I'm off where it's handy, and it busts the story right out of my mind. I have to tell you what a fool I am."

"The whiskey's your side," said Barker. "Go on."

"But, Doc, my courage has quit me. They see what I'm thinking about just like I was a tenderfoot trying his first bluff. I can't stick it out no more, and I'm going to see her, come what will. I've got to. I'm going to ride right up to her window and shoot off 'Neighbor,' and if she don't come out I'll know—"

A knocking came at the Governor's room, and Judge Slaghammer entered. "Not been to our dance, Governor?" said he.

The Governor thought that perhaps he was tired, that perhaps this evening he must forego the pleasure.

"It may be wiser. In your position it may be advisable," said the coroner. "They're getting on rollers over there. We do not like trouble in Drybone, but trouble comes to us—as everywhere."

"Shooting," suggested his Excellency, recalling his hospital practice.

"Well, Governor, you know how it is. Our boys are as big-hearted as any in this big-hearted Western country. You know, Governor. Those generous, warm-blooded spirits are ever ready for anything."

"Especially after Mrs. Slaghammer's whiskey," remarked the Governor.

The coroner shot a shrewd eye at Wyoming's chief executive. It was not politically harmonious to be reminded that but for his wife's liquor a number of fine young men, with nothing save youth untrained and health the matter with them, would to-day be riding their horses instead of sleeping on the hill. But the coroner wanted support in the next campaign. "Boys will be boys," said he. "They ain't pulled any guns to-night. But I come away, though. Some of 'em's making up pretty free to Mrs. Lusk. It ain't suitable for me to see too much. Lusk says he's after you," he mentioned incidentally to Lin. "He's fillin' up, and says he's after you." McLean nodded placidly, and with scant politeness. He wished this visitor would go. But Judge Slaghammer had noticed the whiskey. He filled himself a glass. "Governor, it has my compliments," said he. "Ambrosier. Honey-doo."

"Mrs. Slaghammer seems to have a large gathering," said Barker.

"Good boys, good boys!" The judge blew importantly, and waved his arm. "Bull-whackers, cowpunchers, mule-skinners, tin-horns. All spending generous. Governor, once more! Ambrosier. Honey-doo." He settled himself deep in a chair, and closed his eyes.

McLean rose abruptly. "Good-night," said he, "I'm going to Separ."

"Separ!" exclaimed Slaghammer, rousing slightly. "Oh, stay with us, stay with us." He closed his eyes again, but sustained his smile of office.

"You know how well I wish you," said Barker to Lin. "I'll just see you start."

Forthwith the friends left the coroner quiet beside his glass, and walked toward the horses through Drybone's gaping quadrangle. The dead ruins loomed among the lights of the card-halls, and always the keen jockey cadences of the fiddle sang across the night. But a calling and confusion were set up, and the tune broke off.

"Just like old times!" said his Excellency. "Where's the dump-pile!" It was where it should be, close by, and the two stepped behind it to be screened from wandering bullets. "A man don't forget his habits," declared the Governor. "Makes me feel young again."

"Makes me feel old," said McLean. "Hark!"

"Sounds like my name," said Barker. They listened. "Oh yes. Of course. That's it. They're shouting for the doctor. But we'll just spare them a minute or so to finish their excitement."

"I didn't hear any shooting," said McLean. "It's something, though."

As they waited, no shots came; but still the fiddle was silent, and the murmur of many voices grew in the dance-hall, while single voices wandered outside, calling the doctor's name.

"I'm the Governor on a fishing-trip," said he. "But it's to be done, I suppose."

They left their dump-hill and proceeded over to the dance. The musician sat high and solitary upon two starch-boxes, fiddle on knee, staring and waiting. Half the floor was bare; on the other half the revellers were densely clotted. At the crowd's outer rim the young horsemen, flushed and swaying, retained their gaudy dance partners strongly by the waist, to be ready when the music should resume. "What is it?" they asked. "Who is it?" And they looked in across heads and shoulders, inattentive to the caresses which the partners gave them.

Mrs. Lusk was who it was, and she had taken poison here in their midst, after many dances and drinks.

"Here's Doc!" cried an older one.

"Here's Doc!" chorused the young blood that had come into this country since his day. And the throng caught up the words: "Here's Doc! here's Doc!"

In a moment McLean and Barker were sundered from each other in this flood. Barker, sucked in toward the centre but often eddied back by those who meant to help him, heard the mixed explanations pass his ear unfinished—versions, contradictions, a score of facts. It had been wolf-poison. It had been "Rough on Rats." It had been something in a bottle. There was little steering in this clamorous sea; but Barker reached his patient, where she sat in her new dress, hailing him with wild inebriate gayety.

"I must get her to her room, friends," said he.

"He must get her to her room," went the word. "Leave Doc get her to her room." And they tangled in their eagerness around him and his patient.

"Give us 'Buffalo Girls!'" shouted Mrs. Lusk. . . . "'Buffalo Girls,' you fiddler!"

"We'll come back," said Barker to her.

"'Buffalo Girls,' I tell yus. Ho! There's no sense looking at that bottle, Doc. Take yer dance while there's time!" She was holding the chair.

"Help him!" said the crowd. "Help Doc."

They took her from her chair, and she fought, a big pink mass of ribbons, fluttering and wrenching itself among them.

"She has six ounces of laudanum in her," Barker told them at the top of his voice. "It won't wait all night."

"I'm a whirlwind!" said Mrs. Lusk. "That's my game! And you done your share," she cried to the fiddler. "Here's my regards, old man! 'Buffalo Girls' once more!"

She flung out her hand, and from it fell notes and coins, rolling and ringing around the starch-boxes. Some dragged her on, while some fiercely forbade the musician to touch the money, because it was hers, and she would want it when she came to. Thus they gathered it up for her. But now she had sunk down, asking in a new voice where was Lin McLean.

And when one grinning intimate reminded her that Lusk had gone to shoot him, she laughed out richly, and the crowd joined her mirth. But even in the midst of the joke she asked again in the same voice where was Lin McLean. He came beside her among more jokes. He had kept himself near, and now at sight of him she reached out and held him. "Tell them to leave me go to sleep, Lin," said she.

Barker saw a chance. "Persuade her to come along," said he to McLean. "Minutes are counting now."

"Oh, I'll come," she said, with a laugh, overhearing him, and holding still to Lin.

The rest of the old friends nudged each other. "Back seats for us," they said. "But we've had our turn in front ones." Then, thinking they would be useful in encouraging her to walk, they clustered again, rendering Barker and McLean once more wellnigh helpless. Clumsily the escort made its slow way across the quadrangle, cautioning itself about stones and holes. Thus, presently, she was brought into the room. The escort set her down, crowding the little place as thick as it would hold; the rest gathered thick at the door, and all of them had no thought of departing. The notion to stay was plain on their faces.

Barker surveyed them. "Give the doctor a show now, boys," said he. "You've done it all so far. Don't crowd my elbows. I'll want you," he whispered to McLean.

At the argument of fair-play, obedience swept over them like a veering of wind. "Don't crowd his elbows," they began to say at once, and told each other to come away. "We'll sure give the Doc room. You don't want to be shovin' your auger in, Chalkeye. You want to get yourself pretty near absent." The room thinned of them forthwith. "Fix her up good, Doc," they said, over their shoulders. They shuffled across the threshold and porch with roundabout schemes to tread quietly. When one or other stumbled on the steps and fell, he was jerked to his feet. "You want to tame yourself," was the word. Then, suddenly, Chalkeye and Toothpick Kid came precipitately back. "Her cash," they said. And leaving the notes and coins, they hastened to catch their comrades on the way back to the dance.

"I want you," repeated Barker to McLean.

"Him!" cried Mrs. Lusk, flashing alert again. "Jessamine wants him about now, I guess. Don't keep him from his girl!" And she laughed her hard, rich laugh, looking from one to the other. "Not the two of yus can't save me," she stated, defiantly. But even in these last words a sort of thickness sounded.

"Walk her up and down," said Barker. "Keep her moving. I'll look what I can find. Keep her moving brisk." At once he was out of the door; and before his running steps had died away, the fiddle had taken up its tune across the quadrangle.

" 'Buffalo Girls!' " exclaimed the woman. "Old times! Old times!"

"Come," said McLean. "Walk." And he took her.

Her head was full of the music. Forgetting all but that, she went with him easily, and the two made their first turns around the room. Whenever he brought her near the entrance, she leaned away from him toward the open door, where the old fiddle tune was coming in from the dark. But presently she noticed that she was being led, and her face turned sullen.

"Walk," said McLean.

"Do you think so?" said she, laughing. But she found that she must go with him. Thus they took a few more turns.

"You're hurting me," she said next. Then a look of drowsy cunning filled her eyes, and she fixed them upon McLean's dogged face. "He's gone, Lin," she murmured, raising her hand where Barker had disappeared.

She knew McLean had heard her, and she held back on the quickened pace that he had set.

"Leave me down. You hurt," she pleaded, hanging on him.

The cow-puncher put forth more strength.

"Just the floor," she pleaded again. "Just one minute on the floor. He'll think you could not keep me lifted."

Still McLean made no answer, but steadily led her round and round, as he had undertaken.

"He's playing out!" she exclaimed. "You'll be played out soon!" She laughed herself half-awake. The man drew a breath, and she laughed more to feel his hand and arm strain to surmount her increasing resistance. "Jessamine!" she whispered to him. "Jessamine! Doc'll never suspicion you, Lin."

"Talk sense," said he.

"It's sense I'm talking. Leave me go to sleep. Ah, ah, I'm going! I'll go; you can't—"

"Walk, walk!" he repeated. He looked at the door. An ache was numbing his arms.

"Oh yes, walk! What can you and all your muscle— Ah, walk me to glory, then, craziness! I'm going; I'll go. I'm quitting this outfit for keeps. Lin, you're awful handsome to-night! I'll bet—I'll bet she has never seen you look so. Let me—let me watch yus. Anyway, she knows I came first!"

He grasped her savagely. "First! You and twenty of yu' don't—God! what do I talk to her for?"

"Because—because—I'm going; I'll go. He slung me off—but he had to sling—you can't—stop—"

Her head was rolling, while the lips smiled. Her words came through deeper and deeper veils, fearless, defiant, a challenge inarticulate, a continuous mutter. Again he looked at the door as he struggled to move with her dragging weight. The drops rolled on his forehead and neck, his shirt was wet, his hands slipped upon her ribbons. Suddenly the drugged body folded and sank with him, pulling him to his knees. While he took breath so, the mutter went on, and through the door came the jigging fiddle. A fire of desperation lighted in his eyes. "Buffalo Girls!" he shouted hoarsely, in her ear, and got once more on his feet with her as though they were two partners in a quadrille. Still shouting her to wake, he struck a tottering sort of step, and so, with the bending load in his grip, strove feebly to dance the laudanum away.

Feet stumbled across the porch, and Lusk was in the room. "So I've got you!" he said. He had no weapon, but made a dive under the bed and came up with a carbine. The two men locked, wrenching impotently, and fell together. The carbine's loud shot rang in the room, but did no harm; and McLean lay sick and panting upon Lusk as Barker rushed in.

"Thank God!' said he, and flung Lusk's pistol down. The man, deranged and encouraged by drink, had come across the doctor, delayed him, threatened him with his pistol, and when he had torn it away, had left him suddenly and vanished. But Barker had feared, and come after him here. He glanced at the woman slumbering motionless beside the two men. The husband's brief courage had gone, and he lay beneath McLean, who himself could not rise. Barker pulled them apart.

"Lin, boy, you're not hurt?" he asked, affectionately, and lifted the cow-puncher.

McLean sat passive, with dazed eyes, letting himself be supported.

"You're not hurt?" repeated Barker.

"No," answered the cow-puncher, slowly. "I guess not." He looked about the room and at the door. "I got interrupted," he said.

"You'll be all right soon," said Barker.

"Nobody cares for me!" cried Lusk, suddenly, and took to querulous weeping.

"Get up," ordered Barker, sternly.

"Don't accuse me, Governor," screamed Lusk. "I'm innocent." And he rose.

Barker looked at the woman and then at the husband. "I'll not say there was much chance for her," he said. "But any she had is gone through you. She'll die."

"Nobody cares for me!" repeated the man. "He has learned my boy to scorn me." He ran out aimlessly, and away into the night, leaving peace in the room.

"Stay sitting," said Barker to McLean, and went to Mrs. Lusk.

But the cow-puncher, seeing him begin to lift her toward the bed without help, tried to rise. His strength was not sufficiently come back, and he sank as he had been. "I guess I don't amount to much," said he. "I feel like I was nothing."

"Well, I'm something," said Barker, coming back to his friend, out of breath. "And I know what she weighs." He stared admiringly through his spectacles at the seated man.

The cow-puncher's eyes slowly travelled over his body, and then sought Barker's face. "Doc," said he, "ain't I young to have my nerve quit me this way?"

His Excellency broke into his broad smile.

"I know I've racketed some, but ain't it ruther early?" pursued McLean, wistfully.

"You six-foot infant!" said Barker. "Look at your hand."

Lin stared at it—the fingers quivering and bloody, and the skin grooved raw between them. That was the buckle of her belt, which in the struggle had worked round and been held by him unknowingly. Both his wrists and his shirt were ribbed with the pink of her sashes. He looked over at the bed where lay the woman heavily breathing. It was a something, a sound, not like the breath of life; and Barker saw the cow-puncher shudder.

"She is strong," he said. "Her system will fight to the end. Two hours yet, maybe. Queer world!" he moralized. "People half killing themselves to keep one in it who wanted to go—and one that nobody wanted to stay!"

McLean did not hear. He was musing, his eyes fixed absently in front of him. "I would not want," he said, with hesitating utterance—"I'd not wish for even my enemy to have a thing like what I've had to do to-night."

Barker touched him on the arm. "If there had been another man I could trust—"

"Trust!" broke in the cow-puncher. "Why, Doc, it is the best turn yu' ever done me. I know I am a man now—if my nerve ain't gone."

"I've known you were a man since I knew you!" said the hearty Governor. And he helped the still unsteady six-foot to a chair. "As for your nerve, I'll bring you some whiskey now. And after"—he glanced at the bed—"and tomorrow you'll go try if Miss Jessamine won't put the nerve—"

"Yes, Doc, I'll go there, I know. But don't yu'—don't let's while she's—I'm going to be glad about this, Doc, after awhile, but—"

At the sight of a new-comer in the door, he stopped in what his soul was stammering to say. "What do you want, Judge?" he inquired, coldly.

"I understand," began Slaghammer to Barker—"I am informed—"

"Speak quieter, Judge," said the cow-puncher.

"I understand," repeated Slaghammer, more official than ever, "that there was a case for the coroner."

"You'll be notified," put in McLean again. "Meanwhile you'll talk quiet in this room."

Slaghammer turned, and saw the breathing mass on the bed.

"You are a little early, Judge," said Barker, "but—"

"But your ten dollars are safe," said McLean.

The coroner shot one of his shrewd glances at the cow-puncher, and sat down with an amiable countenance. His fee was, indeed, ten dollars; and he was desirous of a second term.

"Under the apprehension that it had already occurred—the misapprehension—I took steps to impanel a jury," said he, addressing both Barker and McLean. "They are—ah—waiting outside. Responsible men, Governor, and have sat before. Drybone has few responsible men to-night, but I procured these at a little game where they were—ah—losing. You may go back, gentlemen," said he, going to the door. "I will summon you in proper time." He looked in the room again. "Is the husband not intending—"

"That's enough, Judge," said McLean. "There's too many here without adding him."

"Judge," spoke a voice at the door, "ain't she ready yet?"

"She is still passing away," observed Slaghammer, piously.

"Because I was thinking," said the man—"I was just— You see, us jury is dry and dead broke. Doggonedest cards I've held this year, and—Judge, would there be anything out of the way in me touching my fee in advance, if it's a sure thing?"

"I see none, my friend," said Slaghammer, benevolently, "since it must be." He shook his head and nodded it by turns. Then, with full-blown importance, he sat again, and wrote a paper, his coroner's certificate. Next door, in Albany County, these vouchers brought their face value of five dollars to the holder; but on Drybone's neutral soil the saloons would always pay four for them, and it was rare that any juryman could withstand the temptation of four immediate dollars. This one gratefully received his paper, and, cherishing it like a bird in the hand, he with his colleagues bore it where they might wait for duty and slake their thirst.

In the silent room sat Lin McLean, his body coming to life more readily than his shaken spirit. Barker, seeing that the cow-puncher meant to watch until the end, brought the whiskey to him. Slaghammer drew documents from his pocket to fill the time, but was soon in slumber over them. In all precincts of the quadrangle Drybone was keeping it up late. The fiddle, the occasional shouts, and the crack of the billiard-balls travelled clear and far through the vast darkness outside. Presently steps unsteadily drew near, and round the corner of the door a voice, plaintive and diffident, said, "Judge, ain't she most pretty near ready?"

"Wake up, Judge!" said Barker. "Your jury has gone dry again."

The man appeared round the door—a handsome, dishevelled fellow—with hat in hand, balancing himself with respectful anxiety. Thus was a second voucher made out, and the messenger strayed back happy to his friends. Barker and McLean sat wakeful, and Slaghammer fell at once to napping. From time to time he was roused by new messengers, each arriving more unsteady than the last, until every juryman had got his fee and no more messengers came. The coroner slept undisturbed in his chair. McLean and Barker sat. On the bed the mass, with its pink ribbons, breathed and breathed, while moths flew round the lamp, tapping and falling with light sounds. So did the heart of the darkness wear itself away, and through the stone-cold air the dawn began to filter and expand.

Barker rose, bent over the bed, and then stood. Seeing him, McLean stood also.

"Judge," said Barker, quietly, "you may call them now." And with careful steps the judge got himself out of the room to summon his jury.

For a short while the cow-puncher stood looking down upon the woman. She lay lumped in her gaudiness, the ribbons darkly stained by the laudanum; but into the stolid, bold features death had called up the faint-colored ghost of youth, and McLean remembered all his Bear Creek days. "Hind sight is a turruble clear way o' seein' things," said he. "I think I'll take a walk."

"Go," said Barker. "The jury only need me, and I'll join you."

But the jury needed no witness. Their long waiting and the advance pay had been too much for these responsible men. Like brothers they had shared each others' vouchers until responsibility had melted from their brains and the whiskey was finished. Then, no longer entertained, and growing weary of Drybone, they had remembered nothing but their distant beds. Each had mounted his pony, holding trustingly to the saddle, and thus, unguided, the experienced ponies had taken them right. Across the wide sage-brush and up and down the river they were now asleep or riding, dispersed irrevocably. But the coroner was here. He duly received Barker's testimony, brought his verdict in, and signed it, and even while he was issuing to himself his own proper voucher for ten dollars came Chalkeye and Toothpick Kid on their ponies, galloping, eager in their hopes and good wishes for Mrs. Lusk. Life ran strong in them both. The night had gone well with them. Here was the new day going to be fine. It must be well with everybody.

"You don't say!" they exclaimed, taken aback. "Too bad."

They sat still in their saddles, and upon their reckless, kindly faces thought paused for a moment. "Her gone!" they murmured. "Hard to get used to the idea. What's anybody doing about the coffin?"

"Mr. Lusk," answered Slaghammer, "doubtless—"

"Lusk! He'll not know anything this forenoon. He's

out there in the grass. She didn't think nothing of him. Tell Bill—not Dollar Bill, Jerky Bill, Yu' know; he's over the bridge—to fix up a hearse, and we'll be back." The two drove their spurs in with vigorous heels, and instantly were gone rushing up the road to the graveyard.

The fiddle had lately ceased, and no dancers stayed any longer in the hall. Eastward the rose and gold began to flow down upon the plain over the tops of the distant hills. Of the revellers, many had never gone to bed, and many now were already risen from their excesses to revive in the cool glory of the morning. Some were drinking to stay their hunger until breakfast; some splashed and sported in the river, calling and joking; and across the river some were holding horse-races upon the level beyond the hog-ranch. Drybone air rang with them. Their lusty, wandering shouts broke out in gusts of hilarity. Their pistols, aimed at cans or prairie-dogs or anything, cracked as they galloped at large. Their speeding, clear-cut forms would shine upon the bluffs, and, descending, merge in the dust their horses had raised. Yet all this was nothing in the vastness of the growing day. Beyond their voices the rim of the sun moved above the violet hills, and Drybone, amid the quiet, long, new fields of radiance, stood august and strange.

Down along the tall, bare slant from the graveyard the two horsemen were riding back. They could be seen across the river, and the horse-racers grew curious. As more and more watched, the crowd began to speak. It was a calf the two were bringing. It was too small for a calf. It was dead. It was a coyote they had roped. See it swing! See it fall on the road!

"It's a coffin, boys!" said one, shrewd at guessing.

At that the event of last night drifted across their memories, and they wheeled and spurred their ponies. Their crowding hoofs on the bridge brought the swimmers from the waters below, and, dressing, they climbed quickly to the plain and followed the gathering. By the door already were Jerky Bill and Limber Jim and the Doughie, and always more, dashing up with their ponies, halting with a sharp scatter of gravel to hear and comment. Barker was gone, but the important coroner told his news. And it amazed each comer, and set him speaking and remembering past things with the others.

"Dead!" each one began.

"Her, does he say?"

"Why, pshaw!"

"Why, Frenchy said Doc had her cured!"

"Jack Saunders claimed she had rode to Box Elder with Lin McLean."

"Dead? Why, pshaw!"

"Seems Doc couldn't swim her out."

"Couldn't swim her out?"

"That's it. Doc couldn't swim her out."

"Well—there's one less of us."

"Sure! She was one of the boys."

"She grub-staked me when I went broke in '84."

"She gave me fifty dollars onced at Lander, to buy a saddle."

"I run agin her when she was a biscuit-shooter."

"Sidney, Nebraska. I run again her there, too."

"I knowed her at Laramie."

"Where's Lin? He knowed her all the way from Bear Creek to Cheyenne."

They laughed loudly at this.

"That's a lonesome coffin," said the Doughie. "That the best you could do?"

"You'd say so!" said Toothpick Kid.

"Choices are getting scarce up there," said Chalkeye. "We looked the lot over."

They were arriving from their search among the old dug-up graves on the hill. Now they descended from their ponies, with the box roped and rattling between them. "Where's your hearse, Jerky?" said Chalkeye.

"Have her round in a minute," said the cowboy, and galloped away with three or four others to help.

"Turruble lonesome coffin, all the same," repeated the Doughie. And they surveyed the box that had once held some soldier.

"She did like fixin's," said Limber Jim.

"Fixin's!" said Toothpick Kid. "That's easy."

While some six of them, with Chalkeye, bore the light, half-rotted coffin into the room, many followed Toothpick Kid to the post-trader's store. Breaking in here, they found men sleeping on the counters. These had been able to find no other beds in Drybone, and lay as they had stretched themselves on entering. They sprawled in heavy slumber, some with not even their hats taken off, and some with their boots against the rough hair of the next one. They were quickly pushed together, few waking, and so there was space for spreading cloth and chintz. Stuffs were unrolled and flung aside till many folds and colors draped the motionless sleepers, and at length a choice was made. Unmeasured yards of this drab chintz were ripped off, money treble its worth was thumped upon the counter, and they returned, bearing it like a streamer to the coffin. While the noise of their hammers filled the room, the hearse came tottering to the door, pulled and pushed by twenty men. It was an ambulance left behind by the soldiers, and of the old-fashioned shape, concave in body, its top blown away in winds of long ago; and as they revolved, its wheels dished in and out like hoops about to fall. While some made a harness from ropes, and throwing the saddles off two ponies backed them to the vehicle, the body was put in the coffin, now covered by the chintz. But the laudanum upon the front of her dress revolted those who remembered their holidays with her, and turning the

woman upon her face, they looked their last upon
her flashing, colored ribbons, and nailed the lid
down. So they carried her out, but the concave body
of the hearse was too short for the coffin; the end
reached out, and it might have fallen. But Limber Jim,
taking the reins, sat upon the other end, waiting and
smoking. For all Drybone was making ready to follow
in some way. They had sought the husband, the chief
mourner. He, however, still lay in the grass of the
quadrangle, and despising him as she had done, they
left him to wake when he should choose. Those men
who could sit in their saddles rode escort, the old
friends nearest, and four held the heads of the frightened cow-ponies who were to draw the hearse. They
had never known harness before, and they plunged
with the men who held them. Behind the hearse the
women followed in a large ranch-wagon, this moment
arrived in town. Two mares drew this, and their foals
gambolled around them. The great flat-topped dray
for hauling poles came last, with its four government
mules. The cowboys had caught sight of it and cap-
tured it. Rushing to the post-trader's, they carried
the sleeping men from the counter and laid them on
the dray. Then, searching Drybone outside and in for
any more incapable of following, they brought them,
and the dray was piled.

Limber Jim called for another drink and, with his
cigar between his teeth, cracked his long bull-
whacker whip. The ponies, terrified, sprang away,
scattering the men that held them, and the swaying
hearse leaped past the husband, over the stones and
the many playing-cards in the grass. Masterfully
steered, it came safe to an open level, while the
throng cheered the unmoved driver on his coffin, his
cigar between his teeth.

"Stay with it, Jim!" they shouted. "You're a king!"

A steep ditch lay across the flat where he was
veering, abrupt and nearly hidden; but his eye

caught the danger in time, and swinging from it leftward so that two wheels of the leaning coach were in the air, he faced the open again, safe, as the rescue swooped down upon him. The horsemen came at the ditch, a body of daring, a sultry blast of youth. Wheeling at the brink, they turned, whirling their long ropes. The skillful nooses flew, and the ponies, caught by the neck and foot, were dragged back to the quadrangle and held in line. So the pageant started; the wild ponies quivering but subdued by the tightened ropes, and the coffin steady in the ambulance beneath the driver. The escort, in their fringed leather and broad hats, moved slowly beside and behind it, many of them swaying, their faces full of health, and the sun, and the strong drink. The women followed, whispering a little; and behind them the slow dray jolted, with its heaps of men waking from the depths of their whiskey and asking what this was. So they went up the hill. When the riders reached the tilted gate of the graveyard, they sprang off and scattered among the hillocks, stumbling and eager. They nodded to Barker and McLean, quietly waiting there, and began choosing among the open, weather-drifted graves from which the soldiers had been taken. Their figures went up and down the uneven ridges, calling and comparing.

"Here," said the Doughie, "here's a good hole."

"Here's a deep one," said another.

"We've struck a well here," said some more. "Put her in here."

The sand-hills became clamorous with voices until they arrived at a choice, when some one with a spade quickly squared the rain-washed opening. With lariats looping the coffin round, they brought it and were about to lower it, when Chalkeye, too near the edge, fell in, and one end of the box rested upon him. He could not rise by himself, and they pulled the ropes helplessly above.

McLean spoke to Barker. "I'd like to stop this," said he, "But a man might as well—"

"Might as well stop a cloud-burst," said Barker.

"Yes, Doc. But it feels—it feels like I was looking at ten dozen Lin McLeans." And seeing them still helpless with Chalkeye, he joined them and lifted the cowboy out.

"I think," said Slaghammer, stepping forward, "this should proceed no further without some—perhaps some friend would recite 'Now I lay me?' "

"They don't use that on funerals," said the Doughie.

"Will some gentleman give the Lord's Prayer?" inquired the coroner.

Foreheads were knotted; trial mutterings ran among them; but some one remembered a prayer-book in one of the rooms in Drybone, and the notion was hailed. Four mounted, and raced to bring it. They went down the hill in a flowing knot, shirts ballooning and elbows flapping, and so returned. But the book was beyond them. "Take it, you; you take it," each one said. False beginnings were made, big thumbs pushed the pages back and forth, until impatience conquered them. They left the book and lowered the coffin, helped again by McLean. The weight sank slowly, decently, steadily, down between the banks. The sound that it struck the bottom with was a slight sound, the grating of the load upon the solid sand; and a little sand strewed from the edge and fell on the box at the same moment. The rattle came up from below, compact and brief, a single jar, quietly smiting through the crowd, smiting it to silence. One removed his hat, and then another, and then all. They stood eying each his neighbor, and shifting their eyes, looked away at the great valley. Then they filled in the grave, brought a head-board from a grave near by, and wrote the name and date upon it by scratching with a stone.

"She was sure one of us," said Chalkeye. "Let's give her the Lament."

And they followed his lead:

"Once in the saddle I used to go dashing,
 Once in the saddle I used to go gay;
 First took to drinking, and then to card-playing;
 Got shot in the body, and now here I lay.

"Beat the drum slowly,
 Play the fife lowly,
 Sound the dead march as you bear me along.
 Take me to Boot-hill, and throw the sod over me—
 I'm but a poor cowboy, I know I done wrong."

When the song was ended, they left the graveyard quietly and went down the hill. The morning was growing warm. Their work waited them across many sunny miles of range and plain. Soon their voices and themselves had emptied away into the splendid vastness and silence, and they were gone—ready with all their might to live or to die, to be animals or heroes, as the hours might bring them opportunity. In Drybone's deserted quadrangle the sun shone down upon Lusk still sleeping, and the wind shook the aces and kings in the grass.

IV

Over at Separ, Jessamine Buckner had no more stockings of Billy's to mend, and much time for thinking and a change of mind. The day after that strange visit, when she had been told that she had hurt a good man's heart without reason, she took up her work; and while her hands despatched it her thoughts already accused her. Could she have seen that visitor now, she would have thanked her. She looked at the photograph on her table. "Why did he go away so quickly?" she sighed. But when young Billy returned to his questions she was buoyant again, and more than a match for him. He reached the forbidden twelfth time of asking why Lin McLean did not come back and marry her. Nor did she punish him as she had threatened. She looked at him confidentially, and he drew near, full of hope.

"Billy, I'll tell you just why it is," said she. "Lin thinks I'm not a real girl."

"A—ah," drawled Billy, backing from her with suspicion.

"Indeed that's what it is, Billy. If he knew I was a real girl—"

"A—ah," went the boy, entirely angry. "Anybody can tell you're a girl." And he marched out, mystified, and nursing a sense of wrong. Nor did his dignity allow him to reopen the subject.

To-day, two miles out in the sage-brush by himself, he was shooting jack-rabbits, but began suddenly to run in toward Separ. A horseman had passed him, and he had loudly called; but the rider rode on, intent upon the little distant station. Man and horse were soon far ahead of the boy, and the man came into town galloping.

No need to fire the little pistol by her window, as he had once thought to do! She was outside before he could leap to the ground. And as he held her, she could only laugh, and cry, and say "Forgive me! Oh, why have you been so long?" She took him back to the room where his picture was, and made him sit, and sat herself close. "What is it?" she asked him. For through the love she read something else in his serious face. So then he told her how nothing was wrong; and as she listened to all that he had to tell, she, too, grew serious, and held very close to him. "Dear, dear neighbor!" she said.

As they sat so, happy with deepening happiness,

but not gay yet, young Billy burst open the door. "There!" he cried. "I knowed Lin knowed you were a girl!"

Thus did Billy also have his wish. For had he not told Jessamine that he liked her, and urged her to come and live with him and Lin? That cabin on Box Elder became a home of truth, with a woman inside taking the only care of Mr. McLean that he had known since his childhood: though singularly enough he has an impression that it is he who takes care of Jessamine!

In the After-days

The black pines stand high up the hills,
  The white snow sifts their columns deep,
While through the cañon's riven cleft
  From there, beyond, the rose clouds sweep.

Serene above their paling shapes
  One star hath wakened in the sky,
And here in the gray world below
  Over the sage the wind blows by;

Rides through the cotton-woods' ghost-ranks,
  And hums aloft a sturdy tune
Among the river's tawny bluffs,
  Untenanted as is the moon.

Far 'neath the huge invading dusk
  Comes Silence awful through the plain;
But yonder horseman's heart is gay,
  And he goes singing might and main.

THE END